The Mythamöhre

A novel by
Christopher Mark Bessette

***

Print Edition

Cover Design by Michael Bessette
Print Cover Layout Greg Barnes

***

Terrapin Point Publishing
Fonthill, ON Canada

print edition   ISBN 978-0-9681153-2-9
eBook edition ISBN 978-0-9681153-1-2
Terrapin Point Publishing
is a division of Terrapin Point Motion Pictures Ltd.
 http://www.terrapin-point.com

Cover photo: Image © TomaB, 2013
Used under license from Shutterstock.com
Author's photo courtesy: Robert Nowell
Author's Photo © 2013 Christopher Mark Bessette please contact for
permission to reuse. Mail to: info@terrapin-point.com
Printed by CreateSpace, Charleston SC
Available from Amazon.com, CreateSpace.com. and other retail outlets.

Special Thanks:
Toni Wynne Bessette for loving and believing in her husband, the dreamer.
Peter Cuke for his keen eye and wordsmith skills.
Ryan Bundra for the gentle reminder regarding the importance of conflict.
Sue Grierson for encouraging the engaging rabbit trails.
Brian Godawa and Charles G. Pedley for their wisdom
on navigating the seas of publishing.
Robert Nowell for catching a
photogenic moment
and generously giving me the photographs.
Greg Barnes for the technical layout of the print design.
Michael Bessette for his powerful words of encouragement.

Dedicated To:
Rachel, Michael, Melissa, baby "B", William
And especially to my wife and my love Toni; who not only stands by me,
she stands with me.

Table of Contents

Chapter One
FRAGMENTS

The gargoyles stood watch over their city. New York carried on its daily shuffle, oblivious to the stone watchers' subtle movements. It was not by chance they were positioned to watch over the city that carried the title of 'the world's top financial center.' These granite guardians knew the time of the great revealing was coming. They waited in silence and patience for her signal. The signs were all around them. The intensity of the voices that reached the gargoyles' stony ears triggered their readiness. The mixed voices of humanity riding on the winds tickled the stone creatures to life. It had been growing over the centuries alongside the human population. The collective magnitude of humanity's words animated the gargoyles, "I want, I want... I WANT MORE."

It was the fever pitch of the human voices and their carnal desires that called the Queen. The time was coming to unleash the Queen's reign on mankind once again. It would start simple, seem innocent and the humans would not suspect anything was out of ordinary. Humanity was a naive bunch that believed only in what they could see, taste, hear, smell and feel. The Queen knew how to feed mankind's lust... and feed them, she will.

At a little past 8:30 AM, Josh Renfrew stood on the corner of 119 West and 56th Street in Manhattan and checked his watch. I should get there by ten, he thought. Josh looked around him at the madness. Being a writer, Josh's mind shot a variety of rapid-fire exposition that he could use to start his article. He thought, it's a wonder anyone gets to where they are going in New York City, was a good way to start his article. He continued playing with the words in his mind. Josh continued to wrestle with words as he played with an alternate opening, it's somewhat ironic that Dr. Elderidge would bring his latest deep sea discovery to the surface in... in... ARGH! Josh fought with himself for the right words. Why do you do this to yourself Renfrew? Wait till you get into the press junket and the article opening will present itself; Josh tried to comfort himself with that thought.

He stood there for a while and took it all in; somehow most of the people and traffic moved with cohesive symmetry, like schools of synchronized fish. Although the traffic in his hometown of Atlanta could be ridiculous at times, nowhere else in North America had ever seemed this intense.

Kip Somers, a reporter with The Telegraph spotted the fish out of water and decided to rescue Josh. Kip approached his colleague Josh.

"Josh, Josh Renfrew!" Kip called out.

Josh made a full circle in the milieu of people to catch Kip approaching. The first thing to cross Josh's mind was, here he comes! The second thing he wondered was if screaming someone's name out loud is proper 'street etiquette' in Manhattan. Does Kip even know what etiquette means? Josh appreciated Kip's talent, just not the saccharine byline of his blogs, 'always good news'. To Josh, Kip seemed like a reporter from a different era, so it was hard to believe he was so well followed on the internet. It must be all the conservatives hungry for another member of their choir, Josh reasoned.

Kip was only in his 30's yet he towed the conservative line so much that Josh had a hard time believing they were that close in age. Josh was glad his editor didn't make him write Kip's kind of drivel. In Josh's mind, Kip would have attended college around the same time and would have been exposed to the same world events. How could he write a blog that always claimed good news because in this world, there isn't always good news. Josh reasoned, Kip only got the internet blogger job because he probably couldn't land a reputable position... be pleasant with him Renfrew, just be pleasant, he told himself.

"Hey Josh are you in town to cover Elderidge's conference?" Kip questioned.

"Yeah, I was about to flag down a cab. I wonder what Elderidge's deep sea exploration is going to reveal this time, any clues?" Replied Josh.

"No clues but it should be interesting. We can walk to the conference from here. Come on and walk with me, it's only a couple of blocks away. I used to live in this neighborhood."

"Sure," slipped out of Josh's mouth before he caught himself. "You're kidding me? You used to live in New York City?" Josh retorted surprised.

"Yeah, why?"

"I always pictured you as from back-wash Nebraska... you know, small town views... no offense," Josh quickly changed the direction of his comment, attempting to avoid insult.

Kip laughed, "You joining my critics?"

"Someone who always brings 'good news' has critics? Hard to believe. I guess none of us are safe from the critics."

"I think people need to look on the bright side of the clouds," Kip said proudly with a half-smirk on his face. He finished his thought with a, "The sun does shine eventually." Knowing that they could quickly get into a disagreement, Kip changed the subject. "Now they have got the right idea," Kip said as he pointed to the pigeons lined up along the span of a streetlight. "They can see down the road."

"Can't blame them," Josh responded, "Where do you perch when there are no trees?"

"They do the same thing along Central Park, there's no shortage of trees there."

"Waiting to bomb an unsuspecting hansom cab."

"...or person," quipped Kip.

"There's not much good news in that," Josh replied. The men laughed and melded into the morning rush hour crowd.

A few blocks away, Beth closed the drapes on her 15th floor hotel room. She was a small town girl at heart and didn't want any of the neighboring office workers to catch a glimpse of her changing for the press conference. Beth was in her late twenties, an archaeological graduate student; she looked sharp and poised but knew she would feel awkward in her neatly tailored business suit. Getting the suit on and buttoned up, she sat on the bed and struggled with her high heels.

Beth's physical appearance rivaled that of one of the unattainable comic book heroines: hourglass figure, deep red hair framing her silky white complexion and hazel eyes. She was the kind of girl that naturally made any boy take a second look. Dr. Elderidge didn't hire her for her looks, Beth knew that, and she appreciated him for it.

It was exciting to think of the venue for this press conference. The Allen Room of the Jazz at the Lincoln Centre gave a perfect backdrop for Dr. Elderidge's presentation. The room had a spectacular view of the city out of the multi-story high glass wall; a dramatic backdrop for what was sure to be a dramatic presentation. The tiered center-facing seating focused all the attention where it belonged, on Dr. Elderidge. Beth struggled with her high heels and dashed for the door of her hotel room.

Meanwhile, in the Allen Room of the Jazz at the Lincoln Centre, Doctor Philip Elderidge flattened down his bushy hair. It was the type of course hair that only middle-aged men would recognize as problematic. Dr. Elderidge took his seat at the side of the impressive Allen Room. This was not Elderidge's first choice. His assistant Beth had chosen this space. Elderidge considered himself an admirer of historical, classic design and architecture. He hoped that on this trip to New York he would have the opportunity to divert his activities with fun and take a 'Gargoyles of Manhattan' walking tour. If Dr. Elderidge had his way, this press conference would be in one of New York's century old hotels, which he felt held a lot of charm with their ornate crown molding and eleven inch wide baseboards. Even with recent renovations, the musty antique smell of age and tradition lingered. He liked that; it was Dr. Elderidge's preference. To him, the distinct smell of old books seemed to be more in line with academic tradition. For Elderidge, it wasn't hard to imagine the events that went on in rooms like that over the last hundred years. Elderidge noticed Beth's arrival.

It was easy for her to spot Dr. Elderidge, alone, with only a few of the Centre's workers finalizing press conference set-up details. Elderidge stuck out like a sore thumb, he had a way of doing that, even on his best days. Poster sized photographs of deep sea subs and divers were positioned on easels carefully around the room. On other easels, poster sized images depicting a rugged tropical landscape and caves of an unidentified island, were placed. At the front of the room sat a large canvas covered wall-type structure.

Beth walked over and took a seat next to Dr. Elderidge. A couple of TV camera teams had already set up their gear early, ahead of the media group gathered just outside the doors.

"Good morning Doctor Elderidge," Beth said with her usual chirper attitude.

"Morning," replied Dr. Elderidge.

"Is everything to your liking?" Questioned Beth. She knew it would be, she was up late making sure everything was in order.

"Their coffee is a little strong," Dr. Elderidge replied.

Beth smiled and responded, "I'll see what I can do about that."

Beth brushed her pant legs as she nodded her head for the attendant to open both of the doors to the room. Newsmen started to trickle into the room. There was an air of excitement as the groups of reporters filled up the room, chatting and speculating about the content of Dr. Elderidge's findings.

Dr. Elderidge removed his eyeglasses and attempted to scrub the lens clean. The smudges seemed to be permanent, no matter how often he attacked them with his worn handkerchief and a dab of saliva.

Beth leaned in close to Dr. Elderidge, "Can I help you with that?" Beth questioned in a half-whisper. If the last five years had taught her anything, it was the obsessive nature of Philip Elderidge. Beth knew he wouldn't be able to focus on anything else until his glasses were perfectly clean.

Elderidge didn't acknowledge her, he just kept working on his eyeglasses. Beth had grown accustomed to the quirks of Dr. Elderidge, when most people would interpret his actions as rude;

Beth had come to discover that it was merely focus. Beth caught herself laughing as the thought of her dads' mantra flashed through her memory, "You can't leave the porch light on all night without expecting it to burn out eventually." Her father would say that in reference to her teenage late night runs with friends. She now understood it in a different way; Elderidge is so engaged in all he does, eventually he'll burn out too. Beth's laugh caused Dr. Elderidge to pause and look at her. Beth quickly straightened up and leaned closer to him to whisper, "Great turn out," as if that thought had been the cause of her laugh.

Elderidge held his eyeglasses up to the light and squinted as he attempted to see if the smudge had been removed. "There is always a stubborn one. Do you think that they will believe I fabricated this?" Questioned Dr. Elderidge.

Beth raised her eyebrows at the thought. She responded half to herself, "I guess they will have reason to be cynical, I would challenge it if I hadn't seen it with my own eyes." Beth looked around the room and then leaned close to Elderidge once more, "Which one?" Waiting for Elderidge's answer, she began to look around the room for the stubborn person he is talking about.

"Which one who?" Questioned a bewildered Dr. Eldridge.

"Which one is the stubborn one," Beth replied patiently, knowing that Dr. Elderidge was infamous for changing the subject mid-thought.

Dr. Elderidge held up his glasses to the light and pointed at the smudge on the left lens. "This one, right here."

Beth smiled and took the glasses from Elderidge, "Let me help you with that." Beth pulled a tissue from her suit pocket and wiped the lens clean.

Elderidge turned his attention back to the gathering reporters. "These boys are bound to get their monies worth today." The ambient tone of the room rose as the chatter carried indistinctive conversations.

Beth handed Dr. Elderidge his clean glasses back, "I think it is time you addressed everyone."

Elderidge put on his glasses and beamed at the clarity he could now see with. Beth grinned, stood and made her way to the podium. A tuft of her red hair fell across her forehead, and she quickly repositioned her hair before continuing. Beth tapped her finger on the microphone as a test. Like a bull to a red flag, the room filled with mostly male journalists quieted down, fixated on the china doll-like woman that stood before them. Beth felt their looks and for a brief moment became the uncomfortable schoolgirl making a class presentation. She took a deep breath, collected herself and smiled. "Thank you for coming today. I would like to ask that all questions be reserved for the question and answer period that follows the presentation. With your cooperation, we will be able to walk through the amazing discoveries of Dr. Philip Elderidge and his team. At this time, I'd like to bring Dr. Elderidge to the podium for the presentation."

Polite applause filled the room as Dr. Elderidge began his walk to the podium. The chatter in the room picked up for a moment as the last few straggling reporters made their way in, taking their seats. Most of the reporters watched Beth walk back to the side of the room, rather than look at Dr. Elderidge as he approached the podium.

Beth surveyed the crowd of reporters and saw the back door opening with the entrance of the Daily Star's reporter, Josh Renfrew, followed closely by The Graph's Kip Somers. Beth's eyes stayed with Josh. If anyone was in the wrong profession, it was Josh. He didn't have a face for the newspapers, he had a face for television: tall, dark and handsome with piercing blue eyes. He was always impeccably dressed yet sported a day's growth of facial hair. Beth enjoyed seeing Josh as a guest on CNN and believed it would not be long before he was offered his own show on the network.

Perhaps Beth's attraction to him was because he was polar opposite in his views to hers. Beth's eyes met Josh's. Josh smiled and nodded his head. He had been to Dr. Elderidge's press conferences before and his reports were never supportive. However, it was in Dr. Elderidge's best interest that Beth remained cordial with Josh. Beth returned Josh's head nod with a smile, then she turned her attention back to Dr. Elderidge.

Dr. Elderidge adjusted the gooseneck and the microphone responded with a loud squeal. Several chuckles filled the air at the shocked reaction of Dr. Elderidge. Beth acted fast and ran to her bosses aid. She adjusted the microphone in a perfect position, which was slightly lower than what she had required. Dr. Elderidge nodded his head to the reporters as Beth stood off to the side, closer this time and ready to help her boss if he ran into any more trouble. Dr. Elderidge cleared his throat and looked down at his papers, as he shuffled them into the necessary order. The room fell quiet, as the full attention of the reporters focused center stage.

Dr. Elderidge began, "Something has troubled me my entire career... why is it that at the end of every major river in the world we find the same thing, about 4500 years of silt deposit? I have always been a scientist and oceanographer that supported my colleagues' theory of an old earth. However the nagging question remains: If the planet is millions of years old, shouldn't there be deeper silt deposits? I didn't set out to answer that question, but perhaps I have. As you know, our team has been involved in deep-sea exploration for years. Our recent expedition took us to Mangaia, a unique part of the Cook Islands; believed by geologists to be the oldest islands of the South Pacific It was there that we have discovered the remains of a village deep under the sea. It is this new evidence, coupled with the 4500 years of silt deposit at the ends of the worlds major rivers that has caused me to seriously reconsider the 200 cross cultural stories from around our globe... of a cataclysmic planetary flood. The Noah's Flood story if you will," Dr. Elderidge said with a smile. "Perhaps the earth is not as old as my colleagues believe."

There was a rumbling of chuckles around the room, knowing the widely published posture of Dr.Elderidge, most thought he was joking.

With smugness at causing the stir, Dr. Elderidge adjusted his glasses and accidentally touched the lens smudging them again. Dr. Elderidge took off his glasses and examined them in the light.

Beth knew in her gut that Josh would definitely be all over Dr. Elderidge's new belief, what liberal newspaper wouldn't. Dr. Elderidge was always known as the staunch liberal evolutionist, now he was in the other camp. Beth wished that Dr. Elderidge had not spoken his mind, rather just stay to the point. Let the newshound's draw their own conclusions from their discoveries.

One of the reporters leaned towards another, "I like where this is going: Coming from Elderidge, it's like finding out Tupac Shakur was Mother Theresa's love child."

The two burst out laughing.

Most of the other reporters started taking notes while murmuring to each other. A few began to make calls on their cell phones. Television cameras panned the room and settled back on Elderidge. One cameraman began to zoom in on Dr. Elderidge, catching Dr. Elderidge's smirk of satisfaction over the kerfuffle he had caused. A few camera flashes went off, before Dr. Elderidge finally tried to refocus the room, "Ladies and gentlemen please, the best is yet to come," promised Dr. Elderidge as he raised his hands to calm the room. Elderidge mumbled to himself as he surveyed the crowd, "Good, good, good... always start with the sound bite that grabs them."

Josh looked over at Kip who found himself a seat on the opposite side of the room. Did Josh hear things right, he wondered? Kip's smirk told Josh how his colleague felt about Elderidge's comments. Dr. Elderidge admitting to a young-earth view, that's news! He was such a hard line old-earth evolutionist, there has to be more to this story that caused Elderidge to change, Josh thought. Unless the old man has gone bonkers from too many deep-sea dives, Josh reasoned.

Dr. Elderidge cleared his throat, leaned back into the microphone and the murmuring of the reporters ceased. "What prompted my extensive search of this area was the discovery within a cave near Ivirua Mangaia by a local. In this cave we found carvings recording a journey taken by a man of an ancient people. A cast model of the carvings is on display for your examination."

Dr. Elderidge adjusted his physical distance from the microphone and looked at the crowd over his glasses, "Beside the writings we found a Rosetta Stone if you will, a tool that has allowed us to transcribe these ancient writings into modern English. We also found a most interesting image of the life that this man must have lived." Dr. Elderidge held out his hand to point at the canvas-covered wall behind him, "Which I will save for unveiling at the completion of this conference."

Dr. Elderidge continued, "Mangaia has long been believed as the oldest Island in the South Pacific... yes... I've covered that, haven't I... let's see... Mangaia old and... ah yes," Dr. Elderidge looked back at his notes, as he scrambled to find his place. As soon as he was able to locate his place, Dr. Elderidge quickly looked up at the reporters. "It appears that these carvings could be many millennia old, and suggests a people predating the Polynesian culture," Dr. Elderidge stated with an air of confidence.

Beth walked over to a covered glass case and pulled off a black drape covering the case of stone carvings. There was a hum in the crowd as if she had taken off the top of a beehive. A few more flashes from the press went off, as they tried to snag a photo of the artifact.

Dr. Elderidge cleared his throat, "As translated, they are the writings of a man who called himself '... the-Greater.' He may have had a name that preceded that one, but because of its damaged condition the first name is missing. These are remarkable findings. We can tell that this man's journey was of significance to his culture because of the carvings in the cave. His work is poetic in nature and somewhat lyrical, suggesting an advanced form of communication skills beyond anything we expected to find. Since Mangaia juts from the ocean and the writings speak of a valley, this prompted me to dispatch the underwater exploration around Mangaia. Which subsequently led us to the discovery of the ancient remains covered by the ocean."

The reporters hung onto every word Dr. Elderidge was speaking, "We have not been able to place these transcripts in any specific order, but we believe that what you are about to hear are the words of a ruler who lived close to ten thousand years ago. I will verify the dating of our find upon conclusion of my presentation. I believe that if we can find the order it will tell us a great deal more about this ancient civilization. Let me begin by reading the transcript of our findings, we refer to as… Fragment One."

#

FRAGMENT ONE
horizon - tattered clothes - weathered face - wise as mountains - colossal giants - valley people celebrate.
****

IN THE KING'S CHAMBER:

The King lifted up his eyes to see the scribe enter the room. The King had been deep in thought moments before, reflecting on the events that brought him to rule all those years ago. The King didn't fancy wearing his crown but he knew it was expected. He would rather be wearing his warrior's helmet charging the Nephilim that lived in the mountains. It was by the encouragement of his beautiful wife of almost 30 years, that he was going through with this exercise of dictating his adventures to the scribe.

The scribe took note of the King and bowed respectfully before surveying his surroundings. The scribe was nonchalantly looking for a port of quick escape should one be necessary. The room was cavernous but well illuminated by the early morning light that streamed through the second story palace window. There were few furniture pieces in the room, yet each of them was functional. The King sat back in his ornate chair and smiled as the scribe approached a table and nervously prepared his quills to copy every word the King uttered. The King gave a warm welcoming smile but said nothing at first. His shoulder length grey hair and short-cropped beard framed his wise middle-aged face perfectly.

The scribe had been face to face with the King before but he hoped the King would not recognize him. If the scribe lost focus on projecting the appearance of a man, his real identity as Nine the shape shifting creature would become evident. He knew concentration and remaining in solid form as the scribe, was paramount for him to earn the King's trust. The scribe fumbled with multiple scrolls sending most of them to the floor. He scrambled to pick them up and regain his composure. "My apologies your highness, I'm a little nervous or clumsy," confessed the scribe.

"Nothing to be nervous about, so you must be clumsy. Clumsiness can be corrected by calming down. If you are a friend, you should realize that you are with a friend," replied the King.

The scribe bowed and dropped a few more scrolls. He scrambled, picked them up and placed them on the table before taking his seat. "I've come well prepared," said the scribe.

"Very well indeed," replied the King. "There's something familiar about you scribe. Something in your eyes tells me I know you."

The scribe dropped his eyes to his scrolls. "With all respect, it is unlikely your highness," he replied.

"Perhaps it will eventually come to me," answered the King.

The scribe nervously nodded and organized his scrolls, licked the palm of his hand which he used to flattened down his messy hair. He took a big breath before he spoke again, "Shall I begin with your conquests and victories that attest to your greatness; crossing raging rivers, traversing foreign lands or climbing mountains into the clouds to battle the Nephilim giants? Will you share about the imps, the gargoyles or other hellish demons?" The scribe's voice raised in pitch and his eyes widened with excitement knowing what he was about to hear.

The King nodded his head and his smile broadened as he reflected on the adventure he was about to share. He took a long time while he carefully considered his words. He smiled and said, "In due time, all this and more, for now you shall begin with the most important part of my life: Have you ever wondered what lies beyond the next horizon?"

The scribe thought the King was asking him a question. It took a moment before he realized the King had begun his dictation. The scribe hurried his quill and began writing.

The King continued, "I do, always did, especially in those early days when I seemed so much younger than I hoped I appeared. I remember my days as a young boy fondly, I would watch my Papa tend to the sheep as a real master could. He always looked so big and strong -- his tattered clothes and weathered face made him seem as wise as the mountains that

surrounded the grazing highlands where we brought our sheep.
Papa had a gift of gentle leadership, one I would have to learn if
I was to be a master shepherd like him. We had little need for
much of anything the valley people offered. Papa taught me to
appreciate what we had. These simple things: home, family, health
were the truly beautiful things of life. At that age, I had a hard
time believing that there was not something more... especially
standing way up here looking down on the reveling valley people
celebrating their festivals. It seemed that they lived in a constant
state of celebration while we lived in a constant state of just
having enough to get by.

    High up in the mountains, the tall grass of the meadow
swayed, dancing to the cold mountain wind, as if movement was
the only way of keeping warm. It was an attempt to hold on to
summer just a bit longer. The last puffy clouds of the season
would mass into a colossal giant spanning the horizon. I would
often daydream that these colossal giants were another far off
mountain range, stacked on top of one another... somewhere in a
far-away land that was filled with adventure. That's the horizon I
am talking about... can you see it? I soon would, although I had
no idea. I guess none of us really knows the adventure a day
could bring, maybe it is better that way. If I had known then
what I was about to discover, I would have hugged my father
right there and told him how much I loved him."

Chapter Two
THE BROODING PLACE

High on top of the wind-swept outcrop rocks of Mount Crevasse, Thomas looked down on the valley as the Festival of Harvest was just getting under way. The valley was nestled among many mountains that resembled the domed peeks of two-dozen hens' eggs.

Mount Crevasse was a special peek among the hills, not only was it the tallest, It was also the place where the tall grass grew at high elevation. Crops could be grown and indigenous trees grew alongside the coniferous. Few places along Mount Crevasse allowed such a clear view of all below. It was as if certain areas had been charred by an intense fire that solidified the earth to solid rock in a perfect circle of at least 100 feet in diameter. It was on one of these outcroppings that Thomas stood.

The curiosity of a twelve-year-old boy could hardly be contained in his little frame. As he twisted his small shepherds' staff in his hand and caressed a purple pebble in the other, he wondered what it would be like to dance, sing and eat of the fruit of the lush mythamöhre trees in the valley below.

It probably didn't taste anything like the harsh corn and beans Thomas' father would prepare for him and his older brothers. Maybe that's why they moved away, thought Thomas. It had been some time since Kale and Harrow lived at home. They were all grown-up and moved away with their own families. Harrow and Kale each made one trip to the valley lowlands on the inaugural trek with the sheep for grazing. His brothers brought their sheep home, but soon returned to the valley. The valley life can't be all bad, otherwise Harrow and Kale wouldn't have chosen to stay there. Even with the new coat of paint Papa pasted on the inside of their home, the warm walls of comfort seemed dry and pale since Mom died and his brothers left.

High from this vantage point Thomas could see the people of the valley. Music was carried up on the winds and whistled around his head: flute, harp and stringed instruments played as the valley people danced. They danced as if there was no tomorrow... full of joy and happiness. This was the kind of happiness that Thomas longed to feel.

The Festival of Harvest was a wonderful time of year. The valley rumors relayed by travelers passing through his village were retold and whispered amongst his friends. The people of the valley gathered the lush plum colored fruit from the mythamöhre trees. They drank its nectar and became drunk with its sweet intoxicating taste. Thomas had never tasted the mythamöhre fruit, but he had heard the stories. He had heard that they had many ways of preparing the mythamöhre fruit and that each concoction tasted slightly different. Thomas' father and the other adults of his village disallowed any stories of the valley. Still there was no stopping Thomas' imagination once it got started.

There was no fruit in the world like the mythamöhre fruit that grew in the valley. The villagers had the best of the land. Queen Aleah Mythamöhre cared for her subjects, that was obvious. Ever since she brought the mythamöhre plant to the valley, the people of the valley never went without. Thomas had been told stories of Queen Aleah Mythamöhre from his grandfather. The stories had been passed down through the generations. Actually, no one could quite remember how long she ruled over the land, they only knew that the land had always prospered under her. Thomas could never make sense of the stories that claimed generations had past since the queen began her rule. The things that didn't make sense, he discounted as fallacy. Thomas reasoned that parents wanting to keep their sons at home tending sheep probably cooked up these stories. Besides, if none of the highland people ventured into the valley - how would they know what was down there? Their stories were never flattering of the Queen or the people of the valley.

The Queen was young, so how could these stories be true? Thomas had seen drawings from the traders passing through the village and there was no way the Queen was older than Thomas himself. She truly was beautiful, with striking dark hair and deep dark eyes that cut straight to a boy's heart. Being attracted to a girl was not something that Thomas would confess to his friends but it was something that he could feel. If his friends were honest, they would probably admit she was the most beautiful girl anyone had ever seen. Thomas believed that even Talia, a girl from the village who played with Thomas and his friends, would probably admit that the Queen was beautiful. Talia wasn't like the other girls of the village always wanting to learn baking, weaving and such. Although she was adventurous, Talia was a sweet girl and if Thomas were pressed to confess, he'd say she was cute too. Thomas thought her attractive features came about suddenly, right around the time he turned twelve. She had the prettiest sparkling green eyes that had a way of reaching inside Thomas' and tickling him. The sun, causing highlights in it, kissed her curly brown hair that fell on her shoulders. She always had a brilliant smile, as white as the newly fallen snow. Thomas admired the way her nose turned up ever so slightly; it was a perfect tiny point in the middle of her face. Thomas would have been embarrassed to admit that he noticed these things more and more about Talia, just in the last year or so. How was it that she had gotten so pretty? Admitting to liking her was out of the question. She was one of the gang. She had beaten a lot of the boys in the village, in a race climbing trees. However it was more than her physical features or ability that appealed to Thomas; she was a gentle and caring person. For a long time after his mother died, none of his other friends knew how to talk with Thomas, but she did. Thomas often reminisced about the conversation they had on this very rock, where he now stood, it played out in Thomas' memory...

"So now what?" Talia probed. Her shoulder length hair falling across her face as the wind picked up.

Thomas threw rocks over the edge and answered without looking at her, "I dunno, I guess Harrow and Kale and their families will go back to the valley and I'm stuck here."

"No, that's not what I mean," said Talia. "All families go back to their own homes after a funeral, did you expect them to stick around?"

"It would be nice if they had stayed around. Mom would have liked them to stay around with me and Papa," shrugged Thomas.

"I mean, now it's up to you, Thomas Jacob Littlewood. Just because you don't have your mother to remind you to do your chores around the house and to wash your grubby face once in awhile," responded Talia, trying to soften the tense mood.

Thomas looked seriously at her. The corners of her lips turned up in a smirk. Thomas laughed and so did she.

"No one likes you smelling like sheep you know, especially girls."

"What makes you think I care about what girls think?"

"I'm a girl."

"Yeah but you're different," Thomas answered quickly and turned to continue throwing pebbles off the cliff.

He hadn't seen that he had hurt Talia with his words. Although he saw her as one of the guys, she hoped that maybe... just maybe he would start seeing her as something more.

"Now who is going to pick up all those pebbles you're throwing off the cliff?" Questioned Talia, as she attempted to change the subject.

The smile that sparked Thomas' memory of that special day with Talia faded and transported him back to the present. He found himself, once again, standing alone overlooking the valley.

If Thomas mentioned to his friends that Talia was cute he would be ridiculed. No, it was safer to like a girl who was unattainable by all, Thomas thought. It was safer to secretly admire a girl like the Queen. His mind began to reason and assure him of his inadequacies, besides, who could care about a shepherd boy? The smell of sheep was always on his clothes. Sure, people may think that the sheep look cute, but try spending every waking hour with them. They "baaed" their complaints for greener pastures, they "baaed" their complaints for water, they "baaed" their complaints at each other and they were constantly "baaing" their complaints at Thomas. The lambs were another matter, they were like a singing chorus of crying babies, annoying. The noise of the sheep was probably the biggest reason for the pastures being so far from the village; essentially they were far enough away that only the shepherds would have to put up with the sheep and their complaints.

The villagers who migrated to the valley were concerned with the welfare of their families. If Thomas had the opportunity to go to the valley, he wouldn't be concerned for his personal welfare; his concern would be for his heart. He wondered if the Queen would see him as he sees her, even in his smelly sheep-herding cloak. He wondered if she could find one so common as he, attractive? Thomas knew that in her eyes, he would pass as a typical mountain shepherd. There was nothing fancy about his linen tunic, sash, trousers, cloak and boots wrapped in cloth for warmth that laced up to just below his knee... nothing fancy at all. Maybe his striking features would make him stand out in her eyes, or at least that's the way he remembered his mother describing him. Thomas knew his mother had to complement him but In his mind the duties of a shepherd made him unattractive, so how could Talia or the Queen see anything of worth in him? He wondered if he would ever have a chance to meet one so majestic as the Queen.

It was the Queen who introduced the Lottery of Affluence as a gift to her loyal subjects. Once the festival drew to a close, a few lucky villagers would have their lot chosen by the Queen. If a family was picked out of the thousands of entrants in the Lottery of Affluence, suddenly everything changed. No more worries for them or their families, no more planting and harvesting, no more smelly sheep; for the winners life would never be the same.

This night marked the beginning of the Festival of Harvest and the Lottery of Affluence. Three days from now, after the people gorged on mythamöhre fruit, drank the nectar and ate the hot baked sugary pies; the chosen would be announced. They would move away to live in the palace and everything would be...

"Thomas!" The voice of his father almost startled Thomas off his rocky perch overlooking the valley.

Thomas quickly slipped the purple pebble into his pocket. As Thomas' father approached, the mountain wind caught his long white hair and it flittered back off his shoulders. His white beard and weathered face made him look older than he really was. Not even Thomas was entirely sure of his father's age. What Thomas didn't realize was that Papa had a deep heartache, which he wore on his face in every crease, but always hid it behind a mask of smiles.

"Papa, I was just... well wondered if... I could..." Thomas looked for the right words to rescue himself from this awkward situation; caught in the act of daydreaming about life in the valley.

"Iso whurleye Ay?" Papa asked Thomas, in the mountain language the old people spoke.

Thomas hated the mountain dialect, it was so old fashioned. Thomas didn't like talking the mountain dialect because he knew anyone with a little education would certainly make fun of it. All the village kids knew it, but no one used it anymore. Thomas wouldn't even use a word of it, even though the advantage of it was that you could communicate more thoughts with fewer words. Thomas pretended that he didn't understand his father.

"Cum sa lat worta," said Papa. "Cum sa lat worta, tooray!"

Thomas looked puzzled at Papa. He knew exactly what Papa was saying but he also knew that when you go down the road a little with a lie it was hard to backtrack and Thomas wasn't about to give in.

Papa waited for an answer. The longer he waited the more it angered him. He knew Thomas was being stubborn, a trait he had shared with his mother. "Cum sa lat worta tooray. Iso whurleye Ay?

Thomas could see Papa's eyes narrow and he knew what that meant but to give in now was not an option.

Papa took a great inhale and slow exhale to expel his frustration. Papa looked out over the valley. He thought the issue of language was not the most important thing to address at the time. Thomas was probably using his defiance to ignore the pressing issue Papa was trying to address. Papa repeated quietly, "Iso whurleye Ay?" He followed his question immediately in the modern common language, "Is there something so wonderful in that valley?"

Thomas knew that the wrong answer would mean extra chores but the real answer would lead to punishment. Papa always knew when Thomas was lying. It was almost as if he could see right through him with his piercing brown eyes. Papa moved closer to Thomas, close enough for Thomas to smell the distinct smell of his dad: cinnamon and smoke. Papa tended to so many cooking fires since mother died that the smell of the firewood became a permanent part of him. His love of chewing on cinnamon sticks kept his breath minty fresh but the sweetness of it made Thomas' nose twitch.

To avoid eye-contact, Thomas darted his eyes looking for an answer and began to rub his hands as if he was scrubbing them clean.

"Papa why would you think I am wishing that I was in the valley at... at... at the Festival Of Harvest?" Thomas always tripped over his words when he would find himself caught in a bad situation.

Papa's eyes softened and he put his big hands on Thomas' shoulders. Thomas could feel the warmth of his hand through the rough linen section of his wool trimmed cloak.

"Come with me boy," Papa said

Papa led Thomas away from the ledge and back into the high grasslands.

"Run your hand through the grass my son."

Thomas looked puzzled for a moment. Papa took Thomas' hand in his and ever so gently guided it with his across the top of the waste high grass. The wisps of the grass tickled Thomas' palms as they brushed by.

"Do you feel that Thomas?" He asked.

Thomas nodded his head and his father knelt on one knee before him.

"Close your eyes my son... go on and close your eyes." Papa closed his eyes and Thomas followed.

"I want you to imagine the very best things in this world..." Papa said with great concern and confidence.

Thomas closed his eyes and began to daydream. As he dreamt, his father's voice faded and so did the music from the Harvest Festival. He dreamt of playing adventure games with his friends and… and… he dreamt of dancing under a mythamöhre tree with... "NO" Thomas thought and as he stopped himself, Papa's voice became clear again.

"See all the good things that have been given us. You know that Mount Crevasse is the only mountain where crops grow in abundance and tall grass reaches to your waist. These are the good things we have," assured Papa.

Slowly but surely Thomas' mind began to drift off again. His mind went to the lush plum-shaped-fruit that he had seen in the flyers that the traders would sometime bring to the village. Then Thomas thought of the Lottery of Affluence celebration that ended the Festival. Oh, if he could only win that, he'd have the grandest adventure of them all and he'd never have to tend to smelly old sheep again.

No, Thomas thought and quickly his mind raced to the image of his mother. She was so kind and warm, loving and giving. He couldn't really see her face in his imagination anymore but he could still remember her smell. Like the last flower of summer lingered in memory, to him she always smelt like wild flowers in the spring and her hand was so soft. Sometimes the smell of lilacs would fill the air and he imagined his mother was near. He definitely could still feel her hand on his face as she gently stroked his cheek every night before bed.

"Goodnight my Little Falcon", she would say.

That was her name for him and also their secret: Little Falcon. Thomas smiled, how he wished she was still with them... Mom would understand the desires of his heart.

Suddenly tears formed in Thomas' eyes and rolled down his cheeks like the rain on a window pane, spilling over on Papa's hand. Papa opened his eyes to the drips of Thomas' tears.

Papa spoke softly, "Thomas my son, all we have been given and all we possess today, is because we have a thankful heart. A thankful heart will help you find favor in life. Success will not come by unreasonable expectations of winning a chance lottery. I hope you understand."

Thomas nodded his head but knew that Papa didn't understand that he had been thinking about his mother. It would have been cruel to tell him. Papa loved her more than life itself. Thomas knew that admitting to it would only bring his father pain. So he kept his thoughts to himself. Thomas also played along with his Papa but at times he let his philosophy get in the way of his feelings. He knew his Papa meant well but why rub his hands through the grass and think of such things?

The orange glow of the setting sun was painting the skies above it with a ribbon of pink, purple and pale blue. The air had suddenly turned colder and brisker.

"Time to gather the herd and bring them back to the village before night," said Papa.

"Your daydreaming of the valley has let your flock wander close to the upper mountain pass," he said as he pointed to Thomas' sheep in the distance.

Thomas knew the stories about the upper mountain pass: treacherous, twisting roads that lead to the highest points of Mount Crevasse and the caves of the mountain giants. No one from the village that had ventured to the highest points had ever returned and no one who had ventured into the valley from the village had ever returned either. Maybe, Thomas thought, it was because they had found everything they'd ever wanted. All their dreams came true and the beautiful Queen Aleah Mythamöhre generously provided everything for her loyal subjects.

Suddenly Papa ran his hand through Thomas thick curly brown shoulder length hair and ruffled it. Thomas snapped out of his daydream and smiled back at him.

"Hurry boy... we're losing the day," Papa said with a smile that deepened the creases around his eyes.

Papa's wink set Thomas dashing off to gather the flock. Papa had given Thomas his own herd to watch, and Thomas knew them all by name and they knew him. All Thomas would have to do is make the strange clucking sound with his throat, a trick that Papa taught him, and his sheep would come running.

Thomas ran through the meadow as quickly as his feet would carry him. He stretched his staff across his shoulders and dreamt for a moment that he was a bird flying, swooping in and out 'round and 'round, catching the updraft to lift him higher. If he could fly, he would fly to a better place and forget this life that had been handed to him.

"Thomas! The sheep!" his father yelled.

Thomas swung his staff around properly and began to make the clucking sound with his throat. His charge knew the sound. They knew it meant come to their master. Thomas gathered his sheep to his side, each "baaed" and pushed each other into place as they drew near to him. They had all huddled under a grand old oak tree that never grew leaves. Papa called that old oak tree the 'Brooding Place' because it looked as if it was always sad. Maybe it was sad because it stood alone at the foot of the mountain pass? Maybe it was sad because it had no say in where it was planted? The seed was dropped there and now it was bound by its roots to stay. Who could be happy with that? Its branches reached out in twisted form, as if it was reaching to the sunlight, but without leaves, it never realized its goal. Somehow this old oak tree lived without coming to bloom. It would get a few leaves at the start of spring but before any other tree would bloom, it would drop all of its leaves. One might say the elevation was just too high to grow an oak tree. If the leaves nurture a tree, how was it that this tree grew? It was not worth thinking about because the answer was too scary to imagine: witchcraft. One time Thomas cut into the tree with a sharp stone and sap poured out as if it was alive. This was a curious sight and gave credence to the bewitched rumor that Thomas had been accustomed to. No one went by that tree except for Thomas' crazy sheep. Everyone in the village knew why, and so did Thomas. The rumor was that the village Gatekeeper was a mystic who through enchantment cursed the tree. The mountain pass beyond the tree led to a cruel place where evil lurked around every corner. Wolves lived in the caves up there and so did the mountain giants. It was a place that a little boy like Thomas was in danger. A Nephilim giant could cook him for dinner and gobble him up. It was rumored the Nephilim had a taste for human flesh. Thomas didn't believe those fairy tales and superstitions for one second but he kept a sharp eye open, just in case.

Thomas had assured himself that it was just another old-timer's story to keep mischievous boys like him at home. A story designed to keep the boys working because it was free labor for the elders of the village. It was a way of keeping their old values alive. Thomas gave as much credit to these stories as he did to the whispered fables of the valley, that the Queen was really evil. Unlikely thought Thomas, they're just jealous. Eventually he would be old enough to take the sheep to the lowland. It was the right of passage every young man would take. If the young man returned from the valley, he was worthy... another foolish superstition, thought Thomas.

"Come now you dumb sheep," Thomas demanded and the sheep appeared to listen. They made their usual 'baas' in what seemed like protest, but nevertheless they organized themselves and followed the leader to Thomas' side.

"Good that you should listen to me, sheep," Thomas said sternly. "You are off under that old tree and nothing good can come of it. Probably dreaming of better pastures," Thomas mocked doing his best to imitate his father's deep voice. The sheep happily tagged along not taking any notice of Thomas' reprimand.

"And to think that I lead you to this pasture yet you continually embarrass me by going to the foot of the mountain path under that old oak tree, while my father's sheep are so well behaved they stay within sight of him. Why can't you sheep be more like them?" Alas, Thomas was to get no answer. The sheep merrily joined the others as they all journeyed back to the village.

The village lay nestled amongst century old evergreen trees. Tall and majestic pine, which always gave the village a welcoming scent. Beds of pine needles lined the pathways around and through the village.

As Thomas and Papa entered the village with their sheep, Thomas thought to himself, how boring, nothing in this village ever changes.

People were busy finishing their daily chores as Thomas, Papa and the flock came in. From the other corners of the village, shepherds entered with their flocks. Soon they would all be mixed together, safely protected in the towns corral.

By this time, they had passed each of Thomas' friend's homes. Stone and thatch houses gave the village an earthy, welcoming feel. Thomas looked around for a sign of one of his friends, but no one was outside. Aaron's mother was banging a carpet with a broom, Jason's front door was closed. They were probably having supper. Jason's father grew vegetables and other greens that the village would make use of.

Thomas and Papa herded the sheep past Samuel's house, he was Thomas' best friend and they shared everything, hopes, dreams, adventures and all secrets, except for Talia. Thomas couldn't bring himself to tell Samuel he thought she was pretty but they could share their love for the Queen. This feeling about girls was a new and exciting emotion Thomas had. He was glad he had the courage to tell Samuel about it and discover that he also had discovered girls were appealing. Not something either of them would admit to anyone else. Thomas didn't take long wondering why his friends were not out. This was actually a stroke of luck, since their usual greeting always included poking fun at him for having to help his father with livestock. They were just lucky their fathers had other professions that kept them out of the fields tending to animals.

As Thomas and his father approached the center of the village he could see the Gatekeeper standing on some boxes watching the sheep and shepherds file past. He stood with his staff in hand and his heavy linen hooded cloak over his head. The explanation that Papa had given Thomas was that the Gatekeeper wore the hood to keep the sun off by day and the cold out by night. Thomas could not believe the rumors that he had fallen into a fire and as a result, his face was hideously burnt. Thomas thought that maybe he wore the hood because the Gatekeeper was probably just old and ugly.

The Gatekeeper watched as Thomas, Papa and the sheep passed on their way into the pen. Thomas peeked at the Gatekeeper through the corner of his eye. Thomas could see the Gatekeeper's head turn as they passed... he knew the Gatekeeper was watching, he could feel it. Thomas had not looked long enough at the Gatekeeper before to admire how the setting sun caught the fibers of his cloak, picking up flecks of deep purple and royal blue in the seemingly otherwise dark cloth. Thomas started picturing how funny the gatekeeper probably looked under his hood. Thomas' imagination ran wild as he exaggerated facial features making the Gatekeeper's appearance quite comical. Thomas laughed out loud, at the image he had conjured up.

All the shepherds and Papa stopped and looked at Thomas. Thomas' face turned red. He took a quick glance to see if the Gatekeeper was watching him. He was. Thomas returned to helping his father with the last of the sheep.

The sheep entered the pen and seemed as happy here as they did under the old oak tree by the mountain pass. Sheep can be stupid like that, Thomas thought.

The Gatekeeper nodded as Thomas and his father passed by on their way out of the pen. The warm setting sunlight caught the corner of the Gatekeeper's hood and the edge of his mouth with a sliver of light.

Was he smiling? Thomas thought he saw the corner of the Gatekeeper's mouth turned up in a smile... then again... maybe not. The Gatekeeper's head kept in perfect timing with Thomas' passing and Thomas knew it. He hurried up and caught up to his father. The Gatekeeper gave Thomas the creeps and it made the hair stand up on the back of his neck. Thomas knew that the Gatekeeper would be watching him and his Papa as they entered their thatched-roof home. The Gatekeeper was mysterious.

Once inside his home, Thomas ran directly to his bed. Feeling around under his bed amongst the simple wooden toys was his treasure box. Thomas pulled out his treasure box with great excitement.

Papa smiled as he placed his staff in the corner of the room and sat on the little stool by the door to brush the dirt from his boots. Thomas knew Mother would have preferred he would have done that outside but Papa was practical, why stop twice when once will do. Papa removed his cloth strap boots but kept his eye on Thomas.

"Something new for the collection?" Papa quizzed. Papa reached in his pocket and pulled out a tiny purple pebble... but he kept it hidden in his hand.

"New!" Thomas proclaimed. "Have you ever seen one like this?" Thomas pulled the tiny purple pebble out of his pocket and held it up to show his father.

"I'm sure Samuel and the boys have never seen a pebble like this. I'm sure it is the only one in all the land, and I have it. Jason may boast of his collection, Aaron would tell me he has seen a better one and Samuel would pull out all of his beauties from his collection he carries in his satchel, but I would dare to tell my friends that none can compare with this!"

Papa smiled and slipped the purple pebble he had concealed in his hand, back into his pocket.

"Oh my, Thomas, that is beautiful! Obviously you have something very special, " said Papa.

Thomas' grin carried from ear to ear.

"Are you going to give this one to Samuel?" Papa asked.

Thomas thought about it for a moment before he answered.

"I gave him the black pebble with the emerald stripe running through it... I think this one I would like to keep for myself."

"Perfectly fine, you should have one in your collection that is special to you. Now wash up for supper and set the table. Let's celebrate your finding with a special dinner. After that, we'll examine your collection together."

The burning wood crackled in the fireplace. The room smelt of Papa's homemade stew and Mrs. Keel's homemade bread. Since Thomas' mom had died, Mrs. Keel was the widow neighbor who provided Papa and Thomas with homemade bread. Thomas thought Papa and Mrs. Keel might be fancy on each other. He thought Papa always acted a little different around her and she would blush at Papa's compliments about her baking.

As they sat down, Papa bowed his head and gave thanks for the food. It was a good supper. Papa and Thomas laughed and joked together. The fire gave a warm glow to the room as the outside world continued to get darker as evening fell. The night crickets sang outside the window and Thomas loved every second of this time with his Papa. Little did Thomas know that this memory would have to last him for many years to come.

Chapter Three
INTO THE NIGHT

Thomas lay still in his bed. The covers pulled up to his neck and tucked in tightly by Papa, Thomas dare not move. If he moved, that would ruin Papa's 'tuck-in' and then he was guaranteed an awful night sleep. The last time he ruined the tuck, Thomas tossed and turned all night.

Thomas couldn't figure out what was wrong. Here he was wide-awake. Looking through the crack in the shutter, through the wobbly glass window that seemed to make all the stars in the night sky have an unusual glow to them. It was the same kind of glow that a person would experience by squinting his eyes just enough to blur things so they lose their definition. Thomas liked that look, and would often do that while he was out tending his sheep; the edges looked softer on the rocks, the trees, and the clouds. Tonight was an exception to the tuck-in rule. Normally if Papa tucked him in like this, he was sound-a-sleep in no time, but for some reason tonight was different.

Thomas turned his head enough to see Papa across the dark room. He really didn't have to do that, because Papa's snoring sounded like a grizzly bears growl.

Tap… Tap… Tap…

Thomas turned his head to the sound. It was coming from outside his window.

Tap… Tap… Tap…

Thomas looked back across the room. Papa was still sleeping. Didn't he hear the sound outside the window? Surely whoever was tapping outside of his window could hear the grizzly bear that lived in Thomas' house!

Tap... Tap... Tap...

Thomas wriggled his hand out from his side and sat up in bed on his elbows. The back of Thomas' neck was wet from lying perfectly still in one position for what Thomas assumed that must have been hours. A rush of cool air against Thomas's body gave him the shivers that his thin nightshirt didn't protect him from.

Thomas looked over at Papa, "Still asleep," he whispered, half-attempting to wake his father from his slumber.

Thomas turned his attention to the window. He moved further out of the covers, much like a house cat would cautiously approach its prey; Thomas approached the window. Suddenly as Thomas put his eye up to the crack of the shutter to peek out...

Tap... Tap... Tap...

Thomas fell completely out of his bed with a crash on the floor.

Papa gave out a loud snort and turned on his side to face the wall. Papa's snoring always stopped when he lay on his side.

Thomas got to his feet and peeked through the window again. Through the wobbly glass, there in the starry-moonlit-night... stood a figure. The figure started walking away from the window and turned again to face it. The figure motioned with his hand to come. Thomas jumped back from the window.

"How did he know I was peeking at him? " Thomas whispered out-loud.

Thomas ran across the room and made a flying leap for his Papa's bed. Papa sprang straight up as if he was rebounding off a trampoline.

"Thomas Jacob Littlewood, what in the world are you doing!?" Papa demanded.

Thomas could imagine Papa's piercing eyes expecting an answer, even in the dark.

Thomas sat up in Papa's bed and began to wring his hands together, "I... well...." Thomas mumbled.

"Speak up," insisted Papa.

"I dreamt... no I heard... I... I saw someone outside my window calling me... and..."

Papa held up his hand stopping Thomas in mid sentence.

"I would prefer if you went to bed and went to sleep now," Papa said sternly.

"But, but, Papa..." Thomas stammered.

"Son," Papa continued in a softer, calmer tone, "You were only dreaming. There is no one outside, no one under the bed and no one in the closet. It was only a bad dream. Weren't you telling me that you're brave enough to take the flock to the lowland pasture?"

Thomas shivered, took a deep breath and nodded. Thomas got up from Papa's bed and began to head back to his own. Papa thought for a moment and then called Thomas back. He felt Thomas' forehead to see if he had a fever from a sickness that would explain Thomas' unusual actions. Yet there was no fever.

"Sorry Papa I am brave enough," Thomas pleaded.

Papa softened as he saw his youngest boy trying to be a man. "If there is someone lurking outside, perhaps I would feel more secure if you spent the night with me... but I want you to know that I am brave too, it's just better if we sleep back to back. No one can sneak up on us that way." Papa said encouragingly. He pulled back his covers, "That is, if you don't mind, but let's make a pact that no one else will know about this... because we both are truly brave."

Thomas nodded as if he was doing his father a favor. He slipped in his father's bed and they positioned themselves back to back. Soon they were both fast asleep.

In some cultures there is an old saying, 'curiosity killed the cat.' In Thomas' case, it was much more than curiosity that drew him... it was destiny.

Some time later, Thomas opened his eyes. Papa was sleeping soundly, but not snoring, probably because he was sleeping on his side. The bed was warm and comfortable, yet something bothered Thomas. Something was strange and out of place. It was the absence of all sound that woke him.

The room was eerily silent. Strangely enough, even the night crickets that could normally be heard outside the window were not chirping. Thomas wondered if he was dreaming that he was awake. He pinched his own arm. Sure enough, he was awake.

Thomas took a deep breath and knew he had to investigate these strange phenomena. Not wanting to wake his father he carefully slid out of his Papa's bed. Thomas inched his way across the cold stone floor that sent shivers up from the sole of his feet to his pounding anxious heart. He moved toward the window by his bed. To look out that window by his bed, it required he crawl across the bed. The sheets were cool to the touch. Thomas' nightshirt was not made for crawling. It always got caught under his knees when he crawled. He pulled his nightshirt up so it didn't catch under his knees.

Thomas reasoned that he must had been sleeping for quite some time, though it seemed only moments ago, he had crawled into his father's bed.

Thomas slowly moved his eye to the crack in the shutter and peered through the wobbly windowpane, across the garden. There in the still silent moonlit night, sitting on the big rock at the end of the garden was the cloaked figure that beckoned him to come.

Thomas quickly slipped off his bed and back onto the cold stone floor. The pounding of his heart was clearly audible in his ears. He paused for a moment and looked around the room. What to do, he thought. Should he wake his father to help, or face his fear on his own? He was determined to prove to his Papa that he was not afraid of anything. Everything inside him was screaming stop... but his body moved on. If he is to get any sleep tonight he would have to find out who it was that was tapping on his window and sitting on the rock. It was probably one of his foolish friends playing a cruel joke. They would all laugh at him tomorrow for being a 'fraidy-cat.'

Making his way to the big wooden front door of his home, Thomas unlatched it. The door creaked as it opened on its rusty hinges. Thomas looked back but Papa didn't move. Thomas left his home and the security of being inside with Papa, behind.

Thomas decided that it would be far too dangerous to approach the dark figure straight on, just in case it wasn't one of his friends playing a joke. Thomas decided to sneak around the berry shrubs beside the old fence and around the garden to get a closer look at this mysterious figure.

The damp grass was squishy between Thomas' toes as he crouched low and rounded the side of his house. The distance between the house and the old fence was at least four staff long.

The bright moonlight would expose his every move, so he would have to crawl the distance on his belly. It was his only hope of reaching the fence undetected by the veiled figure sitting on the rock.

Thomas wasn't sure what drove him on. Only moments ago he was safe and sound beside Papa in bed, but now, here in the cool night... there was no turning back. He had something to prove and that meant only going forward. If he had the courage to come this far, he could muster the courage to go all the way.

The night was void of all sound, it was surreal: not a cricket, not a lamb, not the goats penned down the lane, not even the wind rustling through the leaves. Safely approaching this figure was a perplexing problem that required the best of Thomas' skills. Thomas decided that what he needed to proceed undetected, was a diversion. For a moment his thoughts were distracted to the weight of the item in his nightshirt pocket.

Thomas reached in and pulled out his purple pebble. That's it! He'll throw the pebble and the sound will attract the figure. His heart was heavy at the thought of making that sacrifice. He admired his special purple pebble in the moonlight. It shimmered with every turn between his fingers. Thomas squinted his eyes to make it glow and to admire its beauty without its form. Thomas heard movement from the direction of the mysterious figure. Thomas believed the figure was coming toward him. He knew it was no longer an option, a diversion was necessary to make his escape; he had to sacrifice his pebble in order to survive.

He knew he could delay no longer; he closed his eyes and lobbed the pebble in the direction of the sheep's pen. The rock was up in the air and Thomas took off making a mad dash for the garden fence. He didn't even stop to hear if the rock landed. He was already on the far side of the fence and around the back of the garden. Crawling on his hands and knees, the soil felt damp and slightly soft, sucking him in place.

Just a few more feet and he would be close enough to identify the figure on the rock. Suddenly the brush rustled ahead. Thomas dropped to his belly and covered his head. He was trapped and he knew it. He felt a gentle nudge on his shoulder. Thomas thought that if he lay perfectly still the shadow figure would think he was dead. With another nudge on Thomas' shoulder, a whispered voice spoke to him. "Come Thomas, get dressed, we must talk," the voice said.

He knows my name, Thomas thought.

And with that, Thomas opened his eyes and found himself staring straight at the ceiling above his bed.

Thomas quickly sat up and discovered he was perfectly tucked in, just like Papa had left him. It had been a dream after all, nothing more. Thomas smiled at the thought, what a silly thing to dream about.

Thomas looked across the room. Although not much more than shapes in the dark could be made out, he could certainly hear Papa and his snoring. Thomas thought it wise to get up and peek though the shutters because Papa always said to him, 'face your fear son and you will find that you are stronger than they are.'

Thomas wasted no time throwing off the covers and hopping out of bed, only to find his nightshirt and his knees covered in brown dirt. He took only a moment to catch his breath and muster his courage. It was not a dream. He really had been outside. This time he wasn't even going to wake his father; he was heading out to face his fears.

Thomas took off his soiled nightshirt and put on his cloak and knee-high laced boots. He lifted both his staff and his father's staff and compared the weight in his hands. Papa staff had the bigger clubbing nub, and would make a better weapon. Thomas swung it as if to strike an invisible foe. It would be his Papa's staff that he took.

Thomas felt in the dark for the front door latch of his home. He found the latch but paused to look at his father and whispered before opening the door.

"You'll be proud of my courage."

Deep down he knew one cry for help and his Papa would be bolting out of bed to his aid.

Thomas carefully opened the old creaky door allowing the sounds of the night air to fill the room: crickets, frogs, sheep and the sound of the wind rustling through the trees. The moonlight streaming in the door illuminated Papa perfectly as he slept soundly. Thomas reassured himself by reasoning that his nightshirt was soiled when he had put it on. Thomas felt proud of himself. He would face his fears and it would prove to be nothing. Thomas looked back on his sleeping Papa.

"He looks so peaceful," Thomas whispered to himself.

"Yes he does," a voice whispered back.

Thomas jumped with a start and readied Papa's staff in his hand.

In the doorway stood the Gatekeeper.

"Shhh, your father needs his rest," said the Gatekeeper.

Thomas lowered his Papa's staff.

"What are you doing?" Thomas forcefully demanded in a whisper.

"You're missing a lamb," responded the Gatekeeper.

"Missing a lamb?" Questioned Thomas. "Did it escape?"

Thomas somehow knew the answer to that question before he asked.

Thomas quickly shot back to the Gatekeeper, "Because if it escaped, my Papa would be very angry at you for not doing your duty."

"Your Papa gets angry at someone who doesn't do their duty?" Queried the Gatekeeper.

"Well... ye...yes," stammered Thomas as the words tripped out of his mouth.

"I see," whispered the Gatekeeper.

Thomas looked back in the room to see if Papa had heard the conversation with the Gatekeeper. The Gatekeeper standing in the doorway blocked the moonlight and made it was considerably darker in the room, so Thomas could no longer make out Papa's form on the bed.

"There is no looking back to where you've been, it's time to look ahead," said the Gatekeeper.

Thomas turned to the Gatekeeper. "You're right... I'm not a little boy any more, I can handle this business myself. Take me to the pen and let us count the sheep together," Thomas said boldly. "You'll be glad that you didn't wake Papa if we find that you've miscounted," Thomas added with a saucy tone.

The Gatekeeper said nothing; rather he turned and walked toward the sheep pen. Thomas stepped out of the hut and closed the door behind him. He was tempted to take one last look at Papa but he was determined to prove his maturity to the Gatekeeper by not looking back.

The mountain breeze rustled though the leaves and through Thomas' hair as he walked tall. Thomas was going to show this Gatekeeper that he was a man and could handle a man's business. As they reached the pen, Thomas thought that the lambs seemed restless.

"Go ahead and count and see if the littlest is not missing," said the Gatekeeper. Thomas counted them twice and sure enough, one was missing.

"If you knew one was missing why didn't you tell us earlier?" Thomas questioned. The Gatekeeper slowly turned his hooded head toward Thomas. Thomas knew he was looking at him although he couldn't see his eyes because of the Gatekeepers hood which hung well over his face. The Gatekeeper let out a sigh, not the type of sigh you hear when someone is frustrated, but the kind of sigh that goes along with a smile. Much like a sigh a parent makes when a child does something foolish.

"Well fine then, I'll just go and wake up Papa," said Thomas.

The Gatekeeper shook his head no and this stopped Thomas mid sentence. "Are you suggesting?... " Thomas' response was again cut short, this time by the Gatekeeper's interruption.

"A good shepherd takes care of his own flock," said the Gatekeeper as he put his hand on Thomas' shoulder. Thomas looked at the Gatekeeper's hand and drooped his shoulder to let the Gatekeeper's hand slide off. Thomas turned and took note of the sheep again. Sure enough, the one missing was the smallest and in Thomas' care as they grazed in the highlands by the brooding tree.

Thomas didn't look back at the Gatekeeper nor at Papa's house, he just turned and walked off into the night with his Papa's staff in hand, determined to retrieve the lamb that was in his charge. As Thomas walked away he said, "Please don't tell Papa I've gone, I'll return before long."

"You will," said the Gatekeeper as he watched Thomas walk over the crest of the hill and beyond the village boundary. "You will," the Gatekeeper repeated to himself in a whisper as he removed a purple pebble from his pocket... the very rock that Thomas had pitched into the pen of sheep.

AT THE ALLEN ROOM PRESS CONFERENCE:

Dr. Elderidge leaned his forearms on the podium as he read the second fragment.

#
FRAGMENT TWO
-- next great thing - life - react - adventure - day to day --
****

IN THE KING'S CHAMBER:

The scribe put down his quill and massaged his hand. He noticed the King was watching him. "I apologize your highness, my hand seems to be cramping."

"We will cover what must be said," assured the King. "If your life is worth living then it is one that is worth sharing and if that takes time, so be it."

"Was the identity of the mystic revealed to you? Are we coming to the point of your first encounter with the Nephilim?" The scribe looked away and asked the next question in an offhanded way, "Did you meet Nine around this time?" The scribe stole a look at the King for his response. When the scribe saw there was no reaction from the King, he was relieved.

"All things in order, carefully and surely we will cover what must be said because there is importance in it all. If any one part matters, then we must consider that each part has its value," replied the King.

The scribe sat knowing he had asked good questions, particularly the question about Nine. It was a risky question but it was a risk he was driven to take.

The King stood and walked behind his ornate chair and looked at the scribe. The scribe caught his inference and picked up the quill again.

"My encounter with Nine would eventually come in the most unassuming way. Just what you might expect from a deceptive creature of his sort."

The scribe swallowed hard and changed the subject quickly, "Are the Nephilim as big as everyone says? I've heard the tallest one spotted was 15 feet!"

The King smiled and continued, "I've often wondered if people knew about the next great thing in their life, how would they react?

The scribe caught the King's inference to continue and he picked up his quill.

"I can look back as I often do and see how I went along in life just day to day. I will admit that sometimes I wished something would happen just for the adventure of it. Little did I know..."

Chapter Four
THE ASCENT

As Thomas rounded the crest of the hill that lay on the boundary of his village, he wondered if the revelers were still celebrating the Festival of Harvest at this late hour. The prospect of seeing them at night when no one would know he was watching was thrilling. Thomas reasoned that first he would find the lamb, then he would take his time on the return and just sit by the ledge to watch the celebrations.

Thomas had it all planned and no one would be smarter for it. This was a great opportunity. A smile crossed his face as Thomas admired his own ingenuity of turning misfortune into fortune. The crickets and bullfrogs serenaded his journey out of the woods and into the high grasslands. Thomas hadn't noticed that clouds began to roll in, dark storm clouds.

Thomas took a moment to pause at the ledge overlooking the valley and the Festival of Harvest. Thomas wasn't sure what time it was but surely it was some time around midnight. Thomas could tell by the position of the moon in the sky. Papa had told him that the moon also made an arc across the sky like the sun and one could tell how far into the night it was by the position of the moon.

In the valley the revelers had not slowed down, in fact, it seemed as if the action had picked up. The dancing was now wild. Frightening screams rose from the valley floor. Thomas thought better of staying around now, he'd have time to watch the activities later. Right now he needed to find that lamb.

If Thomas had stayed just a few minutes longer, he would have witnessed silence fall upon the revelers as the mythamöhre trees began to glow and blossom.

Thomas made his way through the tall grass and up to the base of the brooding tree where he had left the sheep earlier that same day. There, Thomas stood and watched the barren brooding tree blow in the wind. It seemed as if its branches could come alive at any moment and grab an unsuspecting passer-by. That thought frightened Thomas but he wasn't about to let it show. His Papa had once warned him about venturing too high on the mountain because dangerous man-eating wolves were known to frequent the area. Thomas remembered what he told his Papa when he heard that story and he whispered it to himself to boost his own courage, "I may be scared on the inside but I am not scared on the outside."

"Baa... Baa..." the distressed sound of a little lamb came to Thomas' ear.

He looked around hoping to catch sight of the lamb.

"Baa... Baa..." the sound carried on the mountain breeze that sent a chill up Thomas' back.

Thomas looked up the mountain and knew where the sound of the lamb was coming from. In that moment of decision, that second where you can turn around and ignore what you've heard, or follow your heart; Thomas decided to follow his heart and go after the lamb.

This little lamb was his responsibility and Thomas knew it. Rescuing the lamb was the perfect way to prove his readiness to protect the flock in the lowlands?

Thomas kept his eye on the winding ascending path that went up beyond the brooding tree. At this altitude vegetation was sparse. It was usually dry but when it rained he had heard that the trail became slick and dangerous. Thomas climbed the narrowing rocky path and called out to the little lamb using his clucking noise that he made with this throat.

He had never been this high on the path before. As he climbed, the valley and everything below looked much smaller. He was quite familiar with the stories Papa told him about Mount Crevasse and its dangers. Papa told him of the wolves that traveled from one range to another along this trail. He told him of the Mountain Giants that lived in the higher altitudes and served in Queen Aleah's Royal army.

"They are a ruthless and vicious lot," Papa would say... and the sound of Papa's words echoed in Thomas' mind as he carefully navigated his footing on the path.

Thomas climbed higher, as the wind picked up and the storm clouds moved in. The clouds were intermittently blocking the moonlight. Flashes of lightning bloomed in the distance and thunder rumbled.

Maybe coming after this lamb was foolish, Thomas thought. If the lamb is stupid enough to come this far and not come to him by now, then maybe it wasn't worth saving, Thomas reasoned.

"Thomas was a brave boy, he rescued the lamb all by himself" Thomas narrated to himself and thought of Papa saying those exact words.

"Baa... Baa..." the sounds of the lamb reverberated along the mountaintops.

The echo confused Thomas and he wasn't sure just where the sound was coming from. Thomas made some more clucking sounds with his throat... but his clucking sounds reverberated also and the noise was bouncing all around him.

The air suddenly turned ice cold and then with a loud bang, it started to rain. Not a light sprinkle, it was as if the belly of heaven had been split open and all of the water that ever was kept in the clouds came pouring out. This high up on the mountain pass there was nowhere to hide. HIs options were to turn around and disappoint Papa, or going a little further and retrieve the lamb to prove his bravery. Surely the lamb can't be too much farther, Thomas thought. How in the world could a little lamb make it all the way up here by himself anyway, was it part mountain goat? Maybe something was hunting the lamb that caused it to retreat up this path. Thomas dismissed the thought of meeting whatever may have driven the lamb up this trail because it frightened him.

It didn't take long for Thomas' clothes to become drenched. Flashes of lightning sparked up the sky and lit every corner of every rock around Thomas. The path he followed became muddy and slick. One wrong move and he could fall thousands of feet down the cliff. It was dangerous and Thomas knew it. Every step was taken with caution because they became unsure. Thomas started to jam his Papa's staff into the ground for extra stability. Knowing that it was his Papa's staff brought him comfort.

It was extremely dark now. The rain pounded and ran into Thomas' eyes making it difficult for him to see. His own fears argued with him but he knew there was no turning back. His heart began to pound protest and with his every step it shouted, "there is no going forward, you'll never make it!"

Suddenly, in a flash of lightning Thomas saw something just ahead coming toward him. It looked low to the ground but made no sound. Could be the lamb he wondered. Then in a second flash of lighting he saw it briefly... baring fangs at him as if to defy him to take one more step. It was a wolf!

The rain pounded down on them and Thomas readied Papa's staff. The wolf wanted to get by Thomas and Thomas hadn't the choice... he couldn't move on the slippery path. Thomas thought maybe he would speak in a soft reassuring voice to the wolf and the wolf would know he meant it no harm.

"You're probably a mom protecting your young... I understand... I just want to continue up the mountain and find my little one too," Thomas said with a smile on the outside.

The wolf could smell his fear. The wolf snarled and lowered her tail and head.

"You must have young pups around here... in a den somewhere," Thomas offered.

The wolf's growl cut Thomas short.

"Listen to me. I don't want to fight you. I... I.. I'm really good with this staff," Thomas said as he clumsily spun it around in his hands trying to look impressive. Unfortunately the wolf was not impressed.

Thomas tried to take a step back, but his footing slipped and he quickly steadied himself. The sudden move made the wolf edgy. The mud on the mountain ledge was becoming like a sheet of ice.

Too tired to go on, Thomas knew he would not escape without a fight. Thomas readied Papa's staff. The wolf lowered itself on its haunches and lunged. Thomas ducked to the left and held his staff out to block the wolf, but slipped and fell slamming his head hard against a rock.

The rain poured in buckets and lightning flashed in fury on the side of Mount Crevasse that night.

The last image in Thomas' eyes before he blacked out was the wolf in mid air, eyes full of hate, jaws opened with razor sharp teeth coming straight at him.

Chapter Five
UP FOR ADVENTURE

The thunder and lightening woke Talia out of a peaceful sleep. She slipped out of her bed and ventured out of her room. She could see that her parents were woken by the thunder also but their bedroom door was only opened a crack. A lamp from their room told her they were awake. There was a chance she could escape without them knowing she was gone, if she was careful she thought.

Talia loved the rain and even though her parents would scold her for being up, she had to go and see it for herself. There was a special spot where she, Thomas and Samuel hung out in the rain, just to watch it. Tonight, Talia was interested in the light show. She slipped on an outer cloak and boots and carefully opened her door to venture out into the storm.

The air was electric with flashes of lightening all around her. She could see through the tree-line clearing, toward the cloud covered peek of Mount Crevasse that the storm was severe up there. She slightly jogged through the damp grass as she made her way to the tiny cave that was just below the outcrop that she and Thomas liked. It was a place they could safely use to talk about family and friends. It was one of her favorite places, where deep secrets of the soul didn't seem to matter.

Talia got into the cave just as the rain picked up in sheets, lightening flashed. Talia took off her cloak and shook the water from it. Her body was silhouetted in the mouth of the cave that overlooked the valley by a great flash of lightning behind her.

"Great view," came Samuel's voice from the darkness.

Talia jumped, thinking she was alone.

"Samuel, what are you doing here?" She asked.

"Appreciating the view," he replied slowly.

Talia caught his inference and it made her uncomfortable.

"I like the rain," Talia said.

"I know you do, that's why I'm here," replied Samuel.

"Is Thomas with you?"

"Nope, just me," he said.

"Won't your mom and dad get mad at you for being out here?" She asked. She knew she was skirting around a touchy subject with Samuel, but the words were out of her mouth before she could take them back.

"I could ask you the same thing," he replied.

Samuel walked closer and took his cloak off and threw it around Talia.

"I could smell the storm brewing in the air tonight, so I came out to our spot," Samuel said.

Talia knew that was the story he was telling her but the truth was that his father had probably drank too much and was in an angry mood again. She knew that about Samuel and she felt sorry for him.

"You must have been here for a long while, your cloak is dry," Talia said.

"Like I said, I have a nose for these things and I can smell a storm in the air when they are brewing, so I automatically come out here," Samuel replied with a smile.

Talia knew he was also talking about the storm in his home.

"I'm really good a building campfires, let me build you one and we can watch the storm together," Samuel said.

Talia sat down on some rocks and waited while Samuel collected firewood. Talia saw how there was a pile of firewood in the cave, which only confirmed her suspicions that Samuel spent a lot of time out here by himself.

With the fire going, Samuel sat on some rocks beside Talia and looked out into the stormy night with her.

"Oh... I have something I have been meaning to give you," Samuel proclaimed.

He swung his satchel around from his side to his lap; the satchel he always carried with him and he dug deep into the bag.

"I know it's in here somewhere... ah... here it is," he said.

Samuel pulled out a black pebble with an emerald green stripe running through it. He handed it to Talia.

"I got it just for you," Samuel said.

Talia took the pebble in her hand and examined it. The multi-colored pebbles were rare and a collectible item by Talia's friends.

"Didn't Thomas give this to you a few days ago?" She asked.

"Why... I don't think so, I got that for you," he replied.

"I'm sure of it. He had returned to the village from higher on the mountain and he showed me this beauty. He said it was for his best friend." Talia answered.

There was an awkward moment of silence between them.

"Oh... maybe... that's the one he gave me," Samuel searched for an answer, "But it's mine to do with as I please, and I am giving it to you for your collection."

"Won't his feelings be hurt? It meant a lot to him. He thought it would mean a lot to you," Talia answered.

Samuel took a long time before he responded. Talia held the pebble in her open hand and waiting for Samuel's response.

"Talia I know we're all friends and I hope that never changes, but sometimes things in friendships change," he said quietly.

"Sometimes for the better." Samuel looked deeply into her eyes and leaned a little closer with the intent of kissing her.

Talia looked down and away. Samuel caught her rejection. Talia drew her eyes up to meet his.

"You should go home Samuel, your father will be asleep by now and you'll be okay," she said with a gentle smile. She bent forward and kissed him on the forehead and then hugged him. "Thomas and I are your friends Samuel and we always will be," she whispered.

She withdrew from her sisterly embrace and handed him the black and emerald green pebble. "There will come a day when we won't have to sneak out at night to watch the storm... I'm sure," she said softly.

Talia got up and handed Samuel his cloak and picked up her damp one. The rain was subsiding.

"I'll see you tomorrow my friend," she said and slipped out into the night leaving Samuel alone in the cave.

Samuel turned the special black and emerald green pebble over in his hand for a bit. Then he pitched the pebble out of the cave and off the cliff into the valley below.

Chapter Six
THE AWAKENING

As the morning sun rose just beyond the horizon, Thomas opened his eyes for the first time. In the dimly lit surroundings, Thomas could tell he was in some sort of enormous structure made out of wood. Large bales of hay with storage bins of vegetables and fruit were nearby. Apples the size of watermelons filled a bin. He had never seen anything so large in his life. The support beams of the structure he was in were made out of trees that stood hundreds of feet in the air. Who could have built such a structure, Thomas wondered?

Light from the sun streamed in the cracks of the loosely fitted wall planks. Other sections of this gigantic room were very dark. A hazy dust filled the air, which made breathing difficult. A consuming booming sound made it hard for Thomas to focus. His eyes adjusted to his surroundings; he sat up and realized the thumping was in his head, caused by the rather large lump that had risen there. Then he remembered: the storm, the fight, the falling and then darkness. How long had he been unconscious, he wondered? Who brought him here and just exactly where was he?

Thomas slowly battled to his feet. The room seemed to be spinning. He batted his eyes a few times to gain his bearing and equilibrium. The distinct smell of bonfire caught his nostrils but there was no smoke in the area he found himself in. Thomas followed the largest stream of light toward what he thought was the door. Suddenly from somewhere deep in the shadows of this cavernous building, he heard whimpering.

Thomas paused for a moment and listened but heard nothing. As soon as he began to walk forward he heard it again, that whimpering sound that stopped him in his tracks. What was out there in the dark, he wondered? Thomas did his best to control his imagination, which at times could get the better of him.

A memory flashed in his mind and he nodded his head at the realization that this perceived fear could be completely in his imagination. The entire memory replayed in his mind in a flash of a second: a time, not so long ago, when he was out playing on the frozen lake. It was a cold harsh day. The kind of bitter cold day that hurts if you breathe too deeply. Thomas had spent that cold day, sliding on the ice with his friends. They would stand on one shore and through a path that they had made, they would run and then slide on top of the frozen water, sliding as far as they could. The one who slid the furthest would be called the champion of this contest.

Thomas and his friends were always looking for ways to compete against each other, this contest happened to be one of the most entertaining. It was a fun day playing with his good friends from the village. Accompanying Thomas was Aaron, and Thomas's best friend Samuel, Jason the bragger and Talia... she was the reason that the day was memorable. Even on the coldest day of winter, her warmth could melt him.

He had to keep his eyes down and away from her, especially with the others around because if they caught him staring, they would only laugh at him. When Talia smiled, he could feel his heart hurt like frostbite. Talia urged him to come to her house with the others because her mother would make hot cocoa for everyone, but Thomas had a score to settle. Thomas stayed behind to play at the pond even after it was much too late in the day. Jason had beaten Thomas' sliding record. Thomas asked to inspect Jason's boots but he found no difference in them than his own. Thomas thought it might have been Jason's unique takeoff from the shore that allowed him to be propelled so far across the ice. He studied Jason's every move... run, hop, jump takeoff sliding. When Thomas tried Jason's technique, he lost his footing and landed squarely on his bum. At first no one moved, suddenly they all broke out in laughter at Thomas. It was a deeply embarrassing moment. Not only had Thomas lost his crown as the best slider in the village but he had also embarrassed himself in front of his friends and Talia. That's why he wanted to stay behind, to practice. The others lost interest in the game and left for Talia's home and a promised cup of hot cocoa. For what could have been two hours, Thomas tried different techniques of takeoff from shore. Run, hop, slide, jump, jump, jump, hop and slide but he could never gain more distance. Maybe it was the wind that blew just right at Jason's back that propelled him, Thomas reckoned.

So Thomas decided to wait for the wind to help and the more he waited the later it got until finally after hours of practice and waiting without getting any further across the lake, Thomas realized that the sun was setting. It was a cloudy starless night and it would be very dark going home.

Thomas thought it best to begin his journey back to the village. As he walked he heard a crunching sound following him. He walked slower and the crunching sound moved slower. He turned around quickly hoping to catch the one who was following him but no one was there. He called out, "OK guys time to stop following me and come out... I know it is you Jason.

Jason, Samuel, Aaron... stop fooling around come on come out. It is cold out here, let's go home."

It must be Samuel, Thomas thought. He was always playing tricks like this. "Samuel, I will tell your parents that you are acting mean and trying to scare me. Do you realize how angry your father will be when I tell him of your actions?" Thomas threatened.

Yet, there was no answer. The only thing Thomas heard was the wind whistling across the snow carrying with it little funnels of snowflakes, twisting and turning on the empty barren winter wasteland.

"OK Talia... Come on, let's stop fooling around and head back... come on guys!" Thomas said with a quiver in his voice.

Still there was no reply, only the winter wind. Thomas turned and began to run. Not far behind him, the crunching sound followed. Thomas ran quicker, his breath becoming shorter and sharper, tighter, harder to breathe, the cold sucking the very breath out of his lungs. It was like trying to come up above a wave that was in perfect rhythm with him. As he would rise for a breath, the wave would swell and he could never get above it.

Thomas jumped over a snow bank and collapsed. With short puffing breaths he looked over the bank to see only his tracks in the snow. Thomas moved his legs and suddenly the culprit making the crunching sound was revealed!

Thomas laughed out loudly in the dark cavernous building as he remembered how he had frightened himself that day, with the frozen cuffs of his pants rubbing together making the crunching sound.

The sound of whimpering interrupted Thomas' laughter. In the dark of this great building it was clear there was something out there beyond the stream of light he stood in. It was just beyond the edge of what he could see.

"Ha..ha.. Hello," there it was, that quiver in his voice again.

There was nothing funny about the situation he was in now. Thomas remembered he was carrying Papa's staff but he had gone a few steps further, leaving Papa staff behind, somewhere in the dark.

Thomas slowly slid his foot back toward the place he came from. Sliding one foot behind the other, he was trying to follow the stream of light, backing away from the whimpering creature but his own shadow blocked the light and impeded his progress.

Finally he kicked the staff. It rolled further into the dark. Thomas could hear it. It seemed to stop rolling not too far ahead. So Thomas got down on his hands and knees and began to crawl toward the direction of the staff.

The floor felt grimy, slick and damp in places. Thomas would move only a few inches at a time; slowly feeling all around in the dark for Papa's staff. Then he touched it. It felt so good to have Papa's staff in his hands again. Thomas rose to his feet confident that he could meet this whining whimpering creature in the dark. One swift blow of Papa's staff and the creature would be cowering in the dark where it belonged.

Thomas swung around in the direction of the light but it was gone, leaving him in complete darkness. Thomas' breathing started to shorten. He could feel his heart race and pound in his chest. Thomas did not have a clue where he was.

Then Thomas heard scratching on the floor, as if something were dragging itself toward him. Thomas could smell it now, this thing, this creature, its whimpering was low but the smell was horrendous. The smell was worse than the lambs when they were wet. Thomas readied himself and took a step back preparing himself for whatever would emerge from the darkness.

Thomas inhaled deeply, looking for the energy to meet the creature. All he got in return was damp, cold, and stale air that made his stomach queasy.

Suddenly there was a tremendous creaking sound, as if huge doors were swung open on rusty old hinges. Daylight poured into this cavernous room. At first Thomas turned to cover his eyes as he tried to adjust them to the bright light.

Standing in the doorway was an enormous boy. His hair bright red was neatly parted in the middle. The giant boy was grinning foolishly at Thomas. He had two teeth missing in front. The giant boy shuffled his feet and chuckled. He held rope and a 10 foot long metal pole in his hand.

"You live, Meesay!" Proclaimed the giant surprised to see Thomas standing.

"A Nephilim," whispered Thomas to himself.

The giant seemed embarrassed and put the rope and metal pole down. "Dat's youse dog, Meesay!" The giant boy exclaimed. He was talking to Thomas while pointing beyond him.

Thomas turned his attention in the direction to part of the cavernous room to where the darkness once consumed everything, now he could see the source of the whimpering. It was a wolf. The wolf lowered its head and crawled toward Thomas. The wolf was not a mother protecting her cubs; it was only about six months old at best.

The wolf's back leg had been bandaged. Thomas thought that the wolf must have been injured when they first met otherwise why would she be left on the mountain path to fend for herself? Thomas backed up and readied his staff in case of an attack from either side.

"He's not my wolf, th...th... that wolf tried to kill me last night... in... in... th...th...the storm," Thomas stammered.

The giant boy paused for a long moment then burst out laughing.

His laugh was infectious and it made Thomas laugh.

"You talk funny. You have a squeaky voice like a little mouse, Meesay."

Thomas realized that this giant child was much younger than he looked. He was not the same age in his mind as he was in this body. Thomas figured the giant child was telling him, his name was Meesay.

"Is your name Meesay?" Thomas asked.

Meesay smiled broader and he took a few steps forward. "Brother say, don't talk with supper or is it don't talk with mouthful, Meesay wonder?" The giant was confused over the directive he had received from his brother. His quick move forward panicked the wolf. The wolf growled and showed her teeth.

Thomas wondered if he heard the giant right, was he intending Thomas to be supper? The intimidating sight of a wolf growling had been etched into Thomas' memory from the night on the mountain. It was not something he wished to face again. He was trapped between two evils.

Meesay clapped his hands together to get Thomas' attention.

"Squeaky mouse boy take puppy and go before brother gets home, Meesay," Meesay swung out his arm and pointed in the direction of the door.

The giant moved outside of the door and motioned Thomas to come.

"Go, Meesay," demanded the giant.

Thomas was relieved the giant was releasing him but he didn't know where to go.

"Go where?" Questioned Thomas. "I don't know where I am, how will I know where to go?"

"Go down the cloud, Meesay," the giant turned around and counted as a child would playing hide and seek, "one, two, three... when Meesay get to ten, you and you puppy wolf are gone now, Meesay... four, five... six..."

Thomas walked into the sunlight outside of the cavernous building and stood beside Meesay. The view was spectacular. They were above the clouds, higher than he had ever been! Higher than anyone he knew had ever been. He was at the mountaintop and all around him were tremendously large buildings, the giant's village. The buildings were made of enormous cut stone. The giant's village was empty; he seemed to be the only one of his kind in the village. In the near distance he could see the bonfire that he smelt earlier. On both sides of it were supporting poles used for a cooking spit.

"Ten, Meesay," the giant turned to face Thomas with a scowl on his face.

As Thomas looked into Meesay's face, seeing his crooked mouth and scrunched up nose, Thomas couldn't help it, he laughed. Soon Meesay's countenance changed and he began to smile... then his smile broke out into a laugh. The boys laughed and laughed, each taking turns making faces at one another.

It didn't take long before Thomas knew they could be friends. While they were laughing at each other's faces the wolf had crawled close to the door and lay on her side. Thomas took notice of her. The wolf didn't like Thomas looking at her and she snarled and showed her teeth.

"Hey, Meesay, is that really your wolf?" Asked Thomas.

Meesay shook his head no. Then he scratched his head and looked up to the right. Thomas looked up to see what Meesay was looking at. Thomas realized Meesay was only looking up in the air as if he was trying to remember something.

Suddenly Meesay turned back to Thomas with a serious look on his face. "Meesay find puppy wolf on mountain side in storm and little mouse boy too."

Thomas nodded his head and smiled, "Little mouse boy is named Thomas, Thomas," he repeated.

Thomas took Meesay by the baby finger and could barely move the giants' hand but he managed to point at himself with Meesay's hand.

"Thomas," he repeated himself again. Pushing the giants hand toward him.

"You, Meesay, " and then pulling it the other way, "Thomas... I am Thomas."

"Toomas," Meesay pronounced and smiled.

"Brother say don't talk to supper or with mouth full. Time to go Meesay."

"Supper?" Thomas questioned. He stole a glance at the bonfire spit and he suspected the giant had planned to tie him there. Thomas backed away from the giant not knowing where to run. Thomas figured there was no way to outrun this Nephilm even if he wanted to. He had to outwit him to insure his escape.

"Meesay fix puppy wolf and Toomas, see," Meesay pointed to the rags wrapped around the wolf leg and then he pointed to

Thomas' head. Thomas reached up with his hand and felt a rag wrapped around his head and realized that this giant boy had brought him and the wolf up the mountain and out of the storm, dressed their wounds and placed them in the barn overnight.

"No blood makes food dry, not juicy, Meesay."

Just then Thomas' stomach grumbled with a hunger pain. He had only eaten supper with Papa the night before, why should he be so hungry he wondered. He hoped the giant hadn't heard, that might trigger him into thinking about the supper comments he was making.

"How long have we been up here?" Thomas questioned trying to change the subject.

"Two sleeps, Meesay," responded the giant.

Two sleeps thought Thomas! He had been up on the mountain for two days!

"Meesay waited for mouse boy to become stiff and dead. Brother said dead boys stay on cooking pole better, Meesay." Meesay gently poked Thomas and he looked disappointed, "You not dead, Meesay."

Thomas jumped to his feet and did a 360-degree turn looking in all directions - stopping back at Meesay. "No I'm not dead, I'm very much alive and I wouldn't make a good supper because I wouldn't hang from your cooking spit properly. I'm leaving now remember? Before I leave here Meesay, have you seen a little lamb come up the mountain path?" Thomas was concerned as he queried the giant but he had to ask otherwise this journey would all be for nothing if he returned without the lamb. All sorts of thoughts raced through his head. Surely Papa was worried sick by now and had a search party out looking for him. The Gatekeeper must have told Papa where Thomas went.

Maybe Papa would be proud of his son's bravery but until Papa knew of what had happened he would be angry, Thomas thought.

Meesay jumped to his feet and started jumping up and down.

"Oh Meesay know Baa! Meesay save little Baa from scary dark all alone, Meesay."

Saying that Meesay sat down on the ground with a thud.

"Is little baa belong to... Toomas, Meesay?"

Thomas recognized that Meesay had grown attached to his little lamb over the past couple of days.

"Well yes... the lamb belongs to my Papa," Thomas said slowly, hoping to make Meesay understand.

Meesay only looked at the ground and pointed in the direction of his home not far from where they were.

Thomas smiled and took Meesay's baby finger in his hand.

"Thank you my friend for all that you have done for me."

Meesay only raised his eyes to look at Thomas. A smile spread across his face. Meesay tried to contain his joy... Thomas had called him friend. That was significant to Meesay. No one had ever called him friend. Meesay started playing with the rope and fire spit pole; torn by his brother's directions and Thomas' friendly demeanor. How could his family eat these mountain people? They were like cute little pets, Meesay thought.

Thomas raced across the lawn to the giant's home. There behind the huge picket fence was his little lamb grazing. Thomas slipped through the fence slats and the little lamb raised his head to see him. Thomas made the clucking sound with his voice that Papa had taught him. The little lamb was so excited it almost raised itself on its hind legs to spring forward and run to

Thomas. Thomas smiled and held his Papa's staff proudly. He slipped back through the fence and the lamb followed.

Meesay was waiting for him. Thomas looked up at the giant boy and shaded his eyes from the sunlight that was behind Meesay.

"Well Meesay I must head down the mountain path now but someday I hope to return and repay you for the nice things that you did for me." Thomas was being deceptive. He had no intention of ever seeing the Nephilim this close again.

Thomas nodded and moved to walk past Meesay. Meesay stepped in his way and shook his head no.

"I must go home now," Thomas said with a slight quiver in his voice.

"No, Meesay brother and his friends come home from Festival. No like little people up here," said Meesay in a very concerned voice.

Thomas readied his staff and thought he might only have one swing at the giant and it had to be at his head.

"Meesay's family come up path so we go down new way... come, OK?"

Thomas' breathing relaxed for whatever reason this Nephilm was letting him go and showing him the way of escape. Thomas had no other option but to trust him.

Meesay picked up the wolf in his huge arms and carried it like a baby. The wolf wanted to snap but Meesay's size was intimidating even to a wild creature. Thomas clucked and the lamb followed. They went down behind Meesay's house through the garden and under the fence to come out to a narrow winding path. Thomas was amazed at how high they were because he could now gain perspective, a rock he kicked seemed to fall forever before making a sound. Thomas was sure that not even the birds flew this high.

As they descended they would sometimes need to walk in single file because of the narrowness of the path they took. They talked about family and friends, about collecting things like pebbles. It was all small talk about fun things that boys do. Thomas watched the rhythm of his feet in his shadow. It almost appeared musical to him. Thomas began to hum. Meesay smiled. Each one of his big crooked teeth was as large as Thomas' hand. As he walked Thomas' attention turned back to his shadow. Thomas became mesmerized by the rhythm of shadows moving along the trail and he began to daydream. Thomas began to lead on the path down the mountain and Meesay fell in behind. It was then that Thomas decided to be brave and share his biggest dream with Meesay.

"Someday I would love to attend the Festival of Harvest and eat of the mythamöhre tree. I mean, who wouldn't want to be part of the Lottery of Affluence. My brother Kale and his wife journeyed to the valley long ago. They used to write home but when mother died, Papa would just throw Kale's letters in the fire. I don't have many memories of Kale. Once when I was very young, he took me fishing," Thomas said without looking up.

Thomas discovered he was walking alone and spun around to see that Meesay was far up the path, on his way back toward the top. Meesay had let the wolf down on the path and silently left them.

"Meesay, where are you going?" Thomas called out, his voice echoed off the other mountaintops. Thomas patted the lamb on the head and took off running up the path after Meesay.

Running as quick as he could just to catch up to him. Thomas slipped on some of the rocks and avoided the mean wolf by taking a more unstable tenuous way while chasing after Meesay. He needed Meesay to show him where to go. Without him he would have been just as well off facing the other Nephilim of Meesay's village as being abandoned in the wilderness.

"Meesay... where are you going... I thought you were coming?"

Meesay sat down over looking the distant domed mountain range. Thomas didn't need an answer, he could see hurt in Meesay's eyes. Thomas finally made his way to Meesay and sat beside him.

Meesay looked at Thomas with a scowl on his face. Meesay showed his teeth as a child does when he is angry. Thomas could now see that the Nephilim had two rows of teeth, one behind the other. That sent shivers down Thomas' spine but he tried to act brave.

"Meesay should have ate mouse boy before he speak."

Thomas swallowed hard. He put himself in harms way again by coming close to the giant.

"Meesay no like the festival... no...no... no, Meesay!"

Meesay grabbed a rock and pitched it out into the thin mountain air. He looked at Thomas, "Toomas very smart, Meesay." His tone hushed, "Queen no like Nephilim boy like Meesay."

"Nonsense," proclaimed Thomas, "Why not?"

Meesay looked up at Thomas with tears in his big innocent eyes. Thomas knew why.

"Half-wit Meesay," Meesay shook his head in shame.

Thomas put his hand on Meesay's arm.

"They're wrong. I think you are smart. Look at what you did for me, my lamb and the wolf."

Meesay said nothing only hung his head.

"Thank you for saving me," Thomas said quietly.

Meesay smiled and wiped the tears from his eyes.

"Take Toomas home, Meesay. No like squiggly food anyway, Meesay."

Thomas' eyes grew wide at that statement and Meesay laughed. Meesay's joking may have been funny to the Nephilim but Thomas didn't find it funny at all.

Meesay lifted Thomas up on his shoulders. Thomas dare not move for fear of falling off or per chance that the giant boy slip and fall himself. Meesay scooped up the lamb and the wolf on their way down the mountain. Soon they were off, making incredible time moving down the mountain. The group had traveled for about fifteen minutes and the slope of the path had begun to even out when Thomas heard strange cries coming from the valley.

"Meesay, do you hear that?"" Thomas said from on top of Meesay's shoulders,

"Sad people crying, no go there Meesay."

"Who are they?" Asked Thomas.

"People that cry and cry, people that no like Queen, Meesay."

By this time the sun was mid way through the afternoon. Going down this backside of the mountain path was sure exciting but Thomas knew that they had best pick up the pace in order to make it back to his village before nightfall.

Suddenly Meesay stopped and let his traveling companions down on the ground. Meesay crouched by the group he had been carrying. Thomas scrambled to his feet. "We still have a way to go, why are we stopping?" Thomas queried. "Aren't we going to continue down the path to my village? I would love you to meet Papa, my friends and visit with us for a while."

Meeting Meesay was a revelation to Thomas, one that he hoped to share with the entire village. After meeting Meesay, Thomas believed the people of his village had the wrong impression of the mountain giants.

"No, brother not happy for Meesay to be gone too far. Meesay go home now. "Never worry mouse boy Toomas, Meesay always friend. Toomas kind to Meesay." Meesay lifted his finger to his lips as if to say quiet, he was about to share a secret. "Meesay like mouse boy Toomas. Always friend, Meesay." Meesay sprang to his feet and began to dash up the mountain path with the quickness of a mountain goat. Thomas called out to him hoping that Meesay would hear.

"Thank you Meesay, for everything!"

Thomas continued his journey down the mountain path, the little lamb in tow. The injured wolf limped along following at a distance. Thomas turned and threw a rock at the wolf. "Go on, get lost!" Thomas yelled.

The wolf showed her teeth, growled and snarled at Thomas. Thomas yelled at it again, "Get lost or I will club you with my staff!" Thomas swung his staff cutting the air with a whoosh. That caught the wolf's attention and she departed into the woods.

Satisfied that he had scared off the wolf, Thomas turned and began heading back to his village with the lamb. As soon as Thomas was a ways down the path the wolf emerged from the woods and continued following him.

Hours later and exhausted, they were back down in familiar territory. Thomas could see his village from this vantage point off in the distance but there was something strange. No smoke was rising from any of the chimneys in the village. At this time of day, people of the village should be preparing supper. Thomas' mind raced ahead to his village... where was everyone? Thomas hurried the lamb back to his village.

The wolf watched from the ridge and made sure she wasn't noticed before continuing to follow Thomas and the lamb toward the village.

Chapter Seven
LITTLE BOY LOST, LITTLE BOY FOUND

As Thomas arrived in his village he ran from home to home, knocking on doors and opening them to find everyone gone! It was an uneasy sensation Thomas felt. There was no sound of children laughing and playing; no sound of sheep baaing or dogs barking; no sounds of wagons being pulled through the streets by horses; no friendly familiar sounds at all.

There were only the sounds of the birds in the trees, the wind rustling leaves, bullfrogs in the pond nearby but not a single sound of a human in the village.

"Hello! Is anyone here?"

As if on cue the little lamb ran into the pen where all of the other lambs would normally be. Thomas followed his lamb and locked the gate behind her.

"See all the trouble you've caused me," Thomas scolded the lamb.

"I would advise you to stay with the flock from now on," Thomas said as he looked around the empty village. Thomas spoke quietly to himself, "If we can ever find the flock."

If everything is gone, maybe so is Papa. Thomas didn't want to find out. He knew in his heart that he wouldn't know what to do if Papa... he couldn't bring himself to finish the thought: panic began to creep into Thomas' soul.

Thomas turned round and round in the middle of village afraid to take another step in any particular direction. He could hear his heart beating in his chest. He had to have courage again; courage to face whatever was ahead. With that summoning of courage deep within, Thomas went quickly to his house.

"Papa... I'm home, " he shouted as he ran to his house.

Thomas imagined the answer. He imagined that Papa would be there, not like every other house in the village because Papa was always there for him. He swung open the door of his home.

"Papa it is Thomas, where are you?"

The house was empty.

Thomas ran out of the house and into the garden.

"Papa it is me, Thomas! I brought home our little lamb. I swear Papa I don't know how she got lost but I made you proud by getting her... didn't I... Papa?"

Thomas sat in the middle of the garden realizing that his worse fear had come true. He was alone in his village. Everyone had vanished. Thomas cried; not loud and whining cries but tears of pure heartbreak and fear. There was no one to comfort him. There was no one to dry his tears. There was no one to hold him.

The wolf crept up behind the garden fence and kept a watch on him. The wolf's lip curled as she showed some of her fangs.

Sitting there in the garden Thomas was a little boy lost in his own village. Thomas turned his attention to his surroundings, looking around, hoping that someone; anyone might see him as he screamed out through his tears. "Weez-lock neigh, surely so I," Thomas yelled out in his best mountain dialect. "Cum sa lat worta Papa, Cum sa lat worta tooray!" Thomas exclaimed. "I'm sorry Papa that I lied to you, I do understand. Cum sa lat worta, tooray!" Emotions overwhelmed him. "You're right Papa, weez-lock neigh, surely so I. I am too young to take the flock to the grazing lowlands. Did YOU HEAR ME! I said, weez-lock neigh, surely so I"

The only thing that answered him was Thomas' own voice echoing off the houses of the empty village. Thomas' eye caught the movement of the wolf behind the fence. He kept watch on her. Thomas leapt to his feet and shouted at the wolf, "What is it that you want? You want to kill me? Come on do it now... DO IT NOW!"

The wolf growled low and showed more of her teeth.

Thomas sat back down and dropped his head into his hands, "What difference does it make, we've both been abandoned," he whispered quietly.

The wolf found Thomas' actions curious, she caulked her head to the side looking through the garden fence at Thomas.

The next time Thomas looked up she was gone.

That night Thomas made dinner the best he could. Although there were no chickens left, Thomas found many eggs in their roosts. He scrambled them up and served them with bread. Thomas looked out of the window and saw the wolf by garden fence. He watched the wolf for a while before he spoke to himself. "If I don't feed you, you're going to help yourself to my lamb."

Thomas prepared a bowl of raw eggs and some chicken scraps he found from previous meals. He walked out to the garden and faced the wolf.

"Here you go wolf." Thomas threw the chicken scrap to the wolf. The wolf growled and approached it slowly, suddenly grabbing it and returning to the other side of the fence. "You touch my lamb and I will kill you wolf," Thomas mumbled to himself as he watched the wolf rip apart the chicken scrap.

Thomas went to the pen and moved the lamb into the house with him. "Best we spend the night together lamb," Thomas said. "The mess in the house will be easier to explain to Papa then the lamb devoured by a wolf while under my charge," Thomas whispered to himself.

Thomas looked out the window at the wolf in the garden and spoke to himself, "What is it that you want? I will call you Lowen, 'only one' in mountain dialect. Lowen fits you wolf."

Thomas thought that it was best if he didn't go out tonight. Whatever took Papa and all of the villagers could still be lurking in the dark. It was safest if he and lamb stay in with the door locked.

That night Thomas lay on his bed and stared out his window at the stars. He wondered if Papa, wherever he was, could see the same stars that Thomas was now looking at. Soon he was fast asleep.

Morning came quickly. Thomas wiped the sleep from his eyes and pushed the covers back. Thomas' bare toes touched the cold damp floor. He thought of the many times he would get out of bed and Papa would have a morning fire going. The morning fire always warmed the floor. Thomas looked out the window of his home. There was a slight morning mist hanging the in the air but the bright morning sun was sure to burn it off quickly, Thomas thought. Through the window, Thomas spotted the wolf moving on the other side of the fence.

Thomas kept his eye on the wolf and spoke to himself, "Ah Lowen, you are awake. I have my staff ready if you should try anything."

Thomas opened the door of his home, grabbed Papa's staff and went outside. He led the lamb to a patch of grass close to his home keeping a watchful eye for the wolf. He waited for the lamb to have something to eat then herded it back into the house. He spoke to the Lamb, "My little troublemaker, you'll be locked in here for your own safety until I return. I am off to find where everyone from our village went. I will be back soon. He shut the door on the lamb and set off to explore nearby for any clues. That pesky little lamb is the reason he was in this situation. If she would have stayed with the rest of the flock, she would have been in the pen and there would not have been a reason for Thomas to go out in the dark night looking for her. Yes he thought, if it were not for that lamb, he would be with Papa right now. Thomas walked through the empty village, he thought he would also visit the fruit trees and gardens around town to see if there had been anything left behind. That might be a good place to start. As Thomas reached the pen at the center of the village he saw someone standing dressed in a cloak with his back to him. It looked like the Gatekeeper but Thomas couldn't be sure.

"Hello," Thomas said nervously.

Thomas cautiously approached, to not startle the stranger. Thomas gripped his Papa's extra long staff ready to face anything.

The cloaked stranger turned around and to Thomas' surprise it was indeed, the Gatekeeper. Thomas was relieved.

"Where is everyone? I want to know right now!" Thomas demanded.

The Gatekeeper said nothing and sat down by the entrance to the pen, while the little lamb Thomas rescued walked around.

The Gatekeeper picked up some dust from the ground and let it run through his fingers.

"Let me see your fathers staff," said the Gatekeeper.

Thomas took a step forward and dropped to his knees before the Gatekeeper. "Please tell me where everyone has gone, where is Papa? Did he say where he was going and when he would be back?"

"Please, let me see your fathers staff," repeated the Gatekeeper.

Thomas handed him the staff. Tears welled up in Thomas' eyes.

"Please tell me where he is... please," begged Thomas, as he dropped to his face on the ground before the Gatekeeper.

The Gatekeeper rose to his feet and held out his hand for Thomas to take. Thomas looked up sensing that the Gatekeeper had gotten to his feet. Thomas wiped the tears from his eyes and took the Gatekeeper's hand. With that the Gatekeeper took Thomas up in his arms and held him, comforting him.

Thomas had not been this close to the Gatekeeper before, but his cloak had the distinct smell of wild flowers in spring. Thomas sniffled back his tears and the Gatekeeper lifted Thomas higher to his shoulders. Thomas thought that this man was very strong. It had been years since Papa could lift Thomas to his shoulders and let him ride there. It was something that Thomas loved to do as a younger boy. The thought of Papa carrying him like this brought a smile to his face.

The Gatekeeper began to walk, carrying Thomas on his shoulders. Thomas was so overcome with emotions that he didn't think to ask where they were going, he was just along for the ride. Soon they were leaving the village and cutting through the edge of the woods.

They were on the base level of Mount Crevasse before they came to stop by a mountain stream. The Gatekeeper knelt on one knee, allowing Thomas to get off his shoulders. Thomas moved to the waters edge and looked into the crystal clear mountain stream. The Gatekeeper walked over and put his hand on Thomas' shoulders.

"So much weight you carry on these little shoulders," the Gatekeeper said. Thomas turned to face him.

"Where is my Papa? Do you know?" Thomas repeated.

The Gatekeeper sat on a log by the stream.

"I know where they are and I will take you there," nodded the hooded head of the Gatekeeper.

"What are we waiting for? Let's go!" Thomas exclaimed with excitement.

"First there are things you must understand," the Gatekeeper said as he quickly followed up Thomas' statement.

"Look into this stream and tell me what you see," said the Gatekeeper.

"I see water and rocks," replied Thomas.

"Look deeper Thomas and you will see a word or two bubble to the surface." Trying as hard as he could Thomas could only see water and rocks. His eyes were red from crying. Thomas felt like he had no more tears, that his eye ducts had run dry. The pain in his heart was unbearable. Thomas wondered why the Gatekeeper couldn't just take him to his Papa, why are they playing this game? Thomas' mind only focused on Papa. The Gatekeeper put his hand on Thomas' shoulder. Thomas turned to look at him.

The early morning sunshine on the Gatekeeper's back made seeing details of his hooded head and face difficult.

"Come let's go and see your Papa," said the Gatekeeper.

The Gatekeeper turned and walked along the mountain stream. Thomas followed. They did this for some time without a word more about the significance of the Gatekeeper asking him to stare into the water. Thomas thought there must have been some reason for doing this but couldn't figure it out. Little did Thomas know that the simple truth the Gatekeeper was about to teach him, would become a significant weapon for survival.

Chapter Eight
AT THE GATES OF MOURNING

It wasn't long before Thomas looked up at his surroundings to discover that he and the Gatekeeper had covered an incredible distance in a short period of time. The entire area looked different to Thomas than when he last put up his head to take in his surroundings. The lovely wooded area that started the journey had turned to a haggard rocky crag, with stumps of grass growing here and there. It was a dry and barren land.

Thomas wondered if this old Gatekeeper was tired and hot like he was. He wore the hooded robe day and night and since this was past mid-day surely the blazing sun of this barren land was enough for the Gatekeeper to remove his hood, yet he trudged on without complaining.

"Aren't you hot with the long heavy robe and hood over your face? " Inquired Thomas. He remembered what his Papa told him about the Gatekeeper but wanted to see what the mysterious Gatekeeper would say.

"What keeps out the cold, keeps out the heat," responded the Gatekeeper.

The Gatekeeper stopped and turned to face Thomas.

"When we arrive at the camp; the Gates of Mourning, where your father and the others are; I will protect you and shield you from the site of the guards but you must be careful to do exactly as I say. Understood?" Cautioned the Gatekeeper.

"Guards?" Questioned Thomas.

The Gatekeeper didn't answer; he just turned and walked up over a hill into the sun. Thomas called out to him. "I am not going any further until you tell me where my Papa is!"

Thomas' first thought was, why is the Gatekeeper so sparse with his words when it could only be beneficial to share what is going on. Then he thought as he watched the Gatekeeper disappear over the ridge into the sunlight, have they been traveling all day to get to this spot? Time had seemed to race forward as did the sun in the sky. A moment ago it was morning and now the sun was disappearing behind the ridge.

Thomas wasted no more time pondering. He ran up the ridge with all he had in order to catch up to the Gatekeeper. As Thomas rounded the crest of the ridge he couldn't believe his ears or his eyes.

A multitude of people filled up an area miles long. They were caged in a gigantic compound, all pressing together and moping around in the dust as if they were blind. The moaning and crying they made, mixed together and the resulting sound was deafening. The noise ricocheted off the valley walls and bounced around. The collective sound of suffering was one of despair, there was no one to help. The sound of desperation rose with such an intensity, that Thomas covered his ears hoping to block out the sound.

The Gatekeeper put his hand on Thomas' shoulder to reassure and calm him.

The Gatekeeper spoke solemnly, "There is no hiding from this sound Thomas. Once it is in your soul, you will never forget it."

Thomas removed his hands from his ears and looked up at the Gatekeeper. The sound of the prisoners despair ripped into Thomas. It was so painful; tears began to well up in Thomas' eyes.

"Who are these poor people?" Thomas wondered aloud. "Can't someone help them?"

"Lottery of Affluence winners," responded the Gatekeeper. "Lucky winners," he sadly repeated to himself.

The sky above the compound was dark and foreboding. The clouds constantly churned like a witches' cauldron, motivated by an unseen force. Thomas marveled at the peculiarity of the churning clouds because the skies outside the boundary of the compound were not effected, the air was still and the sun shone bright.

The Gatekeeper started down the hill toward the compound of prisoners.

Thomas reluctantly followed the Gatekeeper. Had the Gatekeeper brought him to see his Papa? Would he find his Papa in this multitude? Papa didn't believe in the valley festivities; surely he wouldn't be in there, Thomas reasoned.

As they approached the fence, the Gatekeeper held up his hand and proclaimed, "We've come." The crowd parted, revealing Thomas' father.

Thomas ran to the fence and stuck his fingers through. "Papa it's me Thomas!"

Initially it seemed as if his father didn't recognize him. His father fumbled his way toward the sound of Thomas' voice.

"Thomas are you out there? It's so dark, I can't see you son," Papa pleaded.

Searing pain began shooting up Thomas' arms, emanating from his fingers, which were grasping the fence. He held on to the fence until he could cling no more and reluctantly he relinquished his grip.

Thomas looked squarely into his Papa's eyes, "Papa, it's me Thomas! I am so happy I found you. Please come home."

What Thomas didn't realize was that when he abandoned his grip on the fence, he released the conduit by which his voice travelled into the other realm.

Papa's expression didn't change. It was as if he couldn't hear or see Thomas.

"Thomas, if you can hear me, do what you can to stay healthy and alive. Remember all that I taught you son. Remember my teachings and stay away from the Queen and the valley. Only darkness and sadness follow her... nothing else."

Thomas could not restrain the tears from pouring down his cheeks.

The Gatekeeper put his hand on Thomas' shoulder. "We must go now before the guards return on their rounds. I will explain everything."

Thomas looked into his Papa's eyes but Papa couldn't look back. The pupils of Papa's eyes where as white as snow, he turned and walked into the host of lost souls. The aimless wandering mob engulfed Papa into their multitude until he melded into the moving mass.

Thomas yelled after him, "No!"

Thomas grabbed the fence firmly. His body shook with the pain that coursed through his body because of his contact with the fence. He endured the pain because he was not prepared to let go of the fence or let go of his father. Tears rushed freely from his eyes and his sobbing made it difficult to catch his breath.

The Gatekeeper slipped his hand on top of Thomas' hand. Thomas released his grip and fell back into the Gatekeeper's arms, as if he was propelled back by a violent invisible force. Thomas regained his footing and the Gatekeeper led Thomas away from the compound of prisoners.

They walked silently up the crest of the hill and along the crag rock trail, back to the stream in the forest. Night was descending on the land.

On the shore of the stream, a fire was lit; fish was prepared and waiting at a vacant campsite. The Gatekeeper sat by the fire as if he knew it was waiting for them. Thomas followed the Gatekeeper's lead. They shared the meal in silence.

The lump in Thomas' throat that was caused by the pain in his heart, made swallowing his meal difficult. Images of his Papa replayed in his mind and became too much for him to bear. With his very best efforts, Thomas tried to remain brave, remembering his father's words: Thomas, if you can hear me, do what you can to stay healthy and alive.

"Have you had your fill?" the Gatekeeper broke the silence and woke Thomas out of his daydream.

"Yes," responded Thomas slowly. "How can we free them? Do you have a plan?" Thomas demanded boldly.

"Please look into the stream again and tell me what you see," the Gatekeeper encouraged.

Thomas looked cynically at the Gatekeeper.

The Gatekeeper nodded toward the stream, "You will find your answer."

Thomas got up from the campfire and walked to the stream. He peered into the water and it began to flow slowly, almost as if it were a dream, "I see rocks, I see water and I see me. I see my reflection!" The water returned to its normal pace as it passed by Thomas.

Although Thomas couldn't see the Gatekeeper smile because of the hood he wore over his head, he could hear the smile in his voice.

"As water reflects the face, so a man's heart reflects the man. The eyes are the pool of a man's soul," said the Gatekeeper as he came alongside Thomas and put his hand on his shoulder. "These are the words of truth to those who are true of heart. These are the words that bubble to the surface for everyone to see who has eyes to see."

Thomas wasn't sure what the Gatekeeper's statement meant but he knew it was important, so he committed it to memory.

No one had ever given this much attention to a Littlewood before. Thomas thought that if the Gatekeeper knew his family history, he'd be looking for another compatriot to confide in. Thomas knew the Littlewood family history and it was something of an embarrassment to him. When his great grandparents moved to this mountain with the other families, all of the migrants gathered together in their respective clans. First order of the day for each family was shelter and warmth. Thomas' great grandfather built a lean-to and gathered firewood to keep his expecting wife warm. In the same time that the other families had settled in for the night, Thomas' great grandfather was still out collecting wood for their fire. He had only collected a "little-wood" mostly shrubs and kindling. In the kindling he had collected, there were no larger wood pieces required to keep a fire burning all night. Then the 'Littlewood' name caught on and stuck. When villagers wanted to mock someone's' poor decision, they'd simply say, 'don't be a 'Littlewood.' It became a derogatory identifier for those without the common sense to provide for their family.

What Thomas didn't know, is that the Gatekeeper knew all of the Littlewood family history and more. The Gatekeeper saved the rest of the story for another day.

The Gatekeeper sat with Thomas and they talked for hours on end. The Gatekeeper told Thomas about the Queen, her kingdom and about the history of generations past. He told Thomas about a reigning King that once ruled among his people. The King offered the land for his people to rule while he traveled to the far reaches of his kingdom. Upon his return the King found that the people had relegated him to myths and fairytales. The people were determined to have a ruler and freely chose to follow Queen Aleah Mythamöhre. So the Good King wore a disguise and lived among his people, searching for the warrior brave enough to stand beside him, when the time came to free his kingdom and his people.

"What about my Papa?" Thomas asked.

"Your Papa has been taken by the Queen because of her jealousy. The villages of the mountain plains remained true to the Good King and never participated in the Festival of Harvest and the Lottery of Affluence. They were never among those pledging their allegiance to the Queen."

"But if they were no threat to her, why would she invade my village and arrest everyone?" Thomas asked.

The timing was not right for the Gatekeeper to explain the weakness in Thomas' village defenses that allowed them to be captured. The Gatekeeper paused for a moment as he considered an explanation that Thomas could understand.

"If they do not stand with her, they stand against her. Greed drives the Queen, not compassion for the people. If she gets them to pledge allegiance to her, then all they posses is hers. When they eat the fruit of the mythamöhre tree their eyes are blinded to the truth and opened to a shallow world. They can't comprehend that they have become slaves; enthralled with the mythamöhre, believing that it is the path to happiness and all they have ever desired. The Lottery of Affluence is nothing but a veil that conceals the truth," the Gatekeeper responded.

"What is the truth?" asked Thomas.

"That same question will be asked by many who refuse the answer before they hear it. Still they will all be confronted with the same question you're asking me now, at some point in their lives," the Gatekeeper leaned in a little closer to Thomas to draw his attention before continuing. The Gatekeeper lowered his voice as if he was revealing a powerful mystery, "The truth my dear boy, is that the Queen takes all that rightfully belongs to the people. She has them believing that the way to happiness is to get more things for themselves, which only ends up in her treasury. She believes that by amassing power and glory for herself, no one will be able to stop her. She knows the prophecy; the foretold return of the Good King and of a time when freedom will reign. She knows of the Warrior that will be instrumental in the fulfillment of the Good King's return. This is one reason the Queen has done this ambitious cleansing of those that resisted her. That's why she sent out her troops and captured those standing in defiance. Thankfully she only captured the weak, who believed her lies in some corner of their heart."

"Where Is the Good King and his Warrior? Where are they now? We must find them!"

"You are right, they must be found."

"What are we waiting for?"

"There is a time and place for everything Thomas. Tonight we will go back to the village and rest. I'm sure your little lamb must be wondering where you are," the Gatekeeper answered in a calm voice.

"Please help me find the King and his warrior, my Papa is trapped and..." Thomas rattled his words quickly hoping to raise the same urgency in the Gatekeeper that he felt himself.

"Tomorrow the journey begins," the Gatekeeper replied.

With those brief words the Gatekeeper dowsed the fire and headed toward the village. Thomas followed.

Chapter Nine
SAFE HAVEN

When Samuel came to, he opened his eyes to find that he was alone, in a hole. The area in which he lay was cold damp and dark. It was musty. A sliver of moonlight illuminated the area just around him. As his eyes focused to the little light there was, he could see a hole in the cavern above him.

"Hello," Samuel yelled out.

"Hello," responded a voice as if it was a echo. It was not his own voice he was hearing.

Samuel sat straight up and noticed that his entire body ached as if he had fallen through the hole in the cavern.

"Who said that?" Samuel yelled.

"Me," responded the voice.

"Who are you?" Asked Samuel.

"Of no consequence I suppose," responded the voice.

"That's no answer," replied Samuel.

"A very good one," replied the voice.

Samuel struggled to his feet and peered into the darkness hoping to catch a glimpse of the one talking to him.

"Show yourself," Samuel shouted.

Flashes of light ignited in the darkness and collected in one spot and became the image of a semi-transparent man. He was very plain and ordinary looking with disheveled hair, almost as if he just woke up. His image illuminated the area around him but Samuel could see right through him.

"Who are you?" Samuel demanded an answer.

The apparition hung his head and looked away from Samuel.

"Nine," the apparition meekly responded.

"That's not a name, it's a number," replied Samuel.

"It's my name," said Nine.

Samuel took a step forward.

"What are you? Where are we?" Asked Samuel.

Nine hung his head in his hands. He was dressed in linen clothes, tunic and boots that were similar to Samuel's attire. Samuel thought he might have been from somewhere on the mountain; perhaps from another community where he had never been.

"Too many questions for one little boy. Is that why they dropped you in here?" Asked Nine.

"Dropped me?"

As Samuel thought about it, the image of a broken memory flashed through his mind. He was chained to his friend Jason and they were walking along with others from the village until he woke up here in this spot.

"Yes, did you ask too many questions, is that why they dropped you through the hole in my cave? Asked Nine.

"Answer me one question, where are we?" Replied Samuel.

"Here," answered Nine.

"Of course we are here, where is here?" The level of frustration rose in Samuel's voice.

"Here is on the way to there," relied Nine.

Samuel's legs folded below him and he sat in a heap, dropping his head between his knees. Nausea came over him.

"I am going to be sick," Samuel said quietly.

"I am sick, sick of being alone," replied Nine slowly.

Samuel swallowed hard so as not to throw up.

"Are you a troubling spirit? My father told me about troubling spirits that live on the other side of the mountain. Is that what you are?" Asked Samuel.

"Oh no I don't mean to trouble you, that's not my intention," replied Nine.

"Are you lying to me?" Asked Samuel.

"How could I do that to my only visitor?" Replied Nine.

"Then what are you and where are we? Answer me plainly!" Demanded Samuel.

"I am simply Nine. I don't know how long I have been here but it could be nine years. Nine is all that I know. It has been so long since I have seen my face... that I have forgotten what I look like. Look at my hand." Nine held up his semi-transparent hand.

"See... since I cannot remember what I look like; I cannot see my hand, and since I cannot see my hand, I cannot remember what it looks like, so it has disappeared," replied Nine.

"Will I disappear?" Asked Samuel.

"I don't think so because I can see what you look like," replied Nine.

"I can see what you look like," said Samuel.

"Then I suppose that's enough." replied Nine.

"Enough of what?" Asked Samuel.

"Disappearing... that's enough, disappearing for now," replied Nine.

"Where are we Nine?" Asked Samuel.

"Here. That's the only name for this spot that I know."

"Were you on your way to there?" Asked Samuel.

"Absolutely. Eight companions and me make nine and we were on our way to there when we fell in here. Eight plus one fell in and Nine came out."

As Samuel's eyes became accustomed to the dark, daylight began to find its way into the cave opening and things became slowly brighter.

"You said I was dropped by them into here, who are they?" Asked Samuel.

"The Queen's minions no doubt: giants, gargoyles, imps, I'm unsure but no one else would drop a nice boy in a hole."

"You're right!" Samuel remembered. "There was a raid on our village and they took us captive," Samuel said.

"Oh dear, that could be but it also could be that you just fell in... the ground gives way to holes around here. Holes that strangers suddenly find themselves in."

"No... we were chained and walking toward an extra dark sky."

"Exceedingly dark?" Asked Nine.

"Extraordinarily dark," replied Samuel.

Samuel rose to his feet and looked up at the hole in the roof of the cave he fell into.

"Falling in here may have been what saved me from the raid."

"Nine is good luck for you too. You must be glad to be here instead of there," said Nine.

"Yes I am... wherever there is, cannot be good," said Samuel.

"Indeed not good at all," replied Nine.

Samuel walked around examining his surroundings.

"Is there a way out of here?" Samuel asked. "I have a score to settle."

"From a game. I like games. It's been so long since I've played," responded Nine.

"Yes from a game but not one you would like to play, it's a game of betrayal," replied Samuel.

"It's been so long since I've heard a story. Do you have a story to tell?" Nine queried.

"The story starts the day before my last in the village. I saw my friend Thomas standing before the Gatekeeper for an extra long time. I think they were hatching a plan," said Samuel.

"The best plans can be bad plans if there are bad intentions with them," replied Nine.

"Then the day of the raid, I saw the Gatekeeper go off to the woods just before the raiders entered," said Samuel.

"Suspicious," replied Nine.

"Father told me long ago not to hang around the Gatekeeper because he fancied himself a mystic," said Samuel.

"Very suspicious. Suspicious mystics are never to be trusted," said Nine.

"How come Thomas and the Gatekeeper escaped the raid?"

"Do you have an answer?" Asked Nine.

"I will when I find one of them," replied Samuel. "Will you help me get out of here and find them?"

"Only if you let me stay with you," replied Nine.

"Of course, come along," replied Samuel.

"How do I know you are not a troubling or lying boy? I've heard they exist in villages on this mountain that I have not been to," replied Nine.

Samuel thought for a very long time on how to prove his loyalty and then offered, "You have my word and you know that's true because without me you wouldn't even hear my voice. You see me don't you?"

"Indeed you are right," said Nine. "I see you and I hear you and that is good enough for now." Nine began to chant, "Come along you said. I will, I will, I will."

Chapter Ten
THE JOURNEY

The next morning Thomas woke to bright sunshine streaming in his window. Breakfast was ready at the table.

Thomas got out of bed and touched his toes to the cold floor. Thomas sat at the breakfast table. Corn bread, syrup, eggs, toast, hash browns all the good things that his mother used to make, were right in front of him. His eyes lit up with delight, he hadn't had such a feast since his mother was alive.

"Good Morning Thomas," came a voice from the early morning shadows of the room. It was the Gatekeeper sitting in Papa's rocking chair.

"Good Morning," responded Thomas. "So our journey to find the Good King begins today?" He quickly questioned.

"The journey you desire begins today but in fact your journey began the day you were born Thomas. It was confirmed when you went after the little lost lamb," the Gatekeeper said reassuringly. "I assure you, your lamb will be safe until our return. Hopefully your father doesn't mind the smell of sheep in his home," the Gatekeeper said with a laugh.

After Thomas ate a hardy breakfast, Thomas and the Gatekeeper began to walk out of the village. Without a word they journeyed on the little worn path to the valley below. Thomas tried to stay as close behind the Gatekeeper as possible because he was moving at a pace which required Thomas to jog a few steps. On occasion Thomas attempted to see around the Gatekeeper trying to navigate the path for himself but he could only catch glimpses of the trail. After awhile he rested in the knowledge that the Gatekeeper knew where he was going and

Thomas fell in line behind him. The sun shone overhead, as it progressed across the sky, their path would change but the Gatekeeper seemed to be always directly between Thomas and the sun. Thomas became content to walk in the Gatekeeper's shadow. Little did Thomas know, Lowen the wolf was tracking them.

Soon they were in the valley among the mythamöhre trees. Thomas' excitement was magnified because he had only dreamed of being this close to the beautiful majestic mythamöhre trees. The sweet nectar smell of the lush juicy fruit filled the air. It was almost overwhelmingly intoxicating. Thomas walked up to the tree and put his hand on it. His excitement was quenched as if a cold blanket of fear were laid on his shoulders. Thomas' eyes widened as the tree seemed to pulsate, responding to his touch. There was something moving under the bark of the tree that felt very slimy to the touch. Thomas slowly walked backward to the Gatekeeper, always keeping his eye on the tree, as if something unexpected and frightening could happen at any moment.

"There is something living under the bark of that tree!" Thomas exclaimed.

"This force courses through the sap and into the fruit itself. Are you interested in tasting the fruit Thomas?" The Gatekeeper asked.

"Not if what squirms under the bark finds its way into each fruit," Thomas replied.

"You must never forget this Thomas. What looks beautiful on the outside is not necessarily beautiful beneath," the Gatekeeper warned.

"I will never look at anyone the same," Thomas said with a sigh.

"You will learn to discern. Tonight we will camp in the nearby forests' edge. You will begin the quest under the cover of night."

Thomas and the Gatekeeper sat near the edge of the woods, out of sight of the valley people who came and went to the mythamöhre orchard throughout the day. Thomas and the Gatekeeper quietly watched people coming and going, passing through the orchards to take care of the mythamöhre trees. The orchard caretakers never saw Thomas and the Gatekeeper; they were too focused on their duties.

Thomas and the Gatekeeper spent most of the time talking about Thomas, his hopes and dreams. How he missed his mother and how his father had been very good to him, even though he was overly protective.

As night fell, the activity of the orchard caretakers ceased. Thomas and the Gatekeeper were kept warm by a campfire. Deeper in the woods, out of sight but not out of range of her ability to smell them, Lowen waited for Thomas to be alone.

The Gatekeeper spoke as he stoked the fire with small branches, "You are about to embark on the most amazing journey; May life and peace go with you. When you come to the end, you will find the Good King and his warrior. When the light breaks through, you will find the first of the items necessary to usher in the freedom you desire for your loved ones. Truth will be with you along the way and you will discover the path destined for your life."

Thomas dropped his head, "What if I am not able to fulfill this mission? What about everyone trapped in the Queen's prison, what will happen to them?" Tears filled Thomas' eyes.

"The answer is not in teardrops. It's found in the choice you freely make; one to stand, be strong and courageous. You can never see your destination without looking at the horizon. With your head down and eyes filled with sorrow you can only see where you are standing now, not where you are destined to be," the Gatekeeper encouraged.

Racing though Thomas' mind were all of the things that have happened in the last few days. His Papa was enslaved; was that the fate of his brothers also? What about this journey? He was just a boy. How could he go on a great journey in search of the Good King? This idea of enjoying the Festival of Harvest and to eat the fruit of the mythamöhre trees; what now, what shall he hope for now?

Thomas resented that the hope of enjoying the mythamöhre fruit was taken from him because of the harsh reality revealed by the Gatekeeper. The truth was too ugly; Thomas missed his fantasy of how he would enjoy them. They were beautiful from high above, looking down from the mountainside but now they seemed revolting. What has this Gatekeeper done to everything he hoped for, everything he believed in? With each thought, the anger amplified within him. Thomas jumped to his feet in a burst of anger. He lashed out at the Gatekeeper, "All the days I lived in the village, I have not seen a Good King. Now you... you've caused me to lose hope in everything I believed in!" Thomas could not go on, he fell to the ground on his hands and knees, in total emotional collapse. The Gatekeeper said nothing. He sat silently by and watched. Thomas lifted his eyes to the Gatekeeper, "How did you escape, when everyone else from the village was captured?"

The Gatekeeper kept his eyes on the fire and never turned to Thomas. Thomas sat up but remained on the ground.

"What's the truth Gatekeeper?" Thomas questioned. "You stood by and did nothing as the entire village was captured. You watched them all being taken away and did nothing! Now you expect me to go on some journey to find the king? Well what if I don't want to go, how about that?" Thomas stared at the Gatekeeper for a long time. Not a word was spoken.

Thomas sat back on the log across from the Gatekeeper.

"Your greatest hindrance will be the revelation of the deeds of darkness, but take heart, the night is nearly over and the day is almost here," the Gatekeeper whispered. Thomas didn't understand that the Gatekeeper was talking about something more than the physical shift from night to dawn.

"Deeds of Darkness?" Questioned Thomas.

"Fear is the greatest deed of darkness that stands in your way Thomas," replied the Gatekeeper.

"Haven't I proven myself brave, gone after the lamb and traveled with you to the Gates of Mourning?!" Thomas was insulted and his pride was hurt.

The Gatekeeper was not moved by Thomas' burst of anger, instead he answered in a calm clear tone, "When you decide to let go of the haunting painful past, you will find freedom, then you'll be able to free the ones you love."

Thomas tried to insult the Gatekeeper into taking action, "If not me, then what hope does my father and the others have? Certainly not you!"

"Then you must make this journey," said the Gatekeeper.

Not the answer Thomas wanted to hear.

The Gatekeeper continued, "You've focused on all of the things around you and not on what you know to be true. You question the circumstances; instead, listen to your heartbeat. What is that telling you?"

Thomas exhaled a breath of frustration, "Must you always speak in riddles and mysteries?" In frustration Thomas blurted out the real answer to the Gatekeeper's question. "That I am alive!"

"The lesson of the mythamöhre tree, what did that teach you? How can you wonder about all the things beyond your control without wondering about all the things within you; the very force that courses through you," the Gatekeeper replied.

Thomas hung his head in his hands.

"Inside you there is compassion, giving, caring, bravery, commitment, and the greatest characteristic of all, love. Follow that love Thomas and the rest will come to you," the Gatekeeper encouraged.

The Gatekeeper reached inside his cloak and pulled out a map.

"On this map you will find your path and with it will come the answers to free your family. Be well, be strong, be courageous and you will discover a strength that you never knew you had," said the Gatekeeper. The Gatekeeper stood up and began to move as if he was leaving.

Thomas darted to his feet.

"How can you be so sure that I am able to find the answers I need?" Thomas asked.

"Because my dear boy, I have watched you grow up from a baby to this day. All that I have seen in you is up to this challenge." The Gatekeeper paused for a moment then said, "Come here beside me."

Thomas moved close to the Gatekeeper. The Gatekeeper motioned his hand for Thomas to sit. Thomas did.

"Thomas my dear boy, you were born for a day such as this. Remember these words and walk in their truth. I must leave now and with that, I leave the choice for you to go on this journey or to return to your village."

Thomas was shocked and couldn't speak.

"The choice is totally yours Thomas," the Gatekeeper said.

The Gatekeeper touched Thomas on the head and then left.

"Where are you going? I don't know the way back to my village and I want to return!"

The Gatekeeper kept walking and answered without turning around, "Walk in the direction we came and you will find it. You know the way. It is plain to you."

The Gatekeeper was talking about more than the physical path to Thomas' village. He was talking about the path Thomas would discover within himself.

Thomas wasn't sure about venturing off in the dark toward his village, perhaps he best stay where he was until morning.

The Gatekeeper disappeared into the dark woods and it wasn't long before Thomas couldn't hear his footsteps.

Lowen knew Thomas was alone. She inched closer to him. In the dark of night it was easy for her to remain hidden and wait for her opportunity.

Thomas stared into the fire for a very long time, and nervously rocked himself. Thomas picked up the map and threatened to throw it in the fire. He paused, put the map on his lap and dropped his head in his hands.

Thomas spoke to himself, "Stupid journey, stupid sayings, what's wrong with the Gatekeeper? Why can't he find the Good King and the Warrior? Why me? Why can't he do it himself?" Thomas dropped his head on his knees and sobbed himself to sleep.

After a long while Thomas suddenly woke to find the fire had all but burned out. There were only the embers left smoldering in the pit. Thomas took his drinking canteen and poured a little water to douse the fire. He defiantly stood and walked a few paces. "Fine, fine, fine Gatekeeper, why wait until morning? Let's get on with it!"

Thomas took a moment and breathed in the cool night air. Thomas didn't look at the map; he knew where he was. Across the valley and through the grove was where the Queen's castle stood. Thomas determined he'd do this himself. The thought came to him that if he stood there a moment longer, the Queen would be able to see him from her castle tower and have him arrested as a trespasser. Thomas shook his head and dismissed that thought as being influenced by the mystic nonsense talk of the Gatekeeper.

Thomas moved into the mythamöhre grove. Little did he know just how right he was, the Queen had seen him. Lowen rose quietly to her feet and began following Thomas.

Chapter Eleven
CALCULATED COLLECTION

Nine led the way as Samuel followed, crawling on his hands and knees along the forested craggy mountainside at night. Nine seemed to be more nimble on his hands and knees.

"Is it really necessary to crawl to get to there?" Samuel asked.

"Definitely" replied Nine as he looked back at Samuel.

Nine could turn his head completely around to look backwards without turning his shoulders. This ability made Samuel uncomfortable.

"At this pace we'll never get there," Samuel complained.

Nine kept crawling forward but turned his head around to look at Samuel again.

"Unquestioningly, eventually, we will." replied Nine.

"Can you stop doing that..." Samuel didn't get the entire sentence out of his mouth before he fell into a hole.

"Ah... my back, my legs," complained Samuel as he lay at the bottom of the hole.

"Hello, Samuel?" Jason's voice spoke from the darkness.

"Jason?" Samuel asked as he sat up.

Jason emerged from the darkness. Samuel struggled to his feet and Jason joyfully held on to him for a long while.

"We escaped the raiders," whispered Samuel.

"I'm so glad to see you, to see anyone," replied Jason.

Samuel hugged his friend tighter in celebration.

Jason pulled away from the sharp pain in his own shoulder.

"I think the talon of the Gargoyle pierced my shoulder and my whole arm is in fiery pain. I think it is infected," said Jason

"Come on let's get out of here," replied Samuel.

Samuel peered out of the hole above them, into the night sky.

"Nine! Can you throw us a vine to get us out?" Samuel asked as he yelled up toward the hole.

"Nine, can you hear me?" He repeated.

"I can hear you but I cannot see you." replied Nine from outside of the hole.

"I know you can't see me, but it's me, Samuel. Throw us a vine or something to get out."

"If I can't see you, how do I know you are there and you are really Samuel?" Replied Nine.

"You can hear my voice, now help us out of here," answered Samuel.

Nine turned and sat on his haunches. When he didn't have to project the image that the viewer wished of him, he could relax and appear as himself. His whip-like-pointed-tail twitched and curled as it always did when he was nervous or excited. He scratched the back of his furry head, wiggled his large rodent ears and batted his round bulbous eyes. Nine ran his tongue over his sharp canine teeth and muttered to himself, "Two, I have two, the start of a very nice collection. Seven plus two make Nine and that would make it complete."

"Nine! Are you still there?" Shouted Samuel.

"I'M CALCULATING!" Screamed Nine. "Don't interrupt me when I am calculating."

In the hole, Jason turned to Samuel, "Who is Nine?"

Before Samuel could answer a long vine hit the ground beside them.

Samuel picked it up and tied it around Jason's waist, knowing that his wounded friend couldn't pull himself out of the hole.

"Nine, I have the rope tied around my friend, I will climb up it and when we are together we will pull Jason out of the hole. Do you hear me?" Shouted Samuel.

Samuel turned to Jason and spoke softly, "Don't worry we'll get you out." Samuel turned and addressed the opening above him as he tested the vine. "Nine, make sure the vine is secured because I am climbing out!"

Samuel tugged on the vine and assured himself it was secure. He began to climb the vine.

Chapter Twelve
THROUGH THE GROVE

The moon was as full as Thomas had ever seen it. Thomas walked between the rows of mythamöhre trees. Thomas spoke to himself to calm his own fears, "The night we met on the mountain path started out like this and ended as a stormy dangerous night. Focus on good things Thomas Jacob Littlewood, focus on good."

The full moon gave Lowen something to howl about. It may have given away her position but it was a compelling instinct deep within her. She let out a howl that would wake the dead.

The sound of the wolf startled Thomas. Thomas began walking backward trying to peer into the night. He knew Lowen was out there but he couldn't see her. A terrible sinking feeling of fear in the pit of his stomach filled him. The kind of fear one feels when walking down a dark hallway not knowing what's around the corner. Shadows caught his eye and he believed he saw the wolf creature following him. His imagination began to get the better of him as he looked up at the twisted branches of the mythamöhre trees. It was as if at any moment the trees themselves would come to life, reach down and grab him. Thomas regretted not taking the time to look at the map. He did not even know if he was going in the right direction but he was too afraid to stop. He was in it now and had to get out. He didn't like the idea of being alone.

"Come on wolf! If your fixing for a fight I am ready to give it to you!" Thomas shouted.

The wind picked up and rustled through the mythamöhre trees, turning leaves over and scraping branches together. The sound became an orchestra of moaning.

Thomas raced through the grove, trying to reach the end.

Then Thomas stopped and caught sight of her... the wolf was running scared. With tail between her legs, she was running as fast as she could and Thomas was losing sight of her. Seeing Lowen's reaction made his own fear intensify. She was getting further and further away.

"Lowen, you're afraid to fight I see," Thomas called.

Lowen wasn't about to turn around to look behind her and neither did Thomas.

Children play that game all the time. They cover their eyes convinced that if they can't see you, you can't see them. It is easier to cope by not looking than to confirm your fears. Although Thomas could see Lowen now ahead of him running for her life, he was filled with the uneasy anticipation that someone was chasing him and that at any second they would reach out and grab him.

As Thomas ran past the mythamöhre trees, the fruit and the leaves began to magically light up. The mythamöhre trees' illuminations kept perfect timing with Thomas' approach. Thomas thought the trees took on the appearance of houses adorned with lanterns. He had never seen anything like it before; as fast as he could run, the trees kept up their illumination with him. It was like waves of the ocean rolling into the sand and Thomas was riding the crest. It wasn't a feeling of excitement, rather one of terror and the foreknowledge that eventually he would be crashing on the shore.

Thomas could hear Lowen's whimpering in the distance. It was a sound of panic. Thomas could see the clearing. He ran as fast as he could huffing and puffing with sweat pouring down his face. He prayed silently that he would not trip and fall. The ground was becoming increasingly unstable with roots and rocks to navigate. As he approached the end of the orchard, the pathway narrowed and the trees seemed to be closing in.

Lowen saw him coming and began growling. Thomas was happy to face the wolf; at least he knew what he was dealing with. Thomas could see it, there, just ahead; the clearing and he could see Lowen. Thomas could see that the end of the orchard was only a short distance away, this made him dig deeper, push himself harder, run faster when suddenly, Thomas tripped. Thomas hit the ground hard with a thud that knocked the wind out of him. He rolled over on his back with his eyes closed. Between struggling to catch his breath and his wild imagination; he first wondered if a tree stuck up its root to trip him. He knew that was nonsense and laughed to himself, he was just in too much of a hurry and stumbled on his own accord. He convinced himself it was all in his imagination. Thomas' breathing calmed and so did he.

The soil was damp and cold. With each inhale; the musty smell became deeply embedded in his nose. The sharpness of the scent hurt as much as being winded. Thomas wiped the mud off of his face but kept his eyes closed. He still had the strange impression that someone was watching him and he didn't want to confirm his fears by opening his eyes.

"Thomas my pretty boy, open your sweet brown eyes and let me look in them. I've waited so long for you to come," cooed the young, soft female voice.

Thomas squeezed his eyes shut tighter.

"Come on my sweet we are alone out here... just you and me. Open your eyes my sweet."

Thomas believed that the voice sounded familiar... was it mom or was it Talia? The familiarity of the voice calmed Thomas' apprehension.

"Come Thomas, open your beautiful brown eyes and let me look at you, there's nothing to be afraid of," reassured the female voice.

Slowly Thomas began to open his eyes.

"That's it handsome, let me see you up close."

The first image as Thomas focused his eyes were the fluttering leaves of the shimmering trees, the golden light hued in radiant colors of the rainbow. Thomas had never seen anything so beautiful. Then out of the light came the image of Queen Aleah Mythamöhre. Her crown glittered and her angelic face glowed. Her pitch-black pupils pierced his soul.

She looked no more than maybe eleven or twelve. Thomas smiled and she shyly smiled back as if she was flattered.

"I know you Thomas Jacob Littlewood and I am so happy you finally came to me. You don't think I've seen you before but I have. How could I not notice someone so handsome and brave as you Thomas." She cocked her head to the side but kept her eyes connected with Thomas'. "I know the journey you're on, a journey that will find its fulfillment with me. Take my hand and let me help you."

Queen Mythamöhre reached out her hand to Thomas.

Thomas was mesmerized. He reached out his hand to her. A flood of emotion waved over his body that rushed from the sole of his feet to the top of his head. He liked the feeling.

All of a sudden, loud growling startled Thomas out of his hypnotic state. Lowen stood beside Thomas: growling and baring her teeth, like only wolves can do.

Thomas stole a glance back to find the Queen gone. To his surprise he saw the branches and the leaves of the mythamöhre tree beginning to wrap around his leg and vine their way up his body. The tree was glowing and pulsating. It began to drag him closer to its trunk. Lowen inched closer growling as if she was about to attack. From this position on the ground Thomas was in no position to defend himself from either of his attackers.

Lowen lunged toward Thomas but rather than ripping at him, she sunk her sharp canine teeth into the branch that was snaking up Thomas' leg. A loud SCREECH like the sound of a thousand screams went up into the air and the branch let go of Thomas. It was as if every tree in the orchard began screaming in pain. The sound was deafening.

Lowen continued ripping into the tree as Thomas scrambled to his feet. He was disoriented at first and could not gather his bearings of which way to go. He was lost in the screaming orchard. He picked up his staff and ran for the end of the orchard. Lowen let go of the living mythamöhre tree and yelped as she ran past Thomas and out of the orchard.

Thomas did not realize that he had left behind the map that was given to him by the Gatekeeper. A vine of the mythamöhre tree wrapped around the forgotten map and began to drag it into the darkness.

In the palace at the end of the orchard, the Queen stood up from the dinner table and grabbed her arm. It was as if the bite of Lowen had been directly on her arm. The screams from the orchard swirled around her head and echoed in the palace-dining hall. All of the ladies and lords gathered at the elaborate banquet stopped feasting in shock at what they saw and heard. The dinner party fell silent.

The Queen looked down at her arm as tree sap oozed out of the bite mark that appeared on her arm. Angry and embarrassed, she looked up at her startled guests.

"Out of here, all of you pathetic excuses for life get out!" Screamed the Queen.

Everyone at the table hurriedly put their napkins on their plates and calmly but quickly found their way to the large banquet hall doors that the butler had opened.

With the room cleared, the butler came to the Queen's side. The Queen looked down as a little girl of 12 and when she looked up at the butler, her form had transfigured into a shapely woman in her mid twenties. it was on rare occasions of extreme stress that the Queen allowed anyone to witness her shape-shifting in person. The butler had this rare privilege.

"Someone has violated me and is in the orchard at this very minute. Send out the Guardsmen, hunt them down and bring them to me NOW!" Demanded the Queen.

"Yes mistress," said the butler as he ran for the door leaving Queen Mythamöhre alone in the room.

A wicked smile crossed her lips as she took a sip of the scarlet colored drink in front of her. She sat and calmly continued to eat her dinner alone.

Thomas and Lowen, now a stone's throw out of the orchard, continued running, never looking back. Just as Thomas and the wolf exited one side of the orchard, the Queen's Gargoyle Guard entered the other. The Guards normally made the exterior wall of the Queen's abode impenetrable. Their giant ape-like bodies would secure themselves as stone to the wall. When they were attached to the palace, their individual shapes were difficult to discern because their numbers intertwined and completely covered the texture of the stone they protected. When an impending danger threatened her security, the Queen sent them out on a search and destroy mission. Their bat-shaped wings, sinewy clawed appendages; rat like ears, bulbous head and nose was accentuated by protruding fangs, which made their six-foot tall stature all the more intimidating.

The Head Gargoyle Guardsman stood with his clawed hands crossed. His cold lifeless eyes peered into the darkened orchard. The gargoyle troops began to scour the orchard for the intruder. Like a swarm of locust, the guards descended on the orchard. Drawing their swords, they searched, poked and prodded every possible hiding place. Moving on the ground, the gargoyles used the knuckles of their hands like a gorilla would when agitated and moving quickly. There was no sign of the intruders.

The vine that had collected the map from Thomas, stretched up and delivered it to one of the droopy eyed, drooling Gargoyle Guards.

The tall grass waved in the breeze as Thomas and Lowen passed through it. Dew settled in and it was making Thomas' legs and feet wet. Lowen looked as if she had just taken a bath and nothing smells so discerning as a wet wolf. If it weren't for Lowen, the Queen would have captured Thomas. Instinctively he knew to follow the wolf to safety. She kept leading him on.

In the palaces' master bedchamber, shards of the rising morning sunlight pierced the darkness of the big room. A fire crackled in the massive fireplace. The Queen's door was opened a crack, enough for the head Gargoyle Guardsman to watch his Queen through the opening. She was in her favorite incarnation, the form of a mature woman in her mid-twenties.

The Queen had her back to the door, her robe draped off her naked shoulders. Her head moved slowly up as she soaked in the sunlight; as if she was a living plant absorbing its nourishment.

The Guardsman's eyes widened as he saw vines retracting under the Queens' floor length night robe. Beneath her robe light emanated from her form. She turned her head looking over her shoulder, spotted him watching her and covered herself up. The light beneath her robe dimmed and disappeared.

"Wicked," she said softly with a smile. "I see you watching me. Come in."

The Gargoyle Guardsman bowed his head, opened the door and approached the Queen. He held up his clawed hand and presented her the map.

The Queen took it, unrolled the map revealing its contents. She studied the map for a moment and smiled. She knew what the map meant. The King was returning.

"So he is coming back, all the more time for us to be prepared. Send out the appropriate welcome for the little boy and his vicious dog. Send the Imps ahead of them and wait. We know where they are going. They will eventually come to us."

The Queen looked up at the Gargoyle towering over her.

To appear submissive, the Gargoyle kept his eyes looking down and away from her.

"Well done my faithful and loyal servant," she said with an irresistible charm.

She stroked her hand along the Gargoyle Guardsman's face and let her fingertips trail down his neck.

He smiled a fanged grin.

"Well done," she repeated in a more serious tone.

Then she tightened her hand around the Gargoyle Guardsman's neck and squeezed.

"Gawk at me again, without permission and it will be the last thing your stony eyes ever see in all eternity," threatened the Queen.

By all appearances one would assume the Gargoyle to be flesh but chips of stone crumbled off the Gargoyles neck under the Queen's grip.

The Gargoyle Guardsman began to become week in his knees from the lack of oxygen. The Queen smiled and let go of her stranglehold. The Gargoyle caught his breath and bowed as he backed his way out of her bedchamber.

The Queen turned around to face the sunlight and began to unrobe again. Looking over her shoulder at the Gargoyle she said, "Be a dear and close the door behind you."

The Gargoyle Guardsman did as he was commanded.

Far from the castle, as the sun rose: Thomas and Lowen were fast asleep. The morning sun warmed them awake. Thomas woke with a jump and saw the wolf a short distance away curled up. Lowen raised her head to look at him but didn't give him a second thought. She went back to sleep. Thomas saw a little yellow bird singing on a branch nearby. Thomas whistled back at the little bird's chirping. Lowen lifted her head and cocked it to one side as dogs often do when puzzled by something, then she lay back down. Thomas got up to his feet and lifted his Papa's staff. The little yellow bird flew off into the sunrise.

Deciding to get a look around at the immediate area, Thomas walked away slowly not to arouse Lowen to follow. Thomas walked to the edge of the hill they were on. He sat overlooking the amazing green landscape below him and the massive sky above. Big deep blue and purple morning clouds hung over the valley.

Normally Thomas would have thought of nothing else but what lay beyond the purple clouds, if it were not for his stomach doing twists and turns; he was hungry. His last meal was breakfast from the morning before. Now that he was out here in the middle of nowhere, how was he to get meals? Thomas was not a hunter.

Thomas shivered from the brisk morning air. Immediately his thoughts left his hunger and went back to his village and family. Snow would be arriving soon at the village. It would be a desolate place with the entire village abandoned. There was no one to stoke the fires that usually warmed their village homes. There would be no building snow forts or hurling snow balls at friends this year. This would be different; it was a time for growing up.

He used to always imagine what it would be like to be grown up and to be able to do what he wanted. Now that he was on his own, it was not as much fun as he imagined. It was lonely, suddenly his shoulders felt extremely heavy as if one wrong move and his head would snap off; it hurt. Maybe this is what grown-ups felt when they said things were stressful. Papa suffered from it when Thomas' mother died. If stress is part of growing up; Thomas wanted no part of it.

Lowen appeared and whimpered pacing back and forth. Thomas readied his staff still unsure if he could trust the wolf. She seemed as if she was trying to get him to follow. Thomas did. Back in the place where they had slept Thomas discovered the remains of a rabbit. Lowen had gone hunting while he was daydreaming, Lowen growled and hung her head low as if to say she had first dibs on the kill. She ripped what she wanted and moved away with it. Thomas took the cue that the rest was for him. He approached the fresh kill slowly and lifted it up. "Thank you Lowen. Thank you for what you did last night as well," Thomas said. Although the wolves were no friends of his village he also knew that the Queen's Guardsmen hunted wolves for sport. They were hunted almost to extinction. Thomas knew there was no love lost between the wolves and the Queen's kingdom. "We have a common adversary don't we wolf?" Thomas asked. He smiled at Lowen and set about building a campfire; that much he knew how to do. Papa had taught him how to build a fire. High up in the mountain passes it was not uncommon for shepherds to build fires at this time of year. Once Thomas got the fire going, he began to cook his breakfast.

Thomas was mesmerized as he watched the rabbit cook over the open fire. Thomas' memory drifted to home and another time he had been forced to sleep under the stars; Papa and Thomas had been out in the high country tending to their sheep when the storm blew in. Thomas and Papa were able to find shelter in a cave on mount Crevasse until the storm blew over. When Thomas and Papa returned to their home, they found a patch on the roof had been torn off, right above Thomas' bed. He was younger then and thought that sleeping on his bed under a hole in the roof was a grand adventure. The thought of that night made him smile. His smile faded as his attention came back to the serious nature of the journey he was on.

Thomas' mind wrestled with the thoughts; if only he had not been so stubborn and just followed the map; perhaps they would not have suffered the dangers of the orchard. Thomas' mind began to lament his predicament... here he was, out in the wilderness on his own. The thought of isolation in this great wilderness caused him to look up at his surroundings with a new realization of the danger that could be lurking ahead.

It was then that something in the bushes nearby caught his eye. If it wasn't for that slash of sunlight through the trees he would have never seen it but the sunlight framed the object perfectly. It was a scroll tied with a piece of red ribbon. Thomas got up and carefully took the scroll from the branches that securely held it. It wasn't damp so there was no way that it had been here all night. Everything else was still covered by the morning dew but not this scroll. The scroll was dry to the touch and this made Thomas look around him again because someone must have just placed that scroll there moments ago. Seeing that there was no sign of the messenger that left the scroll, Thomas carefully opened the scroll.

Thomas read the scroll aloud, "Now that you've passed through the grove of fear: lives you must spare. Destiny calls to those who will listen. The difference one person can make is answered by the steps you will take. Follow the valley until the mill, across the river, up the hill to a cave. In that cave is the treasure you seek. Consider it wise to look again. Remember all that has been and all that was seen by the stream."

"By the stream!" Thomas shouted.

He jumped to his feet and looked around. By the stream Thomas thought, that's where he spent time with the Gatekeeper talking over the meal. Thomas worried if he would remember all the details that he needed to.

"Hello!" Thomas shouted. "Gatekeeper if you are near, please help me. I don't know if I can do this on my own. Hello!"

There was no answer only the wind through the leaves of the trees. Thomas looked out across the land for a sign of the Gatekeeper.

He sat back down and took the rabbit from the spit. If they have to go where he has never been before, he was thankful he had Lowen as a companion although he didn't know if he could fully trust her yet. He was thankful that he had breakfast and thankful to hope. Hope that somewhere along this journey he will find the tools he needed to free his Papa and the other villagers.

Chapter Thirteen
HOLES AND MYSTICS

A strong hand reached over the edge of the of the hole and Samuel grabbed on to it. Up and out of the hole, Samuel rolled on the damp night grass. The moonlight made it difficult to tell who the cloaked figure was that rescued him but Samuel witnessed that with little effort the stranger had also pulled Jason up by the vine, over the edge to safety. The cloaked figure untied Jason from the vine and then he squeezed the vine until a liquid dripped on Jason's wound.

"It will heal," said the cloaked stranger.

Samuel recognized the Gatekeeper's voice.

"I know who you are, Gatekeeper. Betrayer!" Samuel accused.

The Gatekeeper rose to his feet.

"Follow me and I will lead you to safety," replied the Gatekeeper.

"Or to the destination that the Gargoyles were leading us," answered Samuel.

"Then you've made a decision. Navigate your way carefully past the holes and you'll find safety," said the Gatekeeper. He turned and began to walk away.

Jason jumped to his feet and yelled after him, "Please wait."

The Gatekeeper stopped.

Jason turned to Samuel, "Why would he rescue us only to betray us?"

"He escaped the raid on our village. How did he know they were coming? I'll tell you how, he tipped them off. Think about it Jason, it makes sense. He's a mystic, they're not to be trusted."

The Gatekeeper began to walk away again and Jason's plea stopped him, "Wait Gatekeeper if you know the way through this dangerous ground, I'm coming." Jason turned to Samuel, "You can stay here and find your way if you wish."

Something caught Samuel's peripheral vision, it moved in the moonlight behind the tree. It was Nine crouched behind the tree. Nine waved for Samuel to follow him and nodded his head like he knew the way.

Samuel turned his attention back to the Gatekeeper and Jason, "You know the way? We can barely see far enough ahead of us to know the way!"

The Gatekeeper answered, "If you knew the whole way, you'd be responsible for the entire journey. You know the next step, isn't that enough?"

Jason responded, "It's enough for me, I've been in that hole long enough." Jason maneuvered his shoulder and realized the pain and infection was gone. He turned to Samuel, as he moved his arm around in full circles, "Look... I'm going, stay here if you want."

Samuel shot a quick glance to see if Nine was around but he couldn't find him. Samuel approached the Gatekeeper and Jason. He pointed his finger at the Gatekeeper, "I know who you are. You can try and conceal your identity with that hood but it doesn't work with me."

Jason was surprised at this revelation. For as long as he could remember, he had heard the stories and rumors that spread around the village. Everyone tolerated the Gatekeeper's presence but hardly anyone spoke to him. Jason was surprised that Samuel claimed to know the Gatekeeper's real identity.

Samuel walked closer to the Gatekeeper, "Why don't you remove your hood and reveal to us your horrible disfigurement. That's right, I know all about you, Gatekeeper. My father told me."

The Gatekeeper sat on a fallen tree nearby and began to grab the edge of his hood to pull lit back.

Jason yelled out, "No wait!" He turned to Samuel, "Disfigurement?"

Samuel proudly threw back his head, "Yeah... he was a drunk, a coward, a low life that was kicked out of his own village so he came to live with us. As my father said, he was so drunk one time that he fell into a fire he had built... face first... causing these hideous burns... melting the flesh from his face. That's why he stays covered."

"Is it true?" Jason asked the Gatekeeper.

Samuel answered quickly before the Gatekeeper could, "Oh it's all true and he's a mystic, he practices the art of black magic. How do you think he knew to squeeze the vine that poured into your wound? Sure the Gargoyles may have infected your shoulder with their talon but the Gatekeeper has infected your mind with his potion and nonsense talk."

Jason sat on the ground and moved his shoulder, "But Samuel, my shoulder. He rescued us out of that hole!"

Samuel shot back, "We were just fine. I had a friend prepared to help us."

Jason hung his head in his hands.

The Gatekeeper nodded and rose to his feet. Both Samuel's and Jason's eyes followed him.

The Gatekeeper spoke, "Your father has taught you much Samuel. It's easy to be offended when you begin from a position of the offensive. Would a man's appearance determine the motives of his actions?"

"Your actions are pretty clear. Our village was attacked and you had conveniently avoided being captured. Hiding somewhere, proof that you are a coward," replied Samuel.

"Will your actions prove your bravery?" Asked the Gatekeeper.

"What are you asking of us?" Samuel moved closer to Jason.

"Help me find the warrior that will rescue your village and usher in the Good King's return to the kingdom," responded the Gatekeeper.

Samuel laughed and mumbled to himself, "Babbling mystic."

Jason rose to his feet and took Samuel by the shoulders, "What options do we have? Where would we go? If we can find the warrior and the Good King we could rescue our families. Please Samuel."

"What's in it for you?" Samuel asked the Gatekeeper.

"Restoration," responded the Gatekeeper.

"What place does an old drunk, disfigured mystic have with a Good King?" Asked Samuel.

Even though the Gatekeeper's hood concealed his face, Samuel could feel his gaze and knew that Jason also waited for an answer.

Samuel broke his stare with the Gatekeeper and then turned his attention back to Jason and affirmed his decision to go.

In the woods nearby, Nine shook his head in disappointment and mumbled, "Dangerous following, dangerous times, dangerous decisions."

The Gatekeeper began to walk and Jason encouraged Samuel to follow first. The boys fell in line behind the Gatekeeper. They were careful to walk only in the Gatekeepers' footsteps. They had been to the bottom of the pit and did not wish to return.

Chapter Fourteen
THE CAVE OF DOUBT

Thomas walked down the rocky valley following the instructions of the scroll to an ever-widening river. Tall pine trees lined the valley. The rocky path Thomas walked was evidence that at one time the river was much larger. Thomas was on the lookout for the mill that the scroll talked about. He was hopeful that he would find the mill soon but he was content to take his time along the peaceful riverbank. The river was moving slowly, in no particular hurry either. Thomas saw a log floating in the river and decided to try and keep step with it. He walked slowly and could easily pass the log. He had to stop and wait for the floating log to catch up.

Lowen was the impatient one. She hated stopping. She bounced and ran ahead, looking for every kind of trouble she could get herself in. A tiny chipmunk squeaked at the sight of Lowen. Lowen pounced but missed and the chipmunk ran up a tree by the rivers edge. Lowen stood at the bottom of the tree and barked after the chipmunk. She circled the tree to see if she could get a better look at the chipmunk but she couldn't. She stood wagging her tail and watching the tree for the chipmunks' appearance.

Thomas laughed, "Hey girl, do you think that chipmunk is going to come down the tree just because you are waiting for her? You are a silly wolf."

Lowen didn't pay attention to Thomas, she had more pressing concerns and her focus was totally on that pesky chipmunk.

Thomas looked back to the river; the log he had been racing, picked up speed and was quite a distance ahead now.

"Hey Lowen come on, we're going to lose the race!"

Thomas took off and ran along the shore. He passed by a pile of pebbles that normally he would have spent time examining. They were pebbles like his favorite rocks he called beauties; multicolored and interesting. Right now, he had no time, maybe once he got to the cave and retrieved whatever treasure the scroll said was there, he would be able to return to this spot and collect some of these great stones.

By the time he had caught up to the log, he was winded. Thomas stopped to catch his breath but the log did not wait for him, it was moving fast.

With Thomas' attention fully focused on the log, he hadn't noticed that the swift current was the reason the log had picked up its pace. It was moving very fast now. Thomas turned back to look for Lowen and sure enough, she came bouncing over the rocks trying to keep up. Thomas sat on the shore to catch his breath and let his new friend catch up to him. Lowen soon did.

She sat beside him and cocked her head to one side, giving him a slight whimper.

Thomas let out a big sigh and inhaled. He smiled as he looked at Lowen with her head at an angle. Thomas matched the angle of her head as he spoke to her. "What's the matter girl, still thinking about that chipmunk?"

Lowen wasn't looking at Thomas, she was looking beyond him across the river. Thomas turned to see what she was looking at.

There, through the tall trees that hung to the craggy ledge of the shore, was the mill. Beyond the mill, a lantern was bobbing through the forest being carried by someone. The forest was too thick to make out the figure carrying the lantern but it was definitely a person.

Thomas bolted to his feet. The curiosity of this was almost too much. Why would they be carrying a lantern in broad daylight? Then the answer flooded his mind.

"This person must be carrying the lantern because they are going to somewhere dark like... a cave," he whispered out loud to Lowen.

Thomas couldn't make out who the figure was that was carrying the lantern, but this person was moving up the hill and into the woods. Thomas thought of yelling out but the river was moving so fast over the rocks, he probably couldn't yell loudly enough for the person to hear him.

Thomas looked down the river and back to where he had come from. How do I cross this thing, Thomas wondered.

The river was moving way too fast for him to wade into it and walk across, he couldn't begin to guess how deep it was. It could be way over his head.

Thomas sat back down on the rocky shore. He put his head in his hand. Lowen whimpered. Thomas turned to her.

"Great we've come this far to stop here."

Lowen barked at him.

"I suppose you are suggesting that we doggy paddle across." Thomas laughed at the thought.

Lowen backed up a few steps and barked again. Thomas looked behind him, maybe someone was in the woods creeping up, but no, she was barking at Thomas. "Since I don't speak wolf, we are going to have to come up with a better way of communicating," Thomas said.

Lowen turned and ran back in the direction that they had just come.

"Lowen where are you going?" Thomas shouted.

Thomas got up and started after her, partly out of friendship and partly out of fear of being left alone. She was the one that saved his life back in the mythamöhre grove; he would never forget her bravery and friendship. In Thomas' mind, he had come to love her like family.

"Lowen wait!" Lowen stopped.

"It's no use going all the way back up the valley! It'll take us an entire day and who knows if the river narrows enough for us to get across," Thomas reasoned.

Thomas ran to Lowen but every time he did, Lowen took off running ahead so he could never catch up. They were retracing all of the ground they had already covered.

"Wait, don't move Lowen, stay where you are," Thomas yelled.

Thomas ran after Lowen. She waited till he almost got to her before she ran away a bit further. This went on for some time before Thomas decided they had gone far enough.

It would have been funny to onlookers, a boy chasing the wolf; to almost catch her and then repeat the entire chase. To Thomas, the fun had worn off. Exhausted he stopped and sat on some logs that had jammed against the rocks. Lowen stopped too. She came over to Thomas and sat on the shore facing him.

"Glad to see that you came to your senses. I am not going all the way back to the beginning, although by now we've run half the way."

Lowen barked at him.

Thomas pushed against a large rock with his feet while he sat on the log. He rocked it back and forth and eventually the log became loose. Then the thought came to him. If the other log travelled down the river, maybe they could ride down the river on this log and direct it to the far shore.

"Come on girl. Get on," Thomas said. Lowen had decided to lay down and watch Thomas. Lowen got to her feet and wagged her tail at Thomas' urging to join him.

"Come on Lowen, once this gets in the stream there is no turning back."

Lowen hesitated, took a few steps forward then backed up. Then she stepped into the shallow water by the rivers edge.

Thomas helped Lowen on the log and gave one final push; out into the river they went. Lowen looked nervous. Her head was low and she kept looking at the water all around her.

Once she went to jump off and Thomas said sternly, "No."

Lowen balanced and lay down on the log.

Thomas had to sit with a leg on either side of the log in the water because it was very easy to roll and both of them would end up in the river. Thomas pushed Papa's shepherds' staff into the water and almost lost it. This river was deep and cold. Thomas brought the staff out of the water and balanced it on the log in front of him. His legs were starting to freeze. Thomas lifted his legs out of the water and attempted to put them on the log behind him but he almost rolled the log over dumping them both into the river. Thomas winced and lowered his legs back into the freezing water. His toes were numb and sharp pains shot up his legs from the cold water, he was losing the feeling in them.

Thomas bent forward on the log and cupped his hands. He plunged his hands in the water and began to paddle to the other shore but they had entered the river too close to the quick current. This log was on a ride that Thomas couldn't direct. The log began to move side to side and something under the surface rubbed Thomas' leg. Startled, Thomas moved his leg as a reaction to the thing that brushed against him. He took his staff and felt into the dark water.

CLUNK.

His staff had connected with something hard and immovable... a rock.

His legs where getting bumped on either side by the rocks in the river. He couldn't see them until he was almost upon them and the log also started bobbing because of the rocks below the surface.

BANG.

The log drove his leg into a boulder just under the surface. Thomas screamed. Lowen whimpered. Thomas looked down at his leg and blood was floating in the water beside him.

He knew that if he fell off, that he and Lowen would be pinned against these huge boulders. Falling in the water meant they would either freeze or drown before they could save themselves.

Without warning the front of the log dipped and flipped Thomas up in the air over Lowen. As he flew overhead it was as if everything was happening in slow motion, he could see his good friend looking up at him with terror in her eyes as she was dumped into the freezing water.

SPLASH.

Thomas was under the water, then out again and back under the water.

BANG.

The water brought Thomas crashing into a rock and he came up for air. Thomas could hardly catch his breath. The water was so cold, his leg and back hurt from smashing into the rocks... the water pushed him onward.

BANG.

He slammed into another rock and looked around for Lowen. He couldn't find her. Thomas tried to swim for the far shore but the river pushed him on downstream. He clung to his Papa's staff. Thomas was weak and battered and fearful thoughts that he wouldn't make it began to fill his imagination.

A rock in the river caught his Papa's staff almost jerking it out of Thomas' hand, pulling it out behind him. It twisted him around and Thomas looked over his shoulder because he was now going down the river backwards. He could see two large rocks on either side of him. He tried to move himself into the stream just a little more...

CLUNK.

His staff caught between the rocks. Like a bridge in the rushing water it held him and he held on. It took all of Thomas' strength but he pulled himself toward his Papa's staff and the rocks. The rocks where cold and slippery but he was able to maneuver himself in front of one of them. The river beat down on him pushing him on the rock. Thomas looked to his right and to his left. Funny, Thomas thought, this is where Lowen and I sat looking across the river at the old mill. The water seemed to be parting again, not quite a shepherd staff away.

"Lowen, Lowen where are you girl?" Thomas screamed.

No sound and no sign of her, just the roaring sound of the quick rushing water.

Thomas lay his head against the rock that supported his upper body. His whole body started to feel numb and coursed with the pain of a thousand needles poking into him. He knew that it was now or never. Thomas looked back to the rock that was a shepherd staff away and knew he must try to swim to it or drown, pinned here against this boulder.

He examined the distance of the next rock from him. Thomas took a deep breath. With all the courage he could muster, he jumped out into the raging river again.

He was only able to get out a couple of feet before the water started pushing him back toward the rocks he had come from, holding his staff out in front of him...

CLUNK.

It worked! He had jammed the staff against the outcrop of rocks. Thomas held on with all he had. The river pushed him, his legs drifting under his staff. Thomas gritted his teeth and worked his way along the pole, finally making it to the next rock. While trying to keep himself against the rock, he carefully drew his shepherd's staff toward him. Thomas' left foot caught something under the surface... it was the shallow bottom. The river was shallow under his left foot but there was no guarantee how far the shallow water continued. Thomas had no choice; he had to go for it. By his best calculations it was only about two staff lengths to the shore.

Thomas braced himself against the rock and pushed with all the might his cold and aching muscles could muster.

Thomas slipped into the shallow water, falling on some rocks. The current almost pulled him back in to the river. Thomas rolled and jammed his staff between some rocks under the surface. His body was partially out of the water now. He stumbled to his feet and made his way to shore. Thomas collapsed in a heap on the shore. He looked down at his leg that was bruised and bloodied. His arms were battered from the beating he took in the river and large welts were rising on his arms. The rocks of the river left huge scratches on his body as if they were scarred by the claws of a monster under the surface that was trying to drag him under.

"Lowen," Thomas yelled feebly.

He hardly had any strength left in him. Thomas lay back on the shore of the river under overhanging rocks and fell asleep.

When he awoke, the sun was far across the sky. By Thomas' best estimate it was late afternoon. He took a moment to examine his surroundings; winter had started on the mountain, earlier autumn by the grove and here there were still verdurous splashes with trees boasting their summer blush.

He reasoned in his mind that he couldn't have travelled so far south not to be touched by winter. He next wondered if he were in some enchanted land that kept the bitter season at bay. Surely, he thought, winter was nipping at the heals of this lush land.

He went to sit upright but could hardly move. His body was stiff and sore all over. When he was in the heat of battle with the current of the river, his muscles hadn't felt this bad. There was nothing that would numb the pain of the beating he took.

Thomas used his staff to support himself to his feet. He had seen the old shepherds leaning on their staffs like a cane, now so would he. This was a new use for Thomas' staff; usually Thomas swung the staff over his shoulder. The sun had dried Thomas' waterlogged clothes. In pain, Thomas limped his way over the uneven rocks toward the hill that rose from the river.

Thomas yelled out, "Lowen!"

Thomas paused because he thought he heard the howl of a wolf. Looking all around he couldn't discern the direction the sound came from. He reasoned that it was either, the wind, the river, or his imagination making him believe he could hear the faint howl of a wolf far away. Thomas hoped above all things in his heart, that his friend was safe.

Thomas stumbled up to the mound of grass that lined the riverbank. Thomas looked up at the abandoned structure. The mill leaned a little on its foundation. Rumors had reached his village of this place. He had heard that in a time before the Queen, men had implemented incredible innovations like this mill. He knew the name of these colossal structures but not their purpose. It was a purpose, which had passed. He couldn't imagine any worthwhile purpose that this derelict structure served. In the front of the mill was a great wheel that spun around, kicked up by the fast river. Thomas didn't take long to look at this structural marvel, he knew he had a mission and he knew what he had to do.

Thomas limped for some distance up the hill and through the woods in the direction of where he had seen the lantern going. The more he walked the more his cuts and bruises hurt. His leg was swollen to twice its normal size. He began to think that he could go no further, it was then that he saw the cave in the side of the hill. Covered with moss and sharp rocks all around its edge, the cave opened its yawning mouth. It looked like a gaping mouth with the rocks forming the sharp teeth. Thomas leaned against a tree and slumped down to the ground. What if I went in there, he thought, would the mouth of the cave close its sharp teeth and swallow me?

"Young man," a woman's voice called out behind Thomas.

Thomas turned and saw an old woman making her way up the embankment behind him. She had a friendly face but it was incredibly wrinkled and she had pointed ears. Thomas had never seen anyone this old before, especially with such peculiar ears.

"Young man, where do you think you are off to?" The old woman questioned.

"Well I, I , I am only sitting here resting," stammered Thomas.

"Don't you know you are trespassing on crown land?" The old woman queried.

"No, oh I, I, well…" Thomas was nervous. "I don't know what crown land is."

The old woman laughed, "Crown land belongs to the crown, the Queen. You shouldn't be here!"

Thomas slowly stood up.

"Well if I am trespassing, are you not trespassing also?" He questioned the old woman.

The old woman thought for a moment and looked down for an answer that she didn't have.

"Hey boy," a deep male voice called from behind Thomas.

Thomas turned and a Hunter was approaching him. He also had pointed ears. He was smiling and much younger than the Old Woman. He was carrying arrows and had a bow slung over his shoulder.

"There is no loitering in these woods by order of the Queen!" said the Hunter

Thomas was surprised. For the entire days journey, he had not seen a soul and now he has encountered two.

"Well I, ah we," Thomas turned around to include the Old Woman but she was gone.

Thomas looked around the forest but couldn't see her anywhere. The way she lumbered along, there was no way that she could have moved that fast. He turned back around to the Hunter.

"Loit... ering, loitering sir?" Thomas asked.

"Loitering lad. It means to just hang around in one spot," the Hunter replied.

Thomas nodded his head and then asked, "Are you a hunter sir?"

The hunter held out his bow and arrows, "As you can see lad I am." I am hunting wolves this day to rid the kingdom of the nuisance."

The Hunter's response caught Thomas' heart for a moment as he thought of his friend Lowen. Thomas instinctively knew how to respond to the Hunter, the answer was on his lips even before Thomas knew fully what he was going to say.

Thomas lifted his finger to his lips as if to say, be very quiet.

The hunter stopped and looked curiously at Thomas.

"If you make too much noise, you are bound to scare away any wolf within a good distance of here. They have very good hearing you know," Thomas said.

"Yes I know," said the hunter. "I am a hunter of wolves."

"That you've said, but if you are a hunter of wolves you must hide in wait to kill these vicious creatures," Thomas pondered aloud.

The hunter smiled his response.

"Then sir if you are waiting in hiding while hunting the wolves you too are loitering in offense to the Queen's orders," Thomas quipped.

The hunter looked down to the ground, looking for an answer he didn't have.

"Thomas Littlewood," a soft sweet voice he recognized had called his name. Standing in the mouth of the cave was Talia, holding a lantern.

Thomas couldn't believe his eyes. It was Talia all right. How did she escape the raid on the village? Thomas turned back to the Hunter but he was gone. Disappeared like the Old Woman. What strange place is this, Thomas wondered? Is Talia also in his imagination? Thomas questioned himself.

Thomas limped his way to the mouth of the cave. Talia took Thomas by the hand.

"Thomas it is so good to see you," Talia said.

Thomas smiled. It was Talia in the flesh. Thomas dropped his staff and threw his arms around her.

"Oh Talia you don't know how happy I..." then he realized they were hugging. This was the first hug he had ever gotten from a girl his age. They both realized it at the same time and immediately let go.

Talia straightened her dirty dress and brushed back her curly matted hair with her hand.

"Come with me Thomas. You must be cold and frightened out here in the dark without a lantern to see or fire to warm you," Talia said.

Thomas looked at her curiously, "Dark? Talia it is daylight!"

Thomas looked around him and saw shafts of sunlight breaking through the trees, all around the forest.

Talia laughed, "You are so silly sometimes. You are just lucky that I was passing by with my lantern or else I never would have found you out here in the dark."

Thomas picked up his staff and took Talia by the hand.

"Talia, listen to me, it's not dark out here!" Thomas exclaimed.

Talia took her lantern and lifted it high into the air and turned back toward the mouth of the cave.

"I am not staying out here in these dark woods Thomas Littlewood. I am going inside. You can stay out here if you wish but I am not," she said.

Talia took a few steps into the mouth of the cave. She stopped and looked over her shoulder to see if Thomas was coming.

"Are you coming or not?" She asked.

Thomas rolled his eyes and shook his head,

"Yeah I'm coming," he responded.

Thomas couldn't see the smile of relief on Talia's lips but she did smile as Thomas followed her deep into the cave.

Thomas could see a bonfire glowing ahead of him.

Talia turned down her lamp and walked toward the bonfire. Talia took a seat on a big log by the fire. Beyond the edge of the fire's illumination it was very dark, pitch black.

Thomas limped to her side and sat down beside her.

"We are the fortunate ones Thomas. Do you know that?" Talia asked.

"Yes I know," Thomas said.

Deep in the shadows a creature moved. Thomas heard it scurry and a mumble of whispers that were made to another creature scurrying in the dark, who responded. He knew it was out there in the dark. Thomas yelled into the dark, "I am not afraid of you. Come closer and you will taste the wood of this staff!"

Thomas swung his staff in front of him, making a swooshing sound as it split the air before him.

The whispering was behind him, then beside him, then in front. Thomas was busy looking around him, trying to see into the dark and identify the whispering entity.

"Talia, we need to leave this place, right now!" Thomas exclaimed.

"Thomas, it's fine, I am happy to be here and you will be too," Talia responded with a great calm.

Then the creature from the shadows showed itself. Not a dwarf, midget, or a small person, this was a full-grown miniature man dressed in the suit of a chef. Thomas had heard of forest imps and wondered if this could be one. They were known as deceiving little creatures that caused many to become lost in the woods forever.

If Thomas had stood beside the chef he would have come up to Thomas' knee. This little man had pointed ears like the others Thomas met outside of the cave.

"You wicked wretched evil girl, how dare you bring him in here," said the little Chef.

Talia turned her head to hide it from Thomas.

"Forgive me," Talia said.

"Forgive you!" Responded the Chef. "You'll have to work this off to prove your repentance, you ugly little one," demanded the chef.

Thomas stood to his feet and readied his staff.

"Enough!" Thomas yelled. "Talia is my friend."

The Hunter emerged from the darkness, also in miniature form.

"Friend?" Questioned the Hunter. He continued, "This wicked little tramp has no friends, no home, no family and no one cares for her but us, because we speak the truth."

The rumble of whispers increased in the cave, all around Thomas. It was as if the whispers grew in intensity when the Hunter or the Chef spoke out their words. Talia hung her head.

The Old Woman emerged from the darkness, also in miniature form.

"And you of all people should see the truth by now Thomas Jacob Littlewood. You are a meddlesome little boy. A boy that failed at every turn," the Old Woman snarled.

The mumbling whispers from the darkness increased.

Thomas sat back down on the log beside Talia. He looked at her but she just cowered away. Thomas looked back at the three accusers and they had grown considerably in size.

"Yeah failure," the Hunter said.

"You are a worthless shepherd. Everyone knows that! If you had been on proper guard with your sheep, the little lamb would never have gone missing. You abandoned your father when he needed you the most!" The Chef proclaimed.

Talia could barely look at Thomas. She mumbled out three words, "I'm sorry Thomas."

"Sorry for what? I messed up with my lamb, it's not your fault Talia, the Hunter is telling you the truth... it is my fault," Thomas quietly admitted.

Thomas looked down at his swollen legs and it throbbed greater than before. Thomas winced from the increasing pain. The mumbling whispers in the darkness magnified. Talia covered her ears. Thomas rocked with the pain from being battered by the rocks and battered by the words of his accusers.

"Yes, the truth is hard to live with, isn't it?" Asked the Chef.

Thomas looked up at their faces. The Chef, the Hunter and the Old Woman had grown in size again and now stood above Thomas and Talia. They all smiled with razor sharp teeth. Thomas could see their teeth resembled the rocks that surrounded the entrance of the cave. He would have never come into this dark place if not for Talia. He didn't blame her. He loved her.

The dark whispers grew and swirled around them. Certain words were discernible, breaking through the rumble of sound, "Failure, liar, ugly, cheater, loser..."

"I didn't mean to leave Papa, but the Gatekeeper..." Thomas pleaded.

"Yes, of course, the Gatekeeper," interrupted the Old Woman. "He is a cowardly liar that deceives stupid children like you."

"Why do you think he sent you on this impossible mission?" Questioned the Hunter.

"He knew that you would fail. He knew it was impossible to cross that river. He was hoping that you would drown just like your dog Lowen did," said the Chef.

Tears began to fall down Thomas' face.

"Failure, liar, ugly, cheater, loser..." shouted voices from the dark.

"Stop crying you weak wicked little boy," said the Chef.

"We have work to do to prepare the banquet of the Queen and you are getting in the way," accused the Hunter.

"What would you know, you've both gotten in the way of everyone in your entire life. It is a good thing your mother is no longer around because she would be ashamed of you. What a failure you are! Get up, both of you and follow us to the mill. You must carry back flower to make the bread for our banquet. Now get up! You lazy sorry excuses for the living," commanded the Old Woman.

Thomas held on to his staff and could hardly gather the strength to get up. His joints felt old and battered.

Talia got up and tried to help Thomas walk. The Chef, the Hunter and the Old Woman walked out of the cave. Thomas and Talia followed.

At their absence, with no one in attendance, the bonfire, which they sat in front of suddenly, blew out, as if extinguished by the breath of a strong unseen force.

Once they reached outside of the cave, Thomas noticed that the night was as pitch black as it was inside the cave. Had night fallen so quickly he wondered? There was not a star in the sky. Thomas and Talia fell into single file following their Accusers back down the hill toward the mill.

As they reached the water's edge, the moon peaked out between the clouds. No one noticed the faint light from the moon except Thomas. He limped along the riverbank following Talia and the three Accusers.

Thomas looked into the rushing water and remembered his friend Lowen, Papa, Samuel and the others from the village. How had he come so far to be so trusting and to be fooled all this time, he wondered. Thomas felt abandoned. The tears ran down his face as he limped along.

As they walked, the Chef shouted orders back to Talia and Thomas, "The flour will be full of worms. Your job is to pick the maggots out and eat them so we can cleanse the flour in preparation of the magnificent pastries I will make."

"You make the most wonderful pastries," added the Old Woman.

"Genius in gluttonous artistry," declared the Hunter.

"And that's why I call them sublime-lime cake," laughed the Chef.

The Hunter and Old Woman cackled with him.

Beside the mill was a pond where the water was still and calm. Beautiful, Thomas thought as they passed the still water. He remembered a time when he felt like that pond. It wasn't so long ago... suddenly Thomas stopped. He counted the reflections. In the still waters of the pond he could see himself and Talia but the others were not ahead of him.

The Hunter noticed Thomas had stopped and turned to face him.

"What's the matter with you lazy boy?" The Hunter questioned.

Then Thomas remembered what the Gatekeeper had told him. The words of the Gatekeeper echoed in his memory. "As water reflects the face, so a man's heart reflects the man," he could almost hear the Gatekeeper's voice.

Suddenly a courage rose up inside Thomas.

"You are creatures of hate and lies." Thomas pointed his staff at the Accusers.

The Old Woman and the Chef stopped and joined the Hunter as they faced Thomas. Talia hung her head and stopped walking. Thomas drew close to her side.

"You are not speakers of the truth because nothing you have said is true," continued Thomas through a shaky and wounded voice.

"You've lied to Talia and you've lied to me," Thomas continued as he fought back the tears.

The wind whipped up and blew hard against them.

"You rebellious foolish little squid; this girl is not safe with you, your dog was not safe with you, your lamb was not safe with you, no one is safe with a Littlewood," the Old Woman snapped in reply.

The Hunter took off his bow and arrows and began to string it up as if he was readying to shoot Thomas.

"I ought to drown you in that pond because your life means nothing," screamed the Chef.

In a small voice, Talia spoke her feelings, "Thomas means something to me."

That comment emboldened Thomas as he stood a little in front of Talia to protect her.

The Hunter joined in, "You can't protect her. You can't even protect yourself. You are destined to fail."

The power of the wind increased. Thomas looked deeply into Talia's eyes and he realized the power of the words they spoke. He heard the words of the Hunter but chose to ignore their impact, at least for the moment. He was struck with Talia's words, she said he means something to her. Before he could process what he was going to say, much like when he first met the Old Woman, the words were on his lips and out for all to hear.

"And she means something to me, I have come for her because..." Thomas faced their accusers, "I... LOVE... HER!"

Talia looked up to Thomas and smiled through tears. She kept her eyes on him, "I love him too."

Suddenly the earth shook and a crack appeared in the dark sky, letting sunlight shine through the darkness.

"Liar!" said the Old Woman. "What do you know of love?"

Talia looked at the Old Woman and for a moment she let her eyes drop, realizing that she may be right. Courage rose in Talia and she lifted her eyes to meet Thomas', she reached out her hand and grabbed his. Thomas readied his staff in his other hand.

"Maybe I don't know everything love means but I know that I care for Thomas. He is my friend and I love him for that," Talia responded.

The ground rumbled and shook with a great earthquake.

Suddenly the Chef, the Hunter and the Old Woman shrunk to half their size. The Hunter shot an arrow at Thomas. The arrow grazed his shoulder and Thomas stumbled back. Talia ran to his side. The Hunter drew another arrow.

"Shoot them quickly, kill them!" Screamed the Old Woman.

Dark clouds made a funnel around them and moved about in a clockwise direction. The ground shook. Accusations of whispers swirled around them in the clouds. Louder than ever, "Liar, ugly, failure, loser..." were the words of multiple voices in the funnel cloud.

Thomas, still in pain from being grazed by the Hunter's shot, stood up with the help of Talia and faced their Accusers. The sky cracked again and darkness began falling away like flakes of dry paint.

Then around the side of the mill came a growl, one that Thomas recognized well. It was Lowen baring all of her teeth!

"We will not fall for your lies... we... will... stand!" Thomas struggled the words out as the winds blew hard against him and Talia. They gripped each other for support.

As fast as lighting disappears across the sky, the Accusers shot off in all directions into the woods. The Accusers were so small; they were like wisps of wind. The swirling funnel cloud of whispering accusations suddenly reversed in direction, counter clockwise and it was gone!

The leaves rattled on trees deep in the forest from the departing winds. Thomas and Talia could no longer see any sign of the Accusers or even feel the wicked wind that had whipped up against them, all was calm. Lowen came up to Thomas wagging her tail. Thomas dropped to a knee and hugged his wolf.

"Talia this is my good friend Lowen," Thomas smiled. Talia dropped to her knees alongside Thomas with tears of gratitude in her eyes.

"Pleased to meet you Lowen., I'm Thomas' good friend Talia," she said.

Lowen put up her paw in submission and Talia accepted her paw, shaking it. Talia and Thomas laughed through their tears.

"How did you find me?" Talia asked.

"The Gatekeeper!" Thomas responded with new excitement. "We'll rescue the others too. We have to go back to the cave! I'm convinced of it. There may be more for us to find, now that we know the truth, how can we ever fear the lie again?"

Thomas was on his way toward the cave before Talia could respond. It was not the lie that Talia feared facing, it was the liar. She tried her best to put on a brave face as she followed Thomas.

Thomas' new found faith in this mission rose deep within him as he led Talia and Lowen back up the hill to the cave.

When they arrived at the entrance of the cave, they discovered that the earthquake that shook the ground when sunlight broke through had closed the entrance of the cave.

There sticking out of the ground, partially buried in rocks was an armored vest and a belt that went around the waist. Thomas and Talia moved the rocks until it was fully uncovered. The armor was finely adorned with jewels and beautifully crafted with gold ribbing around the polished silver. "Wow, this must have belonged to the great warrior I'm searching for," said Thomas.

"Find the one it fits and you will find the great warrior," a familiar voice came from the woods behind them.

Thomas and Talia turned to find the Gatekeeper.

That night Talia, Thomas, Lowen and the Gatekeeper dined on fish by the river edge.

"Why didn't you rescue us?" Thomas asked the Gatekeeper.

"If the ability for the tree to reproduce itself was not there, soon there would be no forests left. Had I rescued you without the truth, what chance would you have from now on? Freedom comes from the truth you know. It becomes living in you," said the Gatekeeper with a smile that was concealed by the hood he wore.

The warrior's silver breastplate and belt shimmered in the firelight. Thomas eyed it with great admiration. The Gatekeeper saw Thomas looking at the armor, he addressed Thomas and Talia, "As you admire the armor, it's with the same admiration that I look at the both of you. Your families would be proud. I am. Your story has joined the valiant stories of long ago. Your children's children will remember them."

It was a good evening. They told jokes and laughed. Thomas was having such a good time that he hadn't noticed that the swelling on his injuries had disappeared. The campfire blazed and kept them warm as they made themselves comfortable to sleep under the starry skies. The flowing water danced over the rocks with a beautiful rhythm that sang to them a sweet melody of adventures to come.

The very last thing the Gatekeeper said to both of them before they all nodded off to sleep was, "Wait here for my return."

AT THE ALLEN ROOM CONFERENCE:

Dr. Elderidge took a sip of water and smacked his lips together as if the water had gotten stale. He re-read a couple words of the second fragment.

#

FRAGMENT TWO

- life - react - adventure - day to day --

****

Dr. Elderidge looked over his glasses at the audience gathered. "You must always keep in mind the extraordinary nature of this discovery. The dating of these artifacts place them close to ten thousand years ago, at the dawn of modern mankind! I've covered that haven't I? Pardon my excitement because we haven't even reached the most amazing part," added Elderidge.

There was a low rumble in the crowd as reporters mumbled to each other. He nodded his head to Beth and lifted the glass of water to signal her to bring him a fresh glass. Beth quickly poured him another glass and brought it to Dr. Elderidge. He smiled at her and then he lifted another sheet.

"The fragments we have are far too delicate to handle. These items that I am reading to you are the transcriptions. An injection molding of the carvings are enclosed in the glass casings to my left. At the conclusion of this presentation there will be a chance for questions. After such time you'll have an opportunity to photograph the fragments under the glass... have I mentioned this before?" Dr. Elderidge questioned the audience.

The audiences' lack of response was response enough for Dr. Elderidge.

Dr. Elderidge paused, took a handkerchief out of his pocket and dabbed the sweat forming on his forehead. He adjusted his glasses that were slipping down his nose.

"Do any of you find it warm in here?" Dr. Elderidge threw out the general question to the reporters as he loosened his tie and collar.

He turned to his assistant, "Beth, ask them about the air conditioning in this room please, it would be helpful."

Without a word, Beth smiled, went toward the door of the packed Allen Room. Dr. Elderidge watched her walk past a number of reporters and just as she was disappearing in the crowd his eye caught something, a movement of what he believed to be a child. He could have sworn he saw a little girl with eyes so dark that the pupils were indiscernible. Dr. Elderidge shook his head as he wondered, what would a little girl be doing in a press conference? Then he reasoned that maybe she was one of the reporters' daughters playing hide and seek. Dr. Elderidge smiled as he recalled that his granddaughter was shy like that.

If Dr. Elderidge had only known who the child was, snaking her way through the audience and the uncanny resemblance to another girl with jet black pupils, he wouldn't have dismissed it so easily.

A murmur of the reporters picked up around the room. A few stood to stretch their legs, others moved closer to their colleagues to engage in conversation.

Dr. Elderidge took a drink of the glass of water that Beth had placed for him on his podium. Something seemed to be affecting Dr. Elderidge's taste buds, this water also had a funny taste to it or else the metallic taste was in his mouth. The face that Dr. Elderidge made was noticeable to some of the reporters.

Josh took the opportunity to slide into an empty chair, a few seats closer to Dr. Elderidge, the podium, and a few seats closer to where Beth was sitting.

Beth re-entered the room with a Jazz at the Lincoln Centre employee who had a key and opened the control box for the air conditioning.

"It's hotter in here than in one of my submarines," Dr. Elderidge commented over the microphone, even though that was not his intention.

A number of reporters laughed.

Dr. Elderidge looked embarrassed. "Did I say that out loud?"

This brought a greater amount of laughter in the room. Dr. Elderidge looked around the room and smiled playing it up as if he intended to make that comment.

Beth made her way back across the room, Josh reached out and touched her arm, he leaned in and whispered, "Stay close to Elderidge he looks a little grey in color. My grandfather had that coloring before his heart attack."

"I've worked with Dr. Elderidge for a few years and I assure you, he's fine. Just a little stress, he can handle it, some say I have a gift for reading him but it's simply that I've seen him like this before."

"Your call, you have the gift," replied Josh.

Beth raised her eyebrow, taken aback by his flirtatious tone.

"I've never known observation to be considered a gift," Beth commented.

"Depends on who's doing the observing," Josh replied with a smile.

Beth smiled.

Josh nervously laughed, "I think it's wise to keep an eye on the good doctor anyway."

Beth pursed her lips and nodded her head cynically.

"Seriously," Josh encouraged.

Dr. Elderidge cleared his throat and the reporters began taking their seats again.

Josh raised his eyebrows to Beth as if to plea with Beth to promise.

"Okay, I will," blushed Beth.

Dr. Elderidge looked down at his notes.

"Very well then, let's go on, shall we?" Dr. Elderidge nodded.

Dr. Elderidge picked up his papers and tapped their edges on the top of the podium to organize them. He leaned on the podium to continue. He looked out at the sea of reporters and said, "Unfortunately from this fragment all that we are able to decipher is few significant words to ponder. The remainder of this was unrecoverable."

#

FRAGMENT THREE

shame - breaking - spirit - seeps into - heart - piece of darkness

****

IN THE KING'S CHAMBER:

The scribe wondered if all would understand the message and he began to daydream how people of the kingdom would respond. The King noticed he had stopped writing.

"Is there something wrong?" Asked the King.

"Remembering what you told me your highness, that I am with a friend, I must ask, what if they don't believe this story?"

The King leaned back in his chair and pondered the question of the scribe before answering. "If we decide never to share with others, then we have made the decision for them," replied the King.

The scribe understood and lifted his quill to the scroll again.

The King continued, "Shame has a way of breaking your spirit. It seeps into your heart and becomes the piece of darkness that never goes away. If I had understood that as a boy, I would have done what I could to stop the shame and the fear that followed close on its heels. Like the whispering winds of Mount Crevasse that I knew so well as a boy, shame blew in and almost divided my life into a season of winter that threatened to never end."

Chapter Fifteen
SHINY ENVY

Jason stood atop the pile of boulders and waved for Samuel to join him. There was something shimmering in the side of the hill, just as they had seen in the map that the Gatekeeper had given them.

"Samuel, come quickly. I am not fooling you, I can see the shield from here!" Jason exclaimed.

Samuel poked around their campsite a while longer. He and Jason had scoured this area since setting up camp many days ago. Samuel wondered, why would they now so easily find what they have been looking for? Could it be all because of the map that the Gatekeeper left for them the night before? It is unlikely, he determined, not wanting to believe. They had diligently searched the entire area before receiving the map and he knew they were thorough.

Samuel looked in the near distance and saw Nine crouching behind some rocks, concealing his identity from Jason as he has always done.

"Samuel are you coming?!" Jason yelled.

Samuel took a big inhale frustrated by his two traveling companions and joined Jason on top of the pile of rocks.

Jason pointed to the shiny object in the distance.

"Look, just as the Gatekeeper's map indicated," Jason said.

A smile crossed Samuel's face, perhaps there was some payoff to this journey after all, he thought.

Jason and Samuel journeyed most of the day across the bolder strewn terrain toward the side of the hill and the shiny object. Samuel let Jason lead because it was easier for him to keep an eye out for Nine who liked to run from outcropping to outcropping of rock, all in an attempt to conceal himself.

As the end of the day approached they reached the shiny object half buried in the hill. Just as the Gatekeeper's map indicated... it was a silver shield. Jason began to dig at the hard soil with his fingers to release the shield. Samuel sat on some rocks nearby and wiped the sweat from his brow. Jason turned to him. "Come on Samuel, I could use some help!" Jason exclaimed.

"It's not going anywhere, what's the rush?" Samuel responded.

Jason ignored his friend and turned back to keep working on releasing the shield from the earth's grip.

Nine crawled up to Samuel and whispered in his ear, "Let him do the work for YOUR shield. He owes you. You deserve the spoils."

Samuel looked questioningly at Nine.

"If it wasn't for you, he'd still be in that hole, good thing you tied the vine around him... one, two, three he was out," said Nine.

"Yes, that's true," responded Samuel.

"Did you say something?" Asked Jason, without turning around.

"Yes... yes... I will be right there," Samuel stumbled over his own words.

Nine leaned in close to Samuel again, "When something is yours, you need to make sure it is ONLY yours!"

Nine held out his hand to revel a large round rock. He looked at Jason and made a swinging motion with his hand as if to illustrate how to strike Jason in the head. Over and over again Nine violently swung the rock in the air and brought it down on an imaginary target. Nine began to mumble to himself, "Take what is yours, take what is yours, take what is yours."

Jason turned around and saw Samuel sitting by himself on the boulders. The rock that Nine had held, teetered in the dirt as if it was just dropped.

"Well, are you going to help?" Asked Jason.

Samuel picked up the rock and walked toward Jason. He looked at him for a long while and contemplated all that Nine had said. Jason's eyes met Samuel's. Samuel lifted the rock high in the air and swung it to the ground just in front of the buried shield. He continued to use the rock as a digging tool.

Jason smiled and picked up a rock to use as a digging tool also.

"You know if we find all the weapons for the warrior then we are sure to find the warrior also," Jason smiled at his statement. "Maybe he will let us be his weapon bearer and we can join him in battle," Jason added.

The two boys worked together to free the shield.

Chapter Sixteen
ODYSSEY BLUE

On the bank of the river, the early morning sunlight tickled Thomas' eyes awake, he looked beside him and there to his surprise was Talia snuggled next to him. She was sleeping peacefully. Thomas was careful not to wake her. He examined the pretty features of her face, the shape of her eyes, her brow, her nose and lips. Thomas thought that this was probably the first peaceful sleep she has had in a long time, away from that cave of the Accusers.

Lowen raised her head when she saw that Thomas was awake. Thomas slowly slipped his arm out from under Talia's head. He went to the rivers edge and dipped his hands in the cold water and splashed it on his face. Lowen came to the water's edge and did her little cock of the head to the side, as she watched him. She bent over and took a drink of the water.

Thomas patted Lowen on her back and turned around to see Talia sitting on a rock smiling at him. She straightened out her matted hair. Talia greeted him, "Good morning Thomas Littlewood."

"Good morning," Thomas said with a smile.

Thomas walked up the embankment to Talia and they moved back to their campsite. They exchanged small talk about their night's rest and their surroundings, both not talking about the obvious issue they should address. Thomas and Talia waited for quite a while by their campsite for the Gatekeeper who had disappeared sometime during the night. Thomas stoked the fire with dry wood four times that morning and kept a sharp lookout for the Gatekeeper but he never showed up. Talia and Thomas never talked about the words of the Accusers that each other heard. It was less painful that way. They sat in silence for a long time before Talia broke the awkward situation by whistling a familiar tune. It was haunting and melodic, a mournful song but hopeful at the same time.

"I love that song. You used to play it on your flute," Thomas said.

"I wish I still had my flute, I loved playing that song," Talia replied.

There was a long moment of silence as she considered her next words carefully.

"Did you mean, what you said?" Talia asked.

Thomas didn't look at her, just smiled and kept playing with the fire. "Did you?" Thomas answered.

"Of course, why say something you don't mean, just to get something you want?"

"It's not unheard of," Thomas joked.

"And it's not practiced by me," Talia replied.

"And not by me, either," Thomas retorted.

She smiled knowing that he was talking about the 'love' statement they made in front of the Accusers. The moment was getting weird again so she changed the subject with the best compliment that came to her mind.

"I missed your smelly sheep cloak," she said hoping he didn't take it the wrong way.

"Still smells like them?" Thomas questioned as he lifted his cloak to his nose.

Talia giggled. "I like it. It smells like home."

The smile dropped from both of their faces at the mention of home.

"Were you there?" Thomas asked.

Talia nodded her head and looked off with a distant stare in her eyes.

She began slowly, "I saw the raid through the crack in our door. The last thing mother said was don't come out from under your bed, no matter what you hear, no matter what you see."

"There wasn't a warning? Didn't they fight?" Thomas jumped in.

Talia looked away for a moment as she decided what to divulge to Thomas.

"I had been collecting eggs and..." she continued.

Thomas interrupted, "Did you see my Papa that day?"

"He was looking for you Thomas, he and most of the men from the village were out looking for you... that's when it happened."

Her last sentence hung in the air and settled like a weight on Thomas' shoulders.

****

Talia's memory replayed the events: a morning misty haze surrounded the village. The type of haze caused by a change in weather, where a warm day follows a cold night. Papa and men from the village are gathered around the Gatekeepers pen in the center of the village.

Papa directed groups of the village men.

"Salo, you take your men up the south ridge and we will follow the north. If anyone sees his tracks send the signal and the other party will join you," Papa commanded.

"Where was the Gatekeeper, didn't he see anything?" Questioned Salo.

"Thomas is not the only one missing this morning. Let's start before more of the day wears on, he can't have more than a few hours on us," Papa answered.

The village men fanned out in their groups.

****

Back at the campsite, Talia turned her eyes to Thomas.

"They couldn't have timed their raid any better. The men were gone but a short time when I saw the raiders. I was the first to see the Mountain Giants descending on our village. I thought the rams horn blowing was the signal that the men of the village had found you," Talia spoke with tears in her eyes and a break in her voice.

****

Talia's mind drifts to the events of that day. Through her minds-eye we see the raid happening.

In the village on that day, Talia was out by the chicken pen. She could see the Giants coming over the horizon.

"They're coming, mother, the giants are coming!" Talia screamed as she ran for her home. The chickens scurried in all directions.

Talia's mother ran to meet her, grabbed her and swung her around.

"Go inside. Hide under the bed and stay there, don't come out, no matter what you see or what you hear... go NOW!" Mother demanded.

Talia obeyed without hesitation. She ran for her house and did not look back. It was a good thing she had not looked back because from the valley side of the village Gargoyle Guardsmen began pouring over the rooftops and around the houses, swinging nets above their heads. Their bat-like wings extended and flapped erratically bobbing the gargoyles up and down in the air. With one swoop, Talia's mother was scooped up in a net before she could utter a word.

Women and children were running in every direction, screaming and yelling. Samuel and Jason stopped Talia just before she entered her house.

"Come with us, we know the perfect place to hide!" Exclaimed Samuel.

"No, mother told me where to go and that's where I am going!" Talia responded.

She broke free of their grip and dashed into her house, slamming the door behind her.

Samuel and Jason watched Talia enter her house. As if almost on cue; their eyes trailed up to an object upside-down, hanging from Talia's roof. The creature watched Talia as she entered. The creature was a Gargoyle Guardsman. The Gargoyle looked up at the boys from his upside-down position and smiled with his large fanged teeth. The Gargoyle spread his leathery wings and made a low growling sound.

The boys screamed and ran in the opposite direction. The Gargoyle Guardsman took one leap from the building and with outstretched arms landed directly on the boys, pushing them to the ground.

****

High on the mountainside, Papa turned to face the village below. The screams of the village had reached them.

"The sound of war is in our village!" Papa shouted.

The men turned en masse and ran for the village, shouting a war cry themselves.

The earth rumbled as if an earthquake began. That stopped the men in their tracks. They slowly began to turn and look back up to the mountain to see an avalanche of Mountain Giants descending on them with war clubs and nets swinging.

****

Back in the village, Talia had slammed the door behind her with such force that it rebounded and opened a crack. Talia slid under her bed and opened a trap door in the floor. She quickly climbed into the opening and peered out... then she saw them... the imps.

First the Hunter entered the door of her house with his bow and arrow ready to shoot. They were so small; they were the approximate size and speed of rodents. The Imps moved with precision and accuracy. The Old Woman imp followed the Hunter into the opened door of Talia's house. First she sniffed the air like an animal looking for Talia's scent, then her eyes locked with Talia. She lifted her bony finger and pointed directly at Talia's hiding place.

"I see the sneaky little coward," cooed the Old Woman imp.

The Hunter approached Talia with his arrow drawn ready to shoot.

****

Back at the campsite, Thomas drew close to Talia and put his arm around her. She buried her head in his shoulder. It was difficult for her to relive those events. They sat in silence and stared at the fire for a long time.

That night Thomas, Talia and Lowen moved into the mill for shelter. Inside its cobwebbed rooms they found blankets, a couple of beds and a little outcrop to the building that had a cooking fireplace. There was also a loom, which Talia knew how to operate. Her mother made linen clothes for many of the villagers. They decided that they would wait inside the mill for the Gatekeeper's return.

Time passed, as did the seasons. In the corner of their room sat the warrior's silver armor chest plate and the belt.

Winter had come and gone as did spring, summer and fall. It actually had come twice and spring was here again. It was early morning; Thomas had dozed off within the last hour from a night filled with troubled thoughts.

Thomas rolled in his bed, straining at the covers. There was no comfortable position for rest, nothing would free him of the internal struggle that troubled his heart. Sweat beads formed on his head. He was not ill... he was dreaming.

Thomas walked down a gauntlet of souls. A multitude of people he didn't know formed the pathway. There was enough room for him to pass by them but not much more. Motionless they stood shoulder to shoulder in a line on either side of Thomas. Out of the corner of his eye, Thomas saw this multitude slowly raising their heads to look at him with their pure white eyes. A pallor shade of death covered their skin. Thomas was afraid to look at them directly; he knew they were straining to open their stitched-closed lips.

Thomas walked on in this nightmare, hopeful and fearful of reaching the end. The ambience in the room beyond his path was dark as far as they eye could see. A pedestal rose from the ground on the path before him. On the pedestal was a chunk of chocolate with a corner cut off. A few of the souls' hands reached for the chocolate.

"Don't touch it, it's mine!" Thomas yelled.

Thomas lifted the chocolate to his mouth and took a bite. Male and female whispers in the wind started floating past him...

"It's poison, it's poison, it's poison," the voices said.

Thomas turned the chocolate over and chalky grey powder poured out.

He looked up and saw his father with the same pallor and eyes as white as the others standing before him.

"I told you, they're trying to poison us," Papa's words were discernible even through his stitched shut lips.

Thomas' eyes darted open and he shot straight up in bed.

He woke up a lot later than usual that morning and he could not get those images out of his mind.

Thomas paced the room of the little mill for what seemed like hours. He was alone in the room and only for a fleeting minute did he wonder about Talia and Lowen; his mind was preoccupied.

The haunting images from last night's troubled dreams kept him busy. He tried to figure out what it all meant. He roamed around for a long time not saying a word. Every three times across the breadth of the room he'd look at the armor, which sat in the corner and he would mutter something under his breath.

Talia opened the door with a freshly picked bouquet of spring flowers.

"Look Thomas, the first bloom for our breakfast table," she said.

He didn't even look at her. His eyes were transfixed on the armor sitting in the corner.

"How can you be out picking flowers when our families are held captive?" Thomas snapped.

Thomas looked at her and she let the flowers down by her side. A look of compassion came over her.

"We've talked about this plenty of times before. You remember what he said to us. Wait here for my return," Talia reasoned.

"That was two and a half years ago Talia! The only thing that has happened in that time is that we have gotten older and our families more oppressed. Maybe they are not even alive by now," ranted Thomas.

Thomas sat down at their table and put his head in his hand.

"Maybe that armor was all I needed. I should've put it on and marched back to the Queen's castle," Thomas stated.

Talia put her hand through Thomas' hair.

"Dear Thomas, the armor is too big for you to wear into battle," she paused and tears welled up in her eyes.

"Besides you are the only family I have now and if I..." Talia stopped herself short of saying what she is thinking.

She bent forward and kissed Thomas' head but he doesn't notice.

"Family! You have an older sister, a mother and a father. Are you afraid to demand their release from the Queen! Well I'm not afraid," said Thomas sternly.

Talia sat in the chair across from Thomas and dried her eyes.

"I miss them too but the Gatekeeper told us to wait here for his return," confessed Talia.

"Who knows if he will ever come back? Maybe the Queen has captured him too and we will stay here till we are old people, waiting for him never to return. Well I am not going to wait anymore. I don't need this armor anyway. Maybe it wasn't the treasure I was after. Maybe the treasure was you!" Thomas blurted out.

Talia blushed.

Thomas quickly got up from the table and before Talia knew it he had the armor in his hand and was half way out of the door.

"Thomas wait, what are you doing?" Talia yelled after him.

Talia followed Thomas out the door and down to the riverbank. Lowen saw them go and ran after them.

Thomas lifted the armor high above his head and prepared to toss it in the river. He moved closer to the edge of the quickly running river.

"This has not been armor for me, it has been an anchor holding me here to a promise that has kept me from saving my family," Thomas angrily shouted.

Thomas drew his arms back and was about to pitch the armor into the river but Talia grabbed him by the arm.

"Thomas please don't do this. Maybe it was for something else that we have waited for. Maybe we waited for the right time in the Gatekeeper's plan. Maybe to learn patience or maybe to learn to really trust him," Talia reasoned.

Thomas lowered his hands and dropped the armor.

"Gatekeeper's plan?" Questioned Thomas. "Are you joking? What does he know of warfare? He guarded the sheep of our village. Are you ready to trust the lives of our families in his hands?" Thomas demanded.

With that Thomas picked the armor up and lifted it over his head as he took one step closer to the edge of the river.

"Thomas, his wisdom saved me. If you had not known that, we would have been captives forever," Talia said softly with confidence.

Thomas paused for a moment, thinking of what she said. Then he took a few steps toward the shore until he could look in the water. Things began to move slowly as if in a dream. Thomas had experienced this once before, years ago, when he was younger. The water had slowed down until it appeared to be almost still, like it was the time the Gatekeeper brought him by the stream. Thomas looked into the water. The armor shone brightly as the sunlight reflected off of it and it became clearly visible in the water. However, Thomas' own reflection was not visible.

The water continued to flow past Thomas' feet for what seemed like hours but actually it was only seconds. Thomas lowered the armor in front of him and looked at it in the bright sunlight. The clouds and sun reflected off of its surface but Thomas could not see his own reflection in the surface of the breastplate. Talia's reflection shone sharp in the armor as she put her hands on Thomas' shoulders.

"Thomas," she said.

Her words broke the trance Thomas was in. Immediately the water rushed quickly by again. Everything seemed normal, except Thomas' own reflection, which appeared to him to be blurred and distorted in the silver finish of the armor.

"Thomas, we have been provided for all these months. We've had warmth, shelter and provisions. You followed your heart and the directions of the Gatekeeper to come and rescue me. Why now are you willing to ignore all that? In my heart I believe his words were true. He proved that," Talia did her best to encourage him.

Talia took the armor from Thomas and moved back from the river's edge. Thomas looked up to the clear sky. White puffy clouds floated by. An eagle soared overhead and the rapids of the river sang their familiar tune. He turned to Talia. She had set the armor breastplate and belt by the area of the campsite they had spent with the Gatekeeper so long ago.

Talia saw the pain in Thomas' eyes. It was the pain of failure. She moved close to him, put her arms around his shoulders and traced the outline of his face with her finger.

"Let's go back to the mill and have breakfast," Talia whispered.

She smiled, turned and walked up the hill toward the mill. Lowen followed her.

Thomas watched her walk away; she had become an amazingly beautiful young woman. Then something else caught Thomas' eye in the woods. It was someone moving. Thomas wanted to scream out to Talia to be careful but Lowen would have been on guard, she could smell danger from a mile away and curiously she didn't react. Thomas watched Talia and Lowen enter the mill. Thomas was alone by the river's edge, just him and the armor. Thomas gazed into the woods to see if he could catch a second glimpse of the moving object.

Emerging from the woods came the Gatekeeper. At first Thomas couldn't believe his eyes and anger welled up. Now he comes, Thomas thought, just as I am about to give up all hope!

"You haven't failed anyone Thomas," said the Gatekeeper.

"Why have you come now, after all this time?" Thomas questioned.

"For everything there is a season. Thomas, for you this season has been patience and trust. For Talia, this season has been faith," said the Gatekeeper.

"So while I was learning patience and Talia was learning faith my father has been suffering in the Queen's prison," demanded Thomas.

The Gatekeeper sat down on a log by the armor.

"For everything and everyone there is a season," he responded.

"Why have you come back then?" Questioned Thomas

"I think you already know the answer to that, Thomas. It shouldn't be a surprise I told you to wait. It's good that you have."

"Are you going to suggest that I continue now?" Thomas said.

"The choice is yours Thomas. It always has been," said the Gatekeeper.

Thomas walked over to the campsite where he, Talia, and Lowen had spent many nights. He sat on the log and looked out at the river.

"I couldn't go now anyway," Thomas said.

The Gatekeeper turned to Thomas. Thomas turned to face the Gatekeeper.

"I have disappeared. I am nothing but a shadow of the boy I once was and I even question if that shadow that I am casting on the ground is actually me. Once the sun goes behind the cloud it is gone and it is like it never existed," confessed Thomas.

"That's partially true Thomas, the shadow you are casting into the future is that of a young man you are today," said the Gatekeeper.

"So why am I not looking for the man that will fit the armor? I am wasting time here," responded Thomas

"I prefer that you win in this fight for freedom," said the Gatekeeper.

Thomas looked puzzled,.

"Was there a question that I would win the fight?" Asked Thomas.

"The choice is yours," responded the Gatekeeper.

"Why didn't you tell me that before?" Questioned Thomas.

"If I had said, wait two and a half years Thomas, would you have listened?"

"No, but I still don't know who the armor belongs to," Thomas responded.

"Wrap it in a blanket from the mill. Take Talia and Lowen with you. Tell them today is a day of great joy because this is the day," said the Gatekeeper.

"Really?" Asked Thomas.

"Really," said the Gatekeeper.

Thomas sprang to his feet and ran to the mill, yelling for his companions.

"Talia come quickly the Gatekeeper has returned and he says this is the day!"

Thomas ran into the mill and grabbed a blanket from his bed as Talia was setting the table.

"Did you hear me? The Gatekeeper has returned and today is the day," Thomas said it so quickly he almost stumbled over his own words.

Thomas ran out of the mill and back to the shore. Talia and Lowen arrived a few seconds after Thomas but saw no one; only the suit of armor sitting by the old campsite, just as Talia had left it.

Thomas looked around but the Gatekeeper was gone.

"Talia I tell you that he was here only a moment ago and on that log," Thomas said.

In the place of where the Gatekeeper sat was another scroll. Thomas picked up the scroll and unrolled it. It read...

#

Crimson is the Eastern Shore; mystery lies behind the door to your destiny. Strands of silver, bands of gold, earthly things to have and hold, what does it mean, what's in it all for you? Listen to the meadowlark and watch for the fall of night. The moon will guide your flight. Across the mountain, past the valley below, rests the place of Hollows Grove.

****

Thomas looked at Talia with a glint of excitement in his eyes.

"We go tonight," Thomas said with a smile.

He lifted the armor. The sunlight caught the brilliant reflection and splashed his face with the warmth of the sun. Thomas squinted his eyes and looked in the armor... there, in perfect reflection, his face smiled back. It was not like before, he could see his razor sharp reflection now.

It didn't take long for Thomas and Talia to pack their belongings. Talia grabbed as many blankets as she could, to be used as a tent to cover them on this journey. Lowen could sense the excitement. She jumped around side to side hardly able to contain herself.

The night came and they began their journey by moonlight. Night turned to day and day into night. They walked for miles every day. Through woods, across streams and across rocky terrain they walked. Pressing forward in the direction and instruction of the scroll. They made their tent at night camping in the woods. They ate what they could catch or gather. It was there at the campfire that Talia confronted Thomas.

"Why didn't we just stay where we were? We were happy in the mill weren't we?" Talia asked.

Thomas stoked the fire and said nothing. He looked over at Lowen who had curled herself up to sleep.

"Thomas Littlewood, why won't you answer me when I ask you a direct question?" Talia demanded.

Thomas looked up from the fire.

"Because you already know the answer," he responded.

Talia raised her eyebrows and cocked her head to one side as she pursed her lips. Thomas knew what that meant; it was her disapproval look. Even to anyone that didn't know her well, it was plain to understand that she was upset with him.

"Oh I know the answer alright. It is because you have some grand idea of adventure and saving a family that we don't even know exists anymore," Talia said sharply.

Talia dropped her head in her hands. Tears formed in her eyes.

"How can you give up hope that our family is okay?" Thomas asked.

"How can you still have hope? We are not on this journey because of family. If that was your reason Thomas, you would of went back to the place you first saw your father in the Queens' prison. The truth is you like adventure and I have been stupid enough to go with you. You are just selfish. All you think about is you and this great quest. Well let me tell you something, I am sick of this and sick of your dreams. That's all you are Thomas Jacob Littlewood, you're a dreamer. What makes you think that you can do anything different? What makes you think that you can find the warrior or this Good King and bring him back to the kingdom. He left it in the first place... didn't he?" Talia questioned.

Thomas' answer came quickly and even surprised him because he had spent no time thinking of these things before.

"You don't know the whole story, so how do you know why the King left. Why Queen Mythamöhre came to our country and why..."

Talia stood up cutting him mid-sentence. She wanted to hear no more of Thomas' excuses.

"We gave up a warm and comfortable home because you believe some old man in a cloak that writes you poetry and leaves you to interpret its meaning. You remember the rumors of the village as well as I do: the Gatekeeper is nothing but an old, disfigured drunk, who believes in magic. Yet you believe in his warrior and this mysterious Good King that will set the people free! Think about that Thomas and wake up," Talia said with bitterness in her voice that surprised Thomas.

Talia went into her tent.

What just happened? Thomas wondered. He thought she was so supportive by the mill and now these comments made him wonder. Thomas looked at Lowen. Thomas thought that If Lowen could talk then she'd tell Talia that she was wrong. Thomas corrected himself in mid-thought, and said to himself, no, if Lowen could talk maybe she would tell me to turn around and go home. Maybe Talia is right, Thomas thought.

He poked his stick in the fire and spark ashes from the burning log flew up in the air. Thomas thought of the fireflies he would watch out of his village home at night. They would spin around, up and down in the air. Thomas thought you could never predict where they would pop up. The ashes were kind of like those fireflies burning for the moment and then extinguishing. Yes, maybe Talia was right... just maybe he was about to extinguish himself. His heart was heavy and self-doubt grew. His heart felt so heavy that he feared if he leaned too far forward, his heart would fall completely out of his chest.

The heat of the flame from the fire danced on his face and kept out the cold night chill. Colder than the night air were Talia's words that echoed in his head and his heart. They cut him like a knife and nothing would stop the bleeding. It was the bleeding of hope, destiny and faith all rolled into one. It was the hemorrhaging of everything he was and all he had come to be: his reason for existence. His main artery was cut.

Thomas threw his stick on the fire and patted Lowen on the head before heading into his tent for the night. So much was on Thomas' mind; he thought it would be a wonder if he would get any sleep at all this night. Thomas believed that Talia and Lowen were all he had left. This journey was not worth losing her. He imagined that in the morning he would tell her that if she wished to turn around, he would go with her. He was not about to go on without her.

He slept soundly that night, and dreams came...

AT THE ALLEN ROOM PRESS CONFERENCE:

Dr. Elderidge took a sip of water and cleared his throat, "I think we'll be fine now... let's see where we are."

"Dr. Elderidge," a voice came from the back of the room.

Dr. Elderidge looked up and saw a reporter stepping forward.

"I wonder if you could answer a few questions to clarify some things."

Beth walked up to the podium. "I believe it is important that we keep the structure of this presentation to form," she spoke into the microphone. Beth turned to Dr. Elderidge but he didn't respond.

Dr. Elderidge had fixed his attention on the little girl with the jet-black hair, fair skin and dark black eyes. She moved in and out of the reporters as if she was almost playing hide-and-go-seek with Dr. Elderidge. A shiver ran down Dr. Elderidge's arms. The tingling sensation didn't stop there; it ran clear up his back. A cold sweat broke out on his brow. Suddenly his knees felt week and just as they were about to give out on him, Beth put her hand under his shoulder.

"Dr. Elderidge, are you okay?" She asked.

Dr. Elderidge didn't answer. He couldn't. He felt nauseous, dizzy and dry in the mouth all at once.

The gathered group of media could smell the story. A shark tank feeding frenzy began. They all positioned themselves for the best photograph. Multiple camera flashes burst out. To Dr. Elderidge the sound of the clicking shutters became garbled as if it where the sound of someone knocking on many doors miles away and the only thing left of their presence was the echo.

Beth helped her employer and friend, into one of the side rooms. Security guards quickly protected their escape. Beth shut the door behind them. Dr. Elderidge sat down on a chair in the storage area.

"Dr. Elderidge do you need me to call the paramedics?" Beth asked.

Dr. Elderidge could feel his heartbeat slowing to a regular pace. His breathing was returning to normal.

"No, no I'm alright," he answered.

"Do you have numbness in your arms, blurry vision, what is it? Dr. Elderidge you could be having a heart attack," Beth said.

She bent down in front of him.

He looked into her worried eyes.

"I guess I've all but ruined it now," mumbled Dr. Elderidge.

Beth knew he was talking about the press conference and she stopped him before he could say any more.

"There is nothing ruined."

"Easy for you to say, you're a young woman and here I am well into my seventies," Dr. Elderidge said in a low voice.

"Look at Whistler's Mother, when did she start painting? So it took years..." she paused, and corrected herself, "... decades of your career for this, but what a find!"

Dr. Elderidge smiled at her optimism.

"I am fine," Dr. Elderidge assured Beth.

"Maybe it was a little stress manifesting itself, probably nothing more," Beth convinced herself.

"Maybe, mixed with the blasted heat in that room," Elderidge nodded.

Beth could see Dr. Elderidge was his old stubborn self

"And you haven't even gotten to the major discovery. Everyone else in that room will be the ones feeling faint when they hear what you've got to tell them," encouraged Beth.

Dr, Elderidged smiled broadly at her.
"Better?" Beth asked.
Dr. Elderidge stood to his feet, inhaled, slowly letting his breath back out again like the steam of a kettle beginning to boil. "I am sorry Beth. I don't know what got into me," Dr. Elderidge said as he made his way to the door. He paused at the door. "Can you see if anyone brought a child with them to the conference? This is not the place for them," Dr. Elderidge said sharply.
He turned toward the door. Beth looked puzzled, 'child' she thought.

Dr. Elderidge opened the door and confidently strode into the pressroom. Flashes of the reporters' cameras went off in quick succession. Beth followed close behind Elderidge.

Dr. Elderidge paused in the doorway and whispered back to Beth.
"Maybe it is that blasted little girl running around the room that has made me dizzy," he said with a smile as he entered into the pressroom.
Beth paused in the doorway now more concerned than ever at his comments as she watched Dr. Elderidge move back to the podium. She was standing there puzzled. Did he say there was a little girl running around the pressroom? She wondered if she heard him correctly. She shook her head and dismissed the comment. She must have misheard him. Maybe because Dr.

Elderidge felt faint from the heat, he imagined things. She was in that room the whole time with Dr. Elderidge, there certainly wasn't any little girl running around, she was positive of that.

Chapter Seventeen
THE LINE IS CROSSED

The wheat field before him radiated with a strange color of blue, purple and green. Thomas looked down at his hands and they were whiter than any thing he had ever seen. He wondered if his face looked the same, maybe Talia could tell him he thought. Just as that thought came to him, he looked around and realized he was alone.

The trees of the forest were gone. The mountains in the distance had disappeared. The sky had turned into a deep raspberry shade with not a cloud in sight. Talia and Lowen were missing. He was indeed alone, standing in this strange colored sea of wheat. The grass was high, up to his chest. It was as if he had waded out into a never-ending vivid ocean of shifting color . As far as he could see the field stretched out in every direction.

"Talia! Lowen!' Thomas screamed.

He yelled their names as loud as he could but the sound of his own voice collapsed as if there was no air to carry it. No air? Yet I am breathing, Thomas thought. Whatever atmosphere he breathed it was stale and dry. When he inhaled it hurt his lungs. Thomas did his best not to breathe deeply because of the pain it caused.

He attempted to lift his foot from the spot he was standing but it was stuck in the oozing soil. Thomas didn't dare look down at his feet because it felt as if he was slowly sinking. He was afraid of what he might see if he looked down. The more that Thomas tried to move the deeper the muck would suck him in. He didn't know which direction to turn. Then across the sky came a peal of thunder and in the crackle, a voice.

"Welcome home Thomas Jacob Littlewood, welcome home," the voice boomed with a laugh.

Thomas couldn't tell if it was the voice of a man, woman or child. It seemed to be a bit of everything.

"Where am I? Who are you?" Inquired Thomas.

"My, my so many questions for such a young boy as you," the voice responded.

"I'm not scared and, and, and... I'm not a young boy. I am almost fifteen going on sixteen," stammered Thomas.

"Almost fifteen going on sixteen," the voice said with a laugh. "And such a pretty boy too."

He was called pretty boy once before. It was at his meeting with Queen Mythamöhre in the grove.

"Why are you hiding in the clouds or on the wind? Why don't you make yourself visible?" Thomas asked.

"Aren't you on a journey in search of the Good King?" Questioned the voice.

Thomas strained his head around looking up to the sky. The voice seemed to be ricocheting off the clouds. Lightning trickled through the clouds as the voice spoke.

"Well you found the Good King. Here I am Thomas. Tell me your plan to rid my kingdom of that naughty Queen and her subjects and we'll rule together," said the voice.

"Well Good King... I feel foolish standing in the middle of this field shouting to the sky. Can you send a helper that I may take them into my confidence on the matter."

"Yes there has been division in your camp hasn't there? You need a reliable helper," replied the voice. "Talia has lost faith in you, that is obvious. I will send you a helper that you can confide your deepest secret to and she will be all you ever dreamed of in a friend and a companion. She has been loyal to me and will be loyal to you," assured the voice.

The clouds of the sky peeled back and were gone. Then there was a long silence.

"Thomas," whispered a female voice that broke the silence.

Thomas turned and he was standing face to face with a young girl about his age, with red hair, ruby colored lips and a scarlet dress.

"Where did you come from?" Thomas asked.

"Did you not ask the Good King for a helper that you could trust? Here I am," said the ruby red haired girl.

Thomas knew there was something very familiar about this red headed girl, standing before him. He could hardly bring himself to look at her eyes because they were dark. Her eyes were so dark, that he could not discern her pupils.

"Take my hand Thomas Littlewood and bring me back with you to your world. I will forever be with you."

She bent close to Thomas and whispered in his ear.

"I can help you get rid of Talia. She never cared for you at all. It was always Samuel, your best friend that she liked better. She is trouble and a liar and must be dealt with quickly. Take my hand and let me comfort you. That wicked Talia hurt your pride and I can make it all better."

She pulled herself back from Thomas.

She reached out her hand and ran her finger up his arm.

"Do it. Take my hand," she said.

Thomas watched her trace her hand up his arm.

"You can change the color of your hair?" Thomas asked.

"I can!" she quickly responded.

With that her hair went from red to blonde to brunette.

Thomas shook his head in disgust.

"Is this not pleasing to you?" She asked.

"You may be able to change the color of you hair, your skin, your clothes the surroundings but a friend once told me, as the water reflects an image so does the eyes reflect a person's soul. In your eyes I see an empty pit. I know who you are," Thomas declared.

Her black eyes grew wide and the corners of her mouth curled up. Thomas could feel his feet sink further into the mire. She opened her mouth and let out a scream that blasted like the force of a hurricane knocking Thomas back into the tall grass of the field. As Thomas fell into the grass it seemed as if he was falling in slow motion. He looked to his side as he fell, up close to the wheat; each blade of grass had a face on it. They were people he once knew long ago from his village. People who were crying and...

Suddenly Thomas was awake in his tent. He was covered in sweat. The tent flap opened, Talia and Lowen stuck their heads inside.

"What has gotten into you Thomas Littlewood?" Talia asked.

Thomas took a deep breath.

"Thomas Jacob Littlewood you better answer me or I'll be more angry than I already am with you, which would be very hard to do," Talia said.

Thomas lifted his hand and motioned that everything was okay.

"You think that by scaring me half to death that you are going to make me not angry at you any more? Well it is not going to work," Talia said.

Thomas shook his head no. Lowen entered the tent and started to lick Thomas' face.

"Then what has gotten into you?" Talia's tone softened.

"Thankfully nothing," Thomas said with a smile.

"Boys! Come on Lowen let's go back to the girl's tent," Talia rolled her eyes and huffed.

Lowen lay down beside Thomas.

"Fine," said Talia and she left Thomas' tent.

"You understand, don't you girl?" Thomas said to Lowen.

Lowen just curled herself up in a ball and went to sleep. Even though Lowen couldn't speak to Thomas, she had a sense of what had happened to her friend. Cainine's have a way of knowing these things.

Thomas patted Lowen's head and lay down beside her. He put his hand on his wolf and went to sleep.

The last thing he remembered before drifting off to sleep was the weight of his body. Thomas was so exhausted that his body felt as if he was under a ton of rocks.

Morning came quickly, too quickly, was Thomas' first thought as he opened his eyes. He immediately began to feel the heat of the day on his tent, which was a sure sign that he had slept in. Thomas crawled out of his tent and looked up, the sun was at its midday position, directly above him. Thomas looked around him to survey their campsite.

Their campfire was out and Talia's tent was gone! Had she packed up and gone back to the mill that they called home for nearly three years, Thomas wondered.

Thomas stood to his feet and saw Talia's tent neatly packed and ready for travel yet there was no sign of Talia or Lowen.

Thomas rubbed the sleep out of his eyes and yawned. He began to pack up his tent and slung the supplies they had brought with them over his shoulder. He didn't want to leave it around an empty campsite; a deadly invitation for a bear to visit and ransack their camp.

Thomas thought that his first objective was to set out to find Talia. Possibly she had gone ahead to scout, Thomas hoped. He thought of all their time together and what a good friend she has been, had she felt that betrayed by him that she just up and left, he wondered. He thought of Lowen's companionship all this time and gratitude filled his heart to have good friends.

Thomas was grateful to be alive and grateful to survive his dream encounter with the Queen. He shivered at the thought of it as he began walking up the rocky hill in front of their camp.

Thomas rounded the crest of the rocky hill to find a massive field of wheat in the valley below. It was like the field in his dream! Streams of wheat waved in the wind. Thomas' imagination built on the dream he had experienced. From this vantage point, it was difficult to tell if the movement of the field was the result of many unseen creatures moving in the tall grass or if it the field was being pushed by the wind. It made him cautious, uneasy.

"Talia where are you?" Thomas called.

Only the wind answered him. A chill went down his spine as he thought about going into the field alone; a chill that he had only felt two other times in his life. First he became familiar with the cold chill of fear in the mythamöhre tree grove and then last night he experienced it in the dream. The thought of facing that deep fear again as he stood before the field, was overwhelming.

Thomas decided that his friendship with Talia and Lowen was all the motivation he needed to overcome the numbing dread he felt. He mustered what courage he could and he waded into the wheat field.

Childhood memories began floating into Thomas' mind. Although this seemed like a strange time to entertain daydreams, he decided, given his current predicament that the distraction was valuable. Thomas remembered the many times he had spent on his uncle's farm as a boy. The wheat field there was always one of his favorite places to play. He remembered fun filled times that his best friend Samuel would accompany him to his uncles' farm. Samuel would always be carrying a satchel that contained some fresh baked goods prepared by Samuel's mother. As soon as they could, it would be off to the wheat field to play hide and seek and discover what fresh baked good Samuel's mother packed.

Reality snapped him back. The field before him seemed foreboding and ominous. Dream images flashed in Thomas' mind and became mixed with the emotions of fear and anxiety; knowing that if Talia and Lowen were out here, it was up to him to find them.

Hours passed as Thomas walked through the field. He wasn't sure if he had been walking in circles but it seemed as if this field had no end. Occasionally he would stop and listen, hoping to hear a sign of his friends that could give him direction... yet nothing.

Thomas stood on his tip toes to look over the tall grass. He looked in all directions. As he tried to look to the horizon and gain perspective on the direction he was walking in, all he could discern was the grass covered hill that he had walked down into this field. To make matters more confusing, the grass covered hill appeared to be on all sides of him. It was as if he was in gigantic bowl.

Just as Thomas was about to give up hope of ever finding them, he heard giggling. He followed the direction of the giggling, hoping that Talia had been playing a joke on him the whole time.

Thomas quickly waded his way through the wheat toward the giggling and came upon a clearing. In the middle of the clearing sat a young girl with long brown hair, just about his age. She was sitting with her back to him.

"Are you looking for someone?" She questioned.

"Yes possibly you've seen them I..." Thomas answered a little bewildered.

"Of course," she responded.

"Great, can you tell me which direction they went?"

"Of course," she said and began pointing in two directions at once.

"They split up?" Thomas asked.

She giggled and pointed in completely different directions.

"You'll never save them both, you have to decide," she said.

"I am sorry to have bothered you miss," Thomas replied.

He turned and began to walk away but not before noticing that his response had displeased the little girl.

She spun around to face him with an angry scowl on her face.

"Can't you stay and play?" She demanded.

"No I can't, I need to find my friends."

Thomas turned and began to re-enter the wheat field when he heard Talia's voice.

"Well here I am, silly!"

Thomas turned around and looked at the little girl. She looked exactly like... "Talia?" Thomas was asking as much as he was surprised.

He began to walk toward her and she smiled. As he got closer he saw that her eyes were black as coal. Her pupils were missing.

Thomas stopped and took a few steps back.

"You're not Talia!' Thomas exclaimed.

She got to her feet and began to walk toward Thomas.

"What is it that you want Thomas Jacob Littlewood?"

The sky above her head began to spin and swirl as if the vault of the firmament itself were being sucked into a drain that emptied out into space. Thomas could hardly breathe. The ground he stood on suddenly became very soft and he felt his feet sinking.

The impostor had no problem walking on the quicksand as she came toward Thomas. She stood face to face with him and spoke with a seductive invitation. "I said what is it that you want Thomas Jacob Littlewood?"

"You... you... don't know me... how do you know my name?" Thomas stumbled as he always did when he was nervous.

"Oh dear pretty boy, I am the one you've been looking for all along. And I have been looking for you," she said.

"You have been looking for me?" Thomas asked.

"Why should you be looking for me when I have no remembrance of ever meeting you? Who did you say you were?"

The disorientation of reality was playing tricks with Thomas' mind. If only his conscious logical mind stepped in and intervened with this subconscious assault. Thomas struggled to make sense of it all.

She smiled and twirled her long curly hair that looked like Talia's around her finger.

"We have met before Thomas Littlewood. It was such a meeting that I shall never forget. The night air was crisp and it was a full moon. You and your dog were walking through an orchard when you came upon..."

"The mythamöhre trees!" Thomas exclaimed.

He struggled with a few steps backward.

"Why are you backing away? We did meet, I was up in the mythamöhre tree picking fruit when I heard a stumble and fall and saw this handsome young pretty boy on his back at the root of the very tree I had climbed. It was you Thomas. It was you!"

"You still have not answered my question. If we met for the first time there and I never introduced myself, then how would you know my name?" Thomas asked. Suddenly a deep sadness swept over Thomas. It felt as if his stomach had fallen and all the parts of his body were suddenly numb. It was the hopeless feeling of being abandoned, much like the feeling he had standing by his mother's grave. Tears welled up in Thomas and he began to sob. Everything around him, in every direction began to melt as if it were a candle that the flame had burnt and melted all the wax.

Each move of his body hurt and became more difficult, as if weights were attached to his every muscle. The impostor moved to him and Thomas' face jerked in her direction, as if being violently moved by some unseen force. He looked into her bottomless eyes.

"Yes we have met my dear sweet pretty boy, take my hand and enjoy pleasures and riches beyond your imagination. This is what you've been looking for," she said in a low seductive voice.

"Come and play with me, take my hand," she whispered.

"I've put away playing games," Thomas responded.

Thomas shook his head and shut his eyes as tightly as he could.

"Do it," she said in a voice that had lost all need for pleasantries.

"I DO NOT accept your invitation, not now, not ever!" yelled Thomas.

Thomas' eyes were shut tight and it was difficult to speak but he forced those words out of his mouth with all of the strength he could muster.

Even with Thomas' eyes shut tight, the evil apparition he faced was burnt in his memory.

"Thomas, Thomas," Talia's distant faint voice called out.

Thomas gasped as if he had been deprived of oxygen. He opened his eyes to find himself in his tent with Talia looking over him. He could barely make her out in the dark of night and he slid himself back away from her in his tent.

"Thomas what's wrong? I heard you crying and came to see if you were all right," Talia said.

Thomas quickly moved to hug her. Lowen poked her head in the door of the tent. Talia awkwardly put her arms around Thomas. She let his embrace sink into her.

Thomas was dripping with sweat.

"I am sorry Talia," Thomas said.

"Sorry that I made you come along on this journey... I... I... know you are right, we should have stayed at the mill where we were safe," Thomas confessed.

"No," Talia quickly responded.

"After the words we had at the campfire, I couldn't sleep. I kept having these awful dreams and I know that you were right and I was wrong. I am the one who should apologize," Talia's voice trailed off in volume as she made her confession.

Thomas let the weight of his head rest fully on Talia's shoulder, realizing that all he had experienced had only been a bad dream. He was exhausted. Feeling safe in each other's arms, they lay down together. Lowen came in the tent and lay between them. Talia lifted her hand to brush the hair back off of Thomas' head.

"No matter what comes, Thomas, no matter what, we are together. I had stood by you, now I will stand with you," she promised.

Thomas reached over and touched Talia's face and then it happened; the passionate kiss they both had secretly hoped for.

The mid-morning sun made the tent uncomfortable. Lowen was panting so hard that it woke Thomas.

"Come on girl, let's get some fresh air," he whispered so as not to wake Talia. Thomas opened the flap and stepped out into the fresh air. The surroundings seemed friendlier in the daylight. He looked back into the open flap of the tent and saw Talia begin to stir.

Lowen wasted no time in exploring her surroundings. She took off sniffing all around and found her way up the hill and over the crest. Thomas did his best to call her back without waking Talia but Lowen was not listening. Typical stubborn wolf Thomas thought.

Thomas walked up the hill after her. As he rounded the top of the hill a chill traveled up his arms and down his spine, there he stood before a sea of wheat rippling in the wind... just like his dream.

Sometime later Talia woke and found herself alone in the tent. She crawled out into the sunlight and stretched. Maybe Thomas and Lowen have gone in search of breakfast, she thought. Talia sat by the coals of their fire that had survived the night and poked them around to stir up the flames. She placed a few dry branches on the coals to stoke the fire and looked out in the distance for any sign of Thomas or Lowen. She whistled her favorite tune; the sweet melody always bought her comfort when she felt troubled.

She looked up to the hill and thought that possibly she would be able to see her friends from that high vantage point. She climbed the hill only to find Thomas sitting just over the crest. Thomas stared straight-ahead not acknowledging Talia's presence, although he knew she was there.

"You know I thought that we would have reached the end of this trail by now," he said.

Talia looked out across the endless wheat field.

"I can't even see the beginning," Talia admitted.

Thinking she was talking about the journey they had been on, Thomas looked back at her and realized that she was talking about the wheat field in front of them. He smiled and placed his head in his hands.

"Yeah," he said quietly to himself.

Talia sat down beside Thomas. He looked at her. She shuffled her foot in the loose soil and then looked up at him.

"What I said last night, I meant it," she said earnestly.

"I know you did," he paused for effect.

"And I also meant the kiss," Thomas said with a smile.

"I know you did," Talia giggled.

Talia shuffled closer to Thomas and he put his arm around her. He looked back out to the field before them.

"Here is the next leg of our journey," Thomas said.

"What are we waiting for?" Talia asked.

"I am waiting for direction, for guidance," Thomas said.

"From whom? We knew we were to come here," Talia remarked.

"Guidance, that's all," Thomas answered abruptly.

Thomas got up and walked back over the hill toward their campsite. Talia stood up and wondered what she had said that caused him to do that. Had her words the night before caused this shift in Thomas' determination, she wondered. She started down the hill after him. Then the thought came to her and out of her mouth before she could think about what she was saying.

"Thomas Littlewood are you proud or embarrassed of your actions? Are you trying to punish me now?" Talia asked.

Thomas turned on his heels.

"Punish you! Punish you? " He repeated.

The words seared his beaten heart.

"Yeah Talia, that's exactly what I am trying to do, punish you... as a matter of fact we came out here so I could punish you," Thomas sarcastically shot back.

She tried to answer but couldn't.

Talia's words choked in her throat and her eyes welled up. She walked to her tent and began to dismantle it.

"What are you doing?" Thomas asked.

Talia didn't look at him, she couldn't and she didn't answer, she only kept on with her task. Just at that moment Thomas knew a confession was necessary.

"Talia please look at me," he said.

Talia took a deep breath and turned to face him.

"Thomas I would follow you to the end of this journey that you are on, no matter what but I, I , said I was sorry last night and you, you still..." she couldn't speak any more so she sat on the ground and let the tears flow.

Thomas came to her and put his arms around her.

"Talia I've had terrible dreams...and I am afraid of what's before us," he admitted.

He wiped the tears from Talia eyes.

"I have seen a great evil that waits for us Talia and, and, I... I don't know if I have the strength or the courage to face it," Thomas looked down in shame.

She kissed his forehead and he leaned into her.

They sat on the ground and held each other for a long time without saying anything more. She knew that Thomas believed in what he said to her and her heart was softened by his actions. She knew in her heart that It was because he truly loved her that he didn't want to take her through this. Thomas didn't know it and she couldn't express it better, but she meant what she said, 'to the end of this journey, she was with him: heart, body and soul.

Thomas helped Talia set up her tent again and they stayed there by the edge of the wheat field for days. Thomas and Lowen hunted in the woods nearby and Talia prepared their catches. Days moved on into months and autumn approached.

Thomas made a makeshift shelter near the edge of the woods and they moved in. Every morning Thomas rose early to watch the sun rise over the wheat field. He waited patiently because over time he could see subtle changes in the field. It was changing slowly as the new season approached.

Thomas thought that if he could wait until winter the field would die away, the ground would freeze and then he and his companions could cross safely.

Chapter Eighteen
THE TURNING POINT

On the turn of summer to fall; while Talia, Thomas and Lowen lay sleeping, a hard knock against the side of the shelter woke him. Thomas darted up in his bed startled. He peered across the moonlit room. Seeing nothing out of the ordinary, he looked back to check if Talia and Lowen were still sleeping, they were. How had he been the only one to hear the sound? Thomas wondered.

Thomas quietly eased out of bed and stepped outside.

Outside of the shelter, Thomas heard the sound of something moving through the thick brush that was about a stones throw away. Thomas looked up to the sky to gauge the time of night by the position of the moon. The sight of the bright full moon shortly after midnight triggered memories; back to the night as a boy and the encounter he had with the Gatekeeper in his village that had started all of these events.

Thomas dismissed the noise as a deer or other woodland creature that came too close to their shelter. That thought turned him on his heels and back into the cabin. He locked the door behind him.

The next day started out much like all of the other days of the past few months. Thomas rose first and opened the door of their shelter to make his trek to the nearby stream to collect water for the day. He picked up the water bucket and shut the door quietly behind him to not wake Talia and Lowen.

The morning air was brisk but the sun was warm which caused a low gentle mist to rise from dew on the grass. Each of Thomas' exhales collected in puffs of white steam. This was the first time that Thomas could remember the air feeling so cold this early in the fall, long since he left his village all those years ago. Thomas smiled as he remembered his Papa and his home.

The frost-covered grass crackled under his feet as he walked across the clearing into the woods. Usually Thomas would have deliberately avoided looking at the wheat field because of all it represented, however this morning his mind was wonderfully distracted by good memories of home.

Thomas entered the woods, which always began this leg of the journey. The branches snapped under the weight of his feet. Thomas was at the water's edge when a voice from behind surprised him.

"As water reflects the face so a man's heart reflects the man," said the voice.

Thomas spun around and stood face to face with the Gatekeeper.

"Thomas," said the Gatekeeper.

"You picked the wrong one for this journey, I warned you," Thomas responded. "It is because of you that I am out here in the middle of this wilderness. It is because of you that I have no family. It would be better for me that I would have been captured with my Papa and taken to the prison camp than left out here," complained Thomas.

Thomas was frazzled with the Gatekeeper. He left his water bucket by the water, walked past the Gatekeeper and began to head into the woods.

"If ever there was a time to hold on, it is now Thomas. Hold on to your faith that you know in your heart to be true," encouraged the Gatekeeper.

Thomas stopped and turned around and walked past the Gatekeeper back to the water's edge.

"I am not turning around because I like what you've said, I forgot my water bucket," Thomas remarked without looking at the Gatekeeper.

Thomas picked up the bucket and turned around but this time the Gatekeeper was gone.

"I hope for good," Thomas said to himself.

He filled his bucket and started back to the cabin, where he hoped that Talia would have breakfast waiting for him. With every step that Thomas took the angrier he became.

"What right did that Gatekeeper have coming in and out of his life?" Thomas mumbled to himself.

The more he thought about it the quicker he walked, carelessly swinging his bucket of water.

As Thomas reached the cabin he slowed himself down and took a deep breath to calm his nerves. It was then that he noticed that the bucket he carried had become light. He looked into his bucket to find that in his anger he had unknowingly spilled more than half of the water he was carrying. Thomas tossed the bucket against the cabin with a clang.

He started marching resolutely toward the wheat field.

At the noise of the bucket hitting the cabin, Lowen started barking and Talia opened the front door to find Thomas marching toward the wheat field.

"Thomas where are you going?" She asked.

"Where do you think," Thomas responded without looking back.

"Maybe if I wasn't so afraid we could've picked the wheat and made bread!" Thomas answered.

"But you said there was a great evil that waited in there," Talia shouted after him.

With Talia's words Thomas' anger grew and he quickened his pace toward the field.

"Maybe I'll get lucky and the evil will put me out of my misery," Thomas complained to himself.

Just as Thomas was about to step into the field, a voice shouted out behind him. "For all the wrong reasons," came the Gatekeeper's voice.

Thomas stopped. Without turning around he knew it was the voice of the Gatekeeper.

"Maybe I only need one reason and that's good enough," Thomas snapped his answer without looking back.

"Okay then," said the Gatekeeper.

"If the reason is good enough for you, then go," the Gatekeeper's words released him.

Thomas took a step, then another, and stopped.

"Why must you always make it so difficult?" Thomas asked.

"Before you have the courage to go on, you must have the courage to let go what is past," said the Gatekeeper.

Unhesitatingly, Thomas turned and marched back to the Gatekeeper.

The Gatekeeper gently put his hand on Thomas' shoulder. Thomas felt his anger subside.

Thomas looked with questioning eyes into the hooded face that concealed the Gatekeeper's identity.

"What have I held on to?" Asked Thomas.

"You faced three doubts when you rescued Talia. Since then, you've carried their words with you. Before you have the courage to go on, you must have the courage to face their words and let them go," replied the Gatekeeper.

The Gatekeeper took a long pause before he spoke.

"To face the past with courage you must also learn to forgive... yourself," said the Gatekeeper

The Gatekeeper pointed to the wheat field.

"The greatest challenges are ahead. It's you that has kept yourself here, no one else," the Gatekeeper admitted.

Thomas turned and looked back over the wheat field as a large dark cloud began to rise up in the distance.

"Here is the turning point, Thomas. The decision is yours, it always has been," said the Gatekeeper.

Thomas stood and pondered the words of the Gatekeeper as he kept his eyes on the looming storm. The storm rolled in churning with rage, as the large dark clouds seemed to be struggling to climb on top of the other. A cold wind kicked up and blew against Thomas. Suddenly it became difficult to stand against the wind.

"What must I do Gatekeeper?!" Shouted Thomas over the gale of the storm.

"You must put on the full armor Thomas," shouted the Gatekeeper back to Thomas.

Thomas turned again and saw that the storm was almost upon them, roaring louder than anything that he had ever heard.

"The armor doesn't fit me, it's for the warrior!" Thomas exclaimed.

"When have you picked up that armor with intention Thomas?" The Gatekeeper asked.

Thomas didn't pause to answer. He rushed into the cabin and threw the belt around his waist, cinching his clothes tighter.

He slipped the breastplate over his head and attached it to his belt. It fit.

Talia was busy securing loose things around their cabin from the wind that was finding its way inside.

"It fits!" Thomas exclaimed.

Talia didn't pay attention because the storm seemed to be the more urgent matter. Lowen was cowering in the corner.

"Talia, it fits!" Yelled Thomas.

She paused for a moment from her duties to see what he was talking about and she saw Thomas admiring the breastplate and belt he wore.

He looked up at Talia. Their eyes met. She smiled at him.

Thomas stepped outside the door and met the Gatekeeper waiting there. The gale continued to blow.

"The breastplate and belt has always fit you Thomas. It was in 'your' eyes that they were too big," said the Gatekeeper.

Thomas nodded his head. He understood. For the first time he really understood.

"I'll pack our things," Talia exclaimed excitedly.

"No, you're not coming... I mean... it's dangerous and if you get hurt... I mean, I don't want to risk putting you in danger," Thomas responded.

Thomas couldn't believe the words hadn't come out of his mouth any plainer. He loved her.

There was a long moment of awkward silence. She didn't break her look into his eyes. She smiled.

"It's best you stop explaining... I think." She knew full well what he was saying.

Thomas stumbled over his words that had tripped out of his mouth.

"Yeah, I think you're right," Thomas admitted.

They both laughed.

She threw her arms around Thomas and they kissed.

The gale blew hard against them.

"You still hold fast to the lie," said the Gatekeeper.

"The lie?" Queried Thomas.

The wind pressed hard against Thomas and Talia.

They did not loose their embrace as they turned their heads to face the Gatekeeper.

"The lie that Talia and Lowen are in danger with you. You were presented with a bunch of half-truths and you believed them. You carried them with you from the mill; you carry them from your dreams. It is time to lay them down and ask yourself, in whom do you really believe," the Gatekeeper challenged.

Thomas looked at Talia. He knew he would not be able to hold her back. She was determined to come. She picked up Papa's staff and handed it to Thomas. Thomas took the staff in his hands for the first time in a long time. Either the staff had shrunk or Thomas had grown.

"I believe," he whispered to Talia.

He giggled at the thought and turned to face the Gatekeeper again.

"I believe... I believe, I am the warrior you seek," he said to the Gatekeeper. Thomas' stance changed to reflect his new confidence.

The Gatekeeper calmly sat by their ember glowing outdoor cooking fire. The wind continued blowing hard against them.

"You have rested here long enough. Tonight you must travel through to the other side. Let the moonlight guide you," the Gatekeeper admonished.

The Gatekeeper stoked their fire with a few twigs and it burst into flame. The Gatekeeper stood to his feet and the gale wind suddenly died down to a gentle breeze.

For the first time Thomas saw more of the Gatekeeper's face than ever before. It was friendly, wise and powerful.

"Why not go now? The sun is up and I can see any enemy that would come my way! The armor fits, I am the warrior," Thomas said as he positioned the staff to defend any unseen enemy.

The Gatekeeper approached Thomas and spoke is a quiet voice.

"The enemy shall see you in due time but this is not it. You must pass through this valley in peace. You once told Talia that you waited here for guidance... this is the wisdom you waited for that I speak to you," the Gatekeeper said.

With that Thomas turned his attention to Talia.

"He's not been wrong before," Talia said with a smile.

Thomas smiled back at her... new hope filling his very being. Their eyes locked for a moment and then Thomas turned around to find the Gatekeeper gone.

In the place the Gatekeeper once stood, now were a pair of silver boots that matched in design of the breastplate and belt. Thomas picked up the boots and looked at them. He looked at Talia and she only shrugged her shoulders.

"They look like shoes made for a man," Talia said with a nod, encouraging Thomas to try them on.

Thomas did. They fit perfectly.

That day, the excitement of the journey kept Thomas light on his feet in his new boots. He bounced around the camp feeling giddy and full of joy. He had a hard time containing himself. The hours of the day passed slowly as the anticipation of the moonlight travel lay ahead.

As evening approached Thomas heard a cry of the meadowlark and knew it was time.

Chapter Nineteen
THE HEART OF THE MATTER

On the other side of the domed mountains, Samuel walked down to the riverbank to draw water. Jason was back at camp cooking fish they had caught earlier that day. Fortunately they had stumbled across a mill that had abundant supplies for them. As Samuel dipped the bucket into the water, he saw a silver sword shimmering just below the surface. He looked around him to see if Jason was watching. Convinced that he was alone Samuel stepped into the river and bent over, dipped his hand in the rocky shallow river's edge to draw out the sword. Just before he could put his hand on it, the voice of the Gatekeeper stopped him.

"When you least expect it, expect it," said the Gatekeeper.

Startled, Samuel shot up straight at those words. The Gatekeeper stood on the shore.

"Did he tell you to say that to me?" Asked Samuel.

"Those words were originally intended for hope, but sadly good words are twisted for wrong intent," replied the Gatekeeper.

Samuel stepped out of the river's edge and approached the Gatekeeper. Tears filled Samuel's eyes.

"When my father said those words it was soon accompanied by a painful whipping," confessed Samuel.

"Your father carried great pain and guilt."

"Was that any reason to beat me?"

"Just like words, actions intended for good can be wrongly justified in the eyes of the abuser. A broken world is populated by broken citizens." The Gatekeeper paused and bent over playing with pebbles on the shore, and then he looked up toward

Samuel. "You don't have to be a member of the broken population, Samuel. You are so much more than you are giving yourself credit for and you have a destiny set for greatness... if you let go of the pain you carry and forgive your father." The Gatekeeper left the pebbles he was playing with on the ground and stood to his feet. "The pain you carry, Samuel, allows other undesirable things to attach to your life, because you invite them."

"Are you talking about my friend Nine?" Asked Samuel.

"There are nine gifts to be had but there are also counterfeits. When you're ready to draw the sword, you'll be ready to discern the difference. Even then, the choice will be yours to follow the truth."

"Maybe I don't want to set the villagers free, did you ever think of that?" Asked Samuel.

The Gatekeeper moved away from Samuel and picked up a rock and threw it into the river.

"Did you see that?" Asked the Gatekeeper.

"Did you hear what I said? 'What if I DON'T WANT TO SET HIM FREE?'"

The Gatekeeper picked up another rock and pitched it into the river. He turned to Samuel and addressed him, "Well?"

"Well what?" Demanded Samuel.

"Did you see that?" Questioned the Gatekeeper.

"Of course I saw you ignore my statement and focus on throwing rocks," replied Samuel.

The Gatekeeper walked toward Samuel and put his hand on his shoulder. Samuel's eyes filled with tears, which rolled down his cheeks. The taste of salt from his tears ran into Samuel's mouth making him lick his lips.

"You saw the pebble fly through the air and you saw it hit the surface of the water but what you didn't see was the ripples caused on both shores from one tiny pebble," replied the Gatekeeper.

Samuel searched the Gatekeeper's hooded face for an answer. A hint of sunlight caught the edge of the hood and for a moment Samuel thought he saw the Gatekeeper's eyes.

"The ripples of your good actions will be felt... even if you can't see them, they will be felt, trust me on this, Samuel," said the Gatekeeper.

The Gatekeeper put his arms around Samuel and held him. Samuel allowed his head to be buried into the Gatekeeper's robe and his nostrils filled with the scent of wild flowers from a beautiful field back home. Samuel closed his eyes and soaked in the moment of release, as he wept.

"Samuel, are you coming?" Jason yelled.

Jason's voice broke the moment, which caused Samuel to wipe the tears from his eyes and turn up-shore to look in the direction of Jason's voice.

Jason appeared by the forest's edge, "Well, what's taking you so long?

"Come quickly, I found the warrior's sword!" Exclaimed Samuel.

He turned around to see the Gatekeeper's response but he was no where to be found. Samuel couldn't believe his eyes, yet he refocused and ran into the water by the shore's edge, where he had spotted the sword.

Jason ran down to meet him. Jason splashed into the water beside Samuel.

"No, no, don't splash around, I swear the warrior's sword was just here moments ago. I saw it right here!" Declared Samuel.

The sword was gone.

In the woods nearby, Nine sat on his haunches and watched the boys splash around in the water near the shore. Nine scratched his ear with his back leg as a dog would scratch for fleas. He stuck his finger in his ear and wiggled it around. He pulled it out and examined it for any earwax residue. He stuck his finger in his mouth and licked it clean. Nine rocked on his haunches as he watched Samuel and Jason search for the sword. Nine mumbled to himself, "You promised Nine, come along, come along you said, Nine promised you I will, I will, I will."

Chapter Twenty
A TIME TO PUT AWAY CHILDISH THINGS

Nightfall couldn't come quickly enough for Thomas. As the moon rose over the crest of the hill Thomas was on his feet and ready to go. Talia grabbed a torch.

"Now stay close behind me," Thomas said to Talia with a smile.

"When have I not?" Responded Talia.

Talia handed the torch to Thomas.

"Especially you Lowen, none of your nosey wolf antics," Thomas warned.

Thomas patted her on the head. Lowen wagged her tail and pranced around like a pup. The night was full of revelation to Thomas. He couldn't stop thinking about the events of the past few days. His thoughts travelled back to the scroll the Gatekeeper left him by the mill and the words on it, now they were fulfilled:

Crimson is the Eastern Shore; mystery lies behind the door to your destiny.
Strands of silver, bands of gold, earthly things to have and hold,
what does it mean what's in it all for you?
Listen to the meadowlark and watch for the fall of night.
The moon will guide your flight. Across the mountain past the valley below,
rest the place of Hollows Grove.

The writing was really in two parts; not to be read as one but as two parts. Thomas realized for the first time that wisdom required deeper contemplation than what could be understood from the first blush of meaning.

His dreams meant so much more too; he understood their symbolism, he understood his conviction with new and deeper meaning that was hard for him to express to Talia. It was hard to express in words that could be uttered, it was a courage and confidence that burned deep within him. He understood things about himself that he couldn't have possibly understood before.

"Are you ready?" Thomas asked as he looked into Talia's eyes.

Talia didn't break his gaze but her eyes softened with admiration for him. Thomas looked more like a man than the boy who played with her on the frozen ponds back home. Thomas' voice had even deepened through the years. He was indeed becoming a man.

They gathered their things and began the walk up the hill. The darkness on this side of the hill was contrasted by the bright moonlight shining on the other side. Thomas had walked up this hill many times before so he was sure of his footing, sure of the path to take. This time he would not stop at the crest of the hill. He would face his fears and walk into the valley of wheat below.

As Thomas rounded the crest of the hill something amazing happened. The moonlight cut through the mountains on the other side of the valley and there before them, the moon had illuminated a path across the valley. It was a clear, safe passage for them to take.

"Why have we never seen this before?" Asked Talia.

"Amazing the difference perspective makes," responded Thomas.

Down into the valley they ventured. The wind flicked the torch that illuminated just enough for them to see one step ahead. The wheat on both sides of the path danced in a devilish movement as if to dare them to venture in.

Along the path were shards of broken wheat. Thomas stooped and picked some of the broken wheat up. He brought it close to his face to examine it.

"Talia," Thomas whispered.

She moved closer to Thomas' back.

"This is not wheat at all, they are nothing but tares, weeds as my uncle would call them," Thomas said.

Lowen started to whimper.

"Be quiet girl," Thomas forcefully whispered without looking back.

"Thomas help!" Talia whispered in a panic.

Thomas turned about to face his friends. Talia was sinking in the soil and sinking fast, just like Thomas' dream.

Thomas looked down at his feet. The mud under his feet was gurgling as if to try and consume him, yet it could not. The boots of the Gatekeeper allowed him to walk on the path without sinking.

"Thomas, hurry!" Yelled Talia.

The mud was already above her ankles. The sound of a thousand evil screams echoed through the wheat field. Thomas moved quickly to her and pulled with all his might to free her from the mud.

"Put your hands on my breast plate and hold on!" Thomas encouraged.

Thomas braced himself, locked his knees and pulled; the mud gave up Talia. Thomas bent forward.

"Climb on my back!" He said.

Talia did as she was told.

Thomas began moving back from where they had come. He paused at Lowen. The mud had swallowed Lowen's back legs. With her front paws she struggled to stay above the sinking ground. Lowen looked up at Thomas. Thomas had never seen fear in a wolf's eyes before now.

"I will be back for you girl, don't move... I will be back Lowen. I am taking Talia to the other side of the valley but I will be back," Thomas said with as brave a voice as he could. Thomas turned quickly from Lowen. Lowen's whimpers echoed in his ears. The wheat swayed and the wind moaned. Shrieks and screams rose from the dancing field as if it held the souls of a million people.

"You'll never save them both." the Queen's voice rose above the screams.

Tears rolled down Thomas' face. He cried tears of having to leave Lowen behind. Talia held on to him tightly, riding piggyback. She knew there was nothing that could be said. In silence they made their way across the valley to the side of the hill. Thomas let Talia down and bent over to catch his breath. Thomas turned to enter the field again. Talia let her grip go for a moment but grasped Thomas' arm.

"No." Talia said as she held him from returning.

Thomas paused and looked deeply into her eyes.

"If the greatest challenges lay ahead, that means we'll make it, we'll all make it. If it was a lie that you and Lowen are not safe with me, then this is the time to prove the words of the Gatekeeper. I will be safe and so will Lowen," Thomas said.

Talia shook her head as if to ask him to please stay.

"You know I must," Thomas said.

Talia let Thomas go and off Thomas ran back along the gurgling mud path holding his torch high.

"Lowen, I'm coming girl!" Thomas shouted.

The screams of the field also rose in intensity as the Queen's voice echoed across the field.

"You'll never save them both, you'll never save them," the Queen's words rang out.

Thomas reached the spot where Lowen was last seen, but there was no sign of her. The mud gurgled and gulped as if it were molten lava. The wheat tares swayed dancing in the wind and the moans of the wind seemed to mock Thomas.

"No... the Gatekeeper's words are true, and I believe!" Shouted Thomas.

With that Thomas planted the torch in the path thrust his arms into the gurgling mud where Lowen was last seen. Pulling them out of the mud with nothing but the slimy goo on his hands, he wasn't going to give up. He thrust them in a second time to pull them out with nothing. A third time he thrust them in the mud and he felt her. Thomas pulled with all of his strength as he braced himself.

"Lowen and Talia are safe with me, Lowen and Talia are safe with me!" Thomas repeatedly shouted.

Suddenly the gurgling mud let go of Lowen and the force pushed Thomas on his back. Lowen lay in Thomas' arms across his chest. Thomas gently caressed Lowen in his arms. She was not breathing and lay limp in his arms.

"NO!' Yelled Thomas.

He held Lowen close to him. Tears rolled down his cheeks.

"No, no, no," Thomas repeated to himself.

Thomas looked around him as the wheat tares danced, the sound of the wind passing through it caused it to have a cackling sound as if it was laughing at him. Thomas ignored the mocking of the field and struggled to sling Lowen's body across his shoulders. The wolf was not light but the adrenaline in Thomas' body gave him the strength to do it. He was not leaving her behind. Thomas struggled to his feet.

Thomas ran back to the side of the hill where he left Talia. Across the field, along the moonlit path, Thomas ran as fast as he could with Lowen laid across his shoulders.

As Thomas reached Talia on the other side of the field, she already had a fire going. Thomas dropped to his knees and he laid Lowen on the ground before her. Talia moved to Thomas' side and put her hands on the mud-covered wolf.

Thomas was crying, tears ran down Talia's face as they both wiped the mud, goo and slime off of Lowen who lay lifeless before them. A glimmer of light caught Thomas' eye. The glimmer of light blinded him for a moment as Thomas turned to see the Gatekeeper standing with a silver shield resting on the ground in front of his feet. The moon reflecting off the shiny surface of the shield illuminated Thomas, Talia and Lowen.

Thomas touched Talia's hand and she turned to face the Gatekeeper.

"Young warrior," the Gatekeeper addressed Thomas.

Thomas stood to his feet and approached the Gatekeeper. Thomas' tear stained face, body mud splattered, looked more like a tattered young man than a warrior.

"You said they would be safe with me," Thomas stated.

"And they were," the pride in the Gatekeeper's voice was undeniable. He held up the shield and presented it to Thomas.

Thomas looked at the shield and held out his hands as the Gatekeeper passed it to him. "Love has brought you this far and chose you. Now faith will carry you to the hope," the Gatekeeper said.

With that the Gatekeeper passed the shield to Thomas. Thomas examined the finely ordained shield. Gold twine ribbing edged the shield. On the center of the shield was a regal royal crest of a lion, a sword of fire and a circle around the sword as a symbol of eternity.

Thomas forgot his present situation for a moment and turned to look at Talia to see if she saw the shield being presented to him. As Thomas turned back to Talia he saw Lowen move and sit up. He ran to her.

Talia turned her attention back to Lowen. Lowen stood to her feet and shook as dogs do when they are wet and dirty, spraying mud and gunk all over Talia and Thomas. Thomas lifted his shield to block most of the spray but Talia got it full force.

Thomas lowered his shield to see Talia squinting from behind her new mud mask. She wiped the mud from her eyes and looked at Thomas. Thomas came to her and sat on the ground beside her and they both started to laugh. She took some of the mud off her face and wiped it on Thomas. Thomas playfully pushed her away and Lowen came between them not wanting to be left out. Lowen started to lick their faces.

In their laughter they hadn't noticed that the Gatekeeper had left as quietly as he came. They were consumed in the moment, consumed in their friendship and consumed in laughter and joy of being together.

The next morning they rose early and climbed the side of the hill. The field of tares behind them seemed peaceful with no signs of the wicked entity that rested within it. The morning sun beat down on them, drying their mud stained bodies to a cake-like coating that began flaking off. As they rounded the last few steps that took them over the crest of the hill, none of them could believe what they saw below.

Chapter Twenty-One
THE GROWING PLACE

Thomas strapped the shield to his back. He looked at Talia and she smiled. He looked at Lowen and she cocked her head to the side as if to ask him, what was he going to do.

Captivated, they all gazed into the valley before them. The valley was lush, green and beautiful with a majestic sequoia forest, edged by ripe fruit trees and a crystal clear stream curving its way through the center. It was an abundant garden. It was as if autumn had stopped at the crest of this hill.

A troop of white wild horses played in the valley. Almost on cue, the stallion that led the herd stood on his hind legs, whinnied and galloped off; followed by the other horses as they disappeared into the forest. The sight of this brought a smile to Thomas and Talia. Lowen started barking and howling.

This place was full on in summer bloom; the difference from one side of the hill to the other was as striking as bleak black and white to full color saturation. Behind them was the autumn forest and the monochromatic beige field of tares; ahead was paradise.

They took one more moment to take in the beauty from their high vantage point, then turned to each other in almost disbelief. They questioned each other with their looks, as if what they were seeing was true. A sure smile on the others face told them it was really there. Simultaneously they started running down the hill as fast as their legs would carry them.

Lowen began hopping and barking to see over the grass. Thomas and Talia were laughing as they raced into the valley and ran along the stream. Thomas jumped up and grabbed an apple off the tree and bit into it, the juice running down his chin. Talia picked some huge grapes, the biggest she had ever seen. Lowen jumped in the streams edge pouncing on a fish. They had discovered a utopia they never had imagined could exist.

The giant sequoia trees were larger than anything they had ever seen. Not far into the woods they came across a cabin that was fully stocked and furnished. It was as much as they had felt at home in three years. They reasoned that whoever lived in the cabin would surly understand their need for shelter and that they would repay the owner for the hospitality.

Later that day, Lowen lay by the outdoor fireside, content with her catch of the day. On the fire Thomas had a fish cooking. The fish was ready. Thomas took it off of the fire and placed it on some large leaves as a dish.

"Talia!" He called.

She was not in shouting distance or she couldn't hear him because she didn't respond. What had gotten into her, she knew from their travel not to wander off without letting the other know; that was their unspoken rule. Thomas rose to his feet and turned to Lowen who sprang her head up from what seemed like a deep sleep.

"You keep guard of the camp girl," Thomas told her. Lowen lay her head back down, obedient to her master's command. Thomas headed out with the fish in hand, looking for Talia.

"Talia. Talia where are you?" Thomas called.

Thomas could hear splashing in the distance, so he made his way along the trail until he came upon a crystal clear lake. Talia's clothes were at the shore but she was nowhere to be found. Thomas saw ripples on the water and moved closer to the shore.

"Talia?" He called.

Suddenly she sprang up out of the water. Her back was to him but she was definitely naked. He turned his eyes down and looked away. He had noticed she was becoming a woman. Talia turned around and saw him looking away. She covered her chest with her arms.

"Thomas Jacob Littlewood, how long have you been standing there?" She asked.

Thomas began to answer but the explanation that stammered out of his mouth wasn't coming with ease. "I... I... just... was worried... thought that... I brought some fish," he answered. Thomas allowed himself to look back up in her direction.

She sunk herself up to her neck in the water.

"I'd thank you kindly to leave the fish on the shore and return to camp, a girls bathing time is not to be shared," Talia said with a smile.

"Of course... I mean... yes... I just brought the... and... well when I... I'll see you back at camp," Thomas uttered. Thomas placed the cooked fish wrapped in leaves on the rock by her clothes and turned up the trail mumbling to himself.

Talia knew she embarrassed him and she liked it.

Thomas mumbled to himself, "You're so stupid Thomas Littlewood, didn't your father teach you manners? Yeah, she caught you staring, no point in denying it!"

Thomas disappeared into the woods on the trail back to camp before Talia allowed herself to laugh at him. Then she felt other eyes watching her... she turned in the water to the other shore to catch a couple of the white wild horses looking at her from behind the trees.

Talia gasped at first, startled to see them. She moved ever so slightly in the water to gain a better view but the horses knew she was slowly moving toward them. They galloped off into the woods.

Talia dressed and made her way back to their camp ringing out her wet hair as she approached. As he saw her coming Thomas shyly looked down to the outdoor campfire he had burning. She smiled.

Lowen trotted off to meet Talia and escort her to the campfire.

She sat next to him holding her fish wrapped in leaves. Lowen sat with them but kept her attention on Talia's wrapped fish.

"Did you think I should eat my dinner alone by the lake? Is that why you brought me dinner there?" She said to Thomas with a smile.

"Not at all... I... just..." Thomas stammered.

Talia broke the tension by pushing his shoulder. They laughed.

"Can a traveler join you?"

The words of the Gatekeeper broke their laughter and startled them. Standing there before them the Gatekeeper smiled as he watched the budding relationship of Thomas and Talia.

"Whoa... you startled me! Even Lowen doesn't raise her head to warn us of your coming... how do you do that?" Questioned Thomas.

The Gatekeeper sat by the fire and crossed his legs to join them on the ground. He smiled, grabbed a stick and stoked the fire.

"The aroma of your dinner is inviting," admitted the Gatekeeper.

"You are always welcome," smiled Thomas.

"That's why I come," responded the Gatekeeper.

"Don't be concerned with repaying the owner of the cabin, you are most welcome to stay here. It has been prepared especially for you," said the Gatekeeper.

He reached up and removed his hood to let it fall on his shoulders.

For the first time in his life, Thomas could fully see the kind eyes of the Gatekeeper was framed by a strong middle aged face. Creases by his eyes spoke of his wisdom. His long brown locks of curly hair cascaded off his head to his shoulders. His beard matched the dark ruddy color of his hair but it was not long and scruffy, it was rather neat. Thomas admired it. The Gatekeeper smiled at Thomas and Talia.

"You're seen glimpses of me before, it's time we see each other face to face, in this safe place," the Gatekeeper said. "Someday soon you will leave this place and set the captives free," the Gatekeeper added. The Gatekeeper smiled at the thought of his statement.

"The captives will be free," the Gatekeeper whispered to himself.

Night fell and fireflies flittered in the woods as the trio enjoyed each other's company by the campfire. None of the challenges that they experienced matter to Talia now. It was a perfect night. She leaned in on Thomas' shoulder as the Gatekeeper kept them laughing with funny stories of Thomas' youth. Thomas laughed along. The Gatekeeper's stories were not poking fun at Thomas, rather they were told as a proud father would tell to his daughter-in-law... at least that's what Talia let herself imagine. Thomas could take the ribbing.

Talia looked up at the twinkling night constellation, everything was as it should be. She allowed herself to forget the purpose of Thomas' calling and enjoy every second of this moment. The night wore on and the Gatekeeper excused himself, promising to see them in the morning. The Gatekeeper walked away into the woods, leaving them by themselves with their wolf companion.

Later that night in the cabin, Thomas sat at the table by the fireplace; reading through the scrolls the Gatekeeper had given him. Talia approached from behind and put her arms around Thomas' neck. She surprised him because she caught him deep in thought. He jumped slightly.

"Sorry, I didn't mean to scare you," Talia giggled,

"No you didn't, just startled me... I didn't hear you enter the room." Thomas chuckled.

Talia smiled. Thomas went back to looking over the scroll.

"Thomas, this place is beautiful. I know I thought we had it good at the mill, but you were right... for all we went through, this place... well, what I'm trying to say is that I could stay here forever."

Thomas appeared to tune her out for the moment as he straightened the scroll.

"You know, if only I would have followed the first map the Gatekeeper gave me and not gone through that orchard then maybe we wouldn't have encountered the Queen along the way. The map could have brought me directly to you," Thomas stated.

"Thomas you're not listening to me. I like it here," Talia said in an elevated tone.

"Yes, I heard you and I agree. It's awesome."

Thomas carried on with his first thought without missing a beat.

"I realized that I have been missing it by not reading these scrolls for their true meaning," Thomas confessed.

Talia exhaled her frustration and reached across the table, grabbed Thomas' hand drawing his attention to her.

"Thomas, tell me why we can't stay here? We've been on this journey for so long. Is it so bad to dream that we could stay here?" She asked.

Thomas stood to his feet.

"Is there anything about this conversation that seems familiar to you? It sure feels that way to me. How many times do we have to go over this?" Thomas asked.

Talia dropped her head and looked away from Thomas. Thomas knew there was something more she wasn't saying. She turned to him and started to speak slowly because she feared what she would say would break Thomas' heart.

"What if I don't want to go back to the village?" She asked.

"Why not?" Thomas inquired.

There was another long awkward pause before she spoke.

"The whole time we spent with the Old Woman, the Hunter and the Chef, I was afraid they'd tell you the truth about me. When you knew the truth you'd agree with them that I should be left alone to rot in their cave."

"Never Talia, I would fight for you."

"The Old Woman was the one who knew what happened and told the others, she was the one who constantly reminded me..."

Thomas sat forward in his chair bracing himself for whatever confession Talia was about to make.

"I'm the one that brought the Queen's raiders to our village," Talia said.

"Nonsense!" Exclaimed Thomas.

Talia was slow and deliberate with her response.

"I told you about the morning raid on the village, what I didn't tell you is what happened before," Talia confessed.

As Talia speaks, her words trigger the vivid memory of the raid in their village.

****

An early morning mist hung on the village. Talia was outside of her front door looking at Thomas' Papa, Salo and the village men gathered, discussing their strategy for finding Thomas. Talia's mother came to the door.

"Perhaps you should be gathering eggs like I asked you," Talia's mother said.

"Thomas is missing mother," Talia responded.

"The men will find him, not to worry; boys have a way of wandering off on adventures. Please collect the eggs," Talia's mother encouraged.

"Yes," Talia responded.

Talia's mother returned inside of their home. Talia began going to the chicken roost to collect eggs but once she was out of sight of her home, she ran and hid behind some rocks nearby.

Talia lay her head back and looked out over the landscape.

"Thomas, I'm worried about you, where are you?" She whispered to herself. Then a person as small as a mouse, the Old Woman appeared on top of the rock.

"Me too," squeaked the Old Woman. "I worry about the trouble Thomas has gotten himself into," The Old Woman added.

Talia jumped a bit startled at the sight of the imp.

"Who are you? What are you? Where did you come from?" Talia asked.

"We live here and there, we live everywhere just waiting to be invited," responded the Old Woman.

"Invited?" Asked Talia.

"Yes you did, dear," responded the Old Woman.

"I don't even know you, why would I invite you?"

"You know me full well, as I know you, it's just how well we know each other. That's the question! That's always the question. We have a way of growing on you, you'll see," the Old Woman said with a smirk.

"I don't know you very well at all," replied Talia.

"All that is about to change," responded the Old Woman.

"I don't even remember meeting you, how is it that I invited you?"

"Noncompliance, unruliness, disobedience, stubbornness... shall I go on?" Asked the Old Woman.

"What are you talking about?" Replied Talia.

"I don't blame you at all, no one would... why should you fulfill your mother's request when there are far more urgent matters at hand... Thomas is missing! You're a freethinking revolutionary, able to make up your own mind and go your own way," responded the Old Woman.

Talia thought long and hard about the Old Woman's statement. There was something freeing about it, something that sounded right.

"Yes, that's what I've told my mother before," Talia admitted.

A slow broad smile crawled across the Old Woman's lips.

"And you say you didn't invite us... nonsense, it's the very call of rebellion and the need for revolt that draws our kind in," the Old Woman said in sweet voice.

"Your kind?" Talia asked.

"Well..." the Old Woman responded. The Old Woman caught herself and rephrased her sentence before she began. "I clearly mean to say that we are here to support your revolt against the uncaring demanding authority," the Old Woman said in an encouraging tone.

"I never said my mother was uncaring or demanding."

"No, no, of course not. Not in those words but your actions demand a verdict and the judgment has been levied," said the Old Woman.

Talia wasn't sure she liked what the Old Woman said. It kind of frightened her.

Talia rose to her feet and ran back to the village, determined to keep her mother's request; to head to the chicken roost and collect the eggs.

The Old Woman shouted after Talia. "You can't stop what you've started!" "We're here for you!" Proclaimed the Old Woman in support. The Old Woman spoke to herself as Talia ran back to the village. "We're here... for... you," she let her words trail off into a threatening cackle.

Just as Talia reached the chicken roost, she looked up on the horizon and saw the Mountain Giants bearing down toward the village.

****

Back in the cabin, Talia leaned forward in her chair and met Thomas' eyes with hers.

"If at first I had been obedient to my mother and gone to the chicken's roost, the Queen's parasites would have never found me... but I didn't listen, I ran away and when I returned it was too late. The Old Woman said it was my rebellion that invited them. I can't go home Thomas, I can never go home," Talia confessed.

Tears welled up in Thomas' eyes as he felt Talia's pain. Thomas rose from his chair and knelt before her. Talia slid off her chair to the ground wrapping her arms around Thomas.

"I've made mistakes too, Talia, but there is a second chance, this is it, my second chance to make things right... I have to go back," Thomas whispered. Talia nodded her head with understanding. Thomas and Talia embraced for a long time as the fireplace consumed the logs placed on it. To Thomas, everything that Talia confessed to him explained so much; why she had always been reluctant to carry on in different parts of their journey. Above all else Thomas wished he could comfort Talia but he knew the pain she had taken on herself would have to be removed in ways that were beyond his words to express or power to change.

The next day Talia was roused from sleep by the clanging of staffs; wood on wood cracked as they hit together. She moved out of the shelter to see a log stretched across the stream. Lowen sat on the shore wagging her tail and watched as Thomas and the Gatekeeper engaged in a mock battle of staff fighting.

Thomas held out Papa's staff. The Gatekeeper showed him how to hold his hands the width of his body apart. The Gatekeeper swung his staff above his head in a twirling motion and brought it in front spreading his hands a body's length apart. He held it firm as if he was being attacked and pushed it out and away from his body. Then he took a quick leap backwards and to the side of the huge log spanning the creek.

"Defend against the blow and sweep into the attack," the Gatekeeper said.

The Gatekeeper demonstrated the move again.

Thomas lifted his staff and swung it above his head and it slipped out of his hand falling squarely on top of his own head before bouncing toward his feet. The Gatekeeper reached out his foot as the staff landed on top of it, he swept his leg up twirling the staff in the air and caught it in his hand.

"Ouch," exclaimed Thomas.

Thomas rubbed the top of his head where the staff had hit him.

Talia giggled but quickly put her hand to her mouth to cover her laughter. It was a funny image. Thomas heard her laugh and spotted her watching. He looked angry at first but then stole a glance at the Gatekeeper and back to Talia and he giggled at himself.

"Let's try it again," said the Gatekeeper.

The Gatekeeper tossed the staff to Thomas and he caught it. Thomas lifted his staff slowly and carefully repeated the move.

Talia watched from behind the cabin and held a branch in her hand. She tried to copy Thomas' moves in secret; little did she know the Gatekeeper knew what she was doing.

Weeks later the staff was swinging high in the air as the Gatekeeper watched, it clumsily fell to the ground.

"That's okay, a good start," encouraged the Gatekeeper.

This time the hands that picked up the staff were Talia's... she was now the one beginning to learn staff fighting. The Gatekeeper stood beside Talia.

"Why did you offer to show me these things?" Talia asked.

"When your desire to understand outweighed your desire to know, you became ready. You see, it is one thing to know the answer to a difficult question but once you understand the answer, you always will," the Gatekeeper replied.

The Gatekeeper was about to say something else but Talia's words interrupted him. She knew he would eventually want to address her failure at the village on the day of the raid. She wanted to avoid that conversation.

"Thomas is so far ahead," Talia protested.

"If you watch those in the race beside you, your eyes will not be focused on the finish line," the Gatekeeper responded.

Talia nodded her head, she understood the Gatekeeper wanted her not to compare herself to anyone but focus on what she's been given to do.

"Thank you," the Gatekeeper said.

"I've not completed a move you showed me correctly yet."

"You completed the first move perfectly."

"I did?"

The Gatekeeper smiled.

"The day at the rock, when the Old Woman joined in the mocking of your mother, you made the right move. You returned to the village to complete the task your mother had given you."

"She said I was the reason they came," Talia confessed

"The mistake was made but the consequence to the right action you took, will be realized," the Gatekeeper softly said.

The Gatekeeper put his hand on her staff and positioned it and held it still while he peered deep into her eyes.

"Talia, you can realize the results of the right action, starting today. The liar is only as big as the lie they tell and as big as the lies you believe. If you know that, you never have to fear facing the liar," the Gatekeeper encouraged.

He smiled at her and put his big gentle hand on her head. He held it there for a moment before letting go. She smiled at him and felt a release in her heart of the guilt and shame she carried with her since the day of the raid. Talia attempted the same move again, this time with success and accuracy.

In the distance Thomas practiced by himself, swinging his Papa's staff with confidence in the moves the Gatekeeper had taught him. A tool used in loving care to guide his sheep on Mount Crevasse so long ago, was now a formidable weapon in Thomas' hands.

Thomas swung his staff in a series of moves: jabs, swings and strikes, hitting a stick-man decisively, he snapped it in two.

The Gatekeeper was now standing beside Thomas and put his hand on his shoulder. In the background Talia continued her staff fighting moves.

The Gatekeeper leaned in closer to Thomas,

"Well done," said the Gatekeeper.

Thomas looked at his broken target and smiled at his accomplishment.

In the near distance Thomas saw a few of the white horses watching him. Thomas would occasionally see them out of the corner of his eye. They were curious about his activity. The white stallion and his troop always spied on Thomas from a safe distance. Thomas had tried on occasion to draw them in by placing a trail of apples to their camp. It was to no avail, the horses were smarter than that.

Months passed: Talia and Thomas grew in age, wisdom and ability as they did their maneuvers in unison both cracking their respective targets with direct blows.

"He asked to meet us tomorrow morning at dawn," Talia said winded from her exercise.

"Do you think?" Thomas asked.

She knew instinctively what Thomas was asking.

"I do," Talia said with a twinkle in her eye.

A gentle morning mist blanketed the forest that morning and a beautiful calm prevailed. Thomas knelt in front of the Gatekeeper on one knee. Talia stood behind him. Lowen stood to the side respecting this moment, somehow she knew it was a special occasion and only watched from a distance wagging her tail in approval.

The Gatekeeper motioned for Talia to kneel beside Thomas. Talia looked surprised, but did as the Gatekeeper instructed. Thomas looked at her, she at him and they smiled at each other. They both looked back to the Gatekeeper.

The Gatekeeper opened a large cloth bag and it revealed two helmets, two swords along with another shield, boots, breastplate and belt for Talia.

The Gatekeeper lifted the helmet into his hands and held it over Thomas' head. "This helmet is not earned by you, it is freely given by me," the Gatekeeper said.

With that the Gatekeeper lowered the helmet on Thomas' head. The helmet had a nose bridge and covered his head with the royal crest with the gold braiding matching his shield. He repeated the helmet placing ceremony with Talia.

The Gatekeeper lifted a sword into the air. The blade glistened in the sunlight that was streaming through the tall sequoia trees.

"Hold this in your right hand with humility and respect the power and authority I am giving to you to serve the Good King," the Gatekeeper admonished.

Thomas and Talia took the sword in their right hands. Although the blade looked heavy it was light in their hands and the handle seemed custom fit. Talia admired the sword while Thomas swung the blade around with ease in a crisscross manner. Thomas was amazed how he was able to handle the sword. The sword was like an extension of his body. Thomas admired the workmanship of the sword he held in his hands. It was all new to him, yet it was like he had handled the sword his entire life.

Weeks later at sunrise, Thomas, Talia and Lowen stood at the edge of the woods. Thomas and Talia had on their warriors' vestments, with their helmets attached to the belts at their side, their swords sheathed and hanging off the belt as well. Their meager belongings were cinched in cloth and attached to their staffs. The Gatekeeper stood beside them. A gentle breeze blew through the valley. The wildflowers around them were abundant and in full bloom of deep purple, a fitting color for a royal moment like this.

"We shall be together again in a short time," the Gatekeeper promised.

He looked over his shoulder as three white horses appeared from the edge of the woods. They were saddled and bridled.

"My friends here will carry you back to Mount Crevasse where you will meet the Good King," said the Gatekeeper. "He will be waiting there for you." the Gatekeeper added.

Two of the white horses approached them.

The Gatekeeper held the bridle of one horse as he held out his hand to Talia. She took the Gatekeeper's hand and he led her to the horse. She put her foot in the stirrup and swung her leg over the horse and settled into the saddle. Thomas followed on the other horse.

"Ride well my friends," the Gatekeeper shouted.

At his voice, as if on command, the horses took off. Lowen barked, howled and followed behind, trying to keep up.

The horses galloped out of the valley and over the rolling hills that lay to the east. Thomas and Talia rode into the rising day.

Chapter Twenty-Two
RETURN TO MOUNT CREVASSE

Thomas, Talia and Lowen's journey took them a month, but they had finally reached the mountain village they once called home. It was still in the distance as they rounded the last crest of the mountain range. The close of day was fast approaching. It was now autumn and the Festival of Harvest was ramping up in the valley below. The festival's music had not changed in all the time he had been away but Thomas had. Thomas also knew it would be soon time for the Lottery of Affluence. None of this concerned him now. His first and greatest passion was for the welfare of his family.

Thomas and Talia broke out in full stride on their horses as they raced to the village. Thomas arrived first and hopped off his horse in front of his house. The weeds and wildflowers had overgrown their little village and the door on his thatched roofed house was still sticky as he had remembered but the house was barren and cold.

Only the sound of his own footsteps echoing off the walls came back to him. He had hoped his father might have made a break from the prison camp and had been able to return; alas it was as empty as he remembered. The scent of the pine trees surrounding his village was the only familiar friend to welcome him home. It had been over five years since Thomas stood in this exact spot; so much has happened, Thomas thought. The sound of approaching footsteps snapped Thomas out of reminiscing. Thomas turned around to face Talia standing in the doorway. She held her flute in her hand. Talia lifted it up to show Thomas.

"No one left in my home, just the flute where I had left it on my bed. It seems like so long ago," Talia said as she looked down, as if to remember. She looked up at Thomas. "Where do you believe the Good King will be?" She asked.

Thomas shook his head. "Let's stay here tonight and explore the area in the morning. I think I know where to find him," Thomas answered.

That night Thomas made a fire in the fireplace of his home. Although so much had changed it was good to be home. Talia and he exchanged stories from the days they were young. Talia played her flute and Thomas admired her. A few rough notes to start but she soon fell back into the sweet melodies he remembered hearing come from her home when they were children.

Thomas closed his eyes and reminisced as Talia played. With his eyes closed he dreamed of the many occasions and days they spent together as children. He could see Talia walking toward him laughing as she came through the tall wildflowers which grew on the mountain... and then he said it, in words that seemed to naturally fall out, "I've always loved you," Thomas blurted.

Talia stopped playing and lowered her flute. She looked at Thomas. The first thing Thomas noticed was that her music stopped. The second thing that flashed in his mind was the words that came out of his mouth. He replayed it in his mind, "I have always loved you, I have always loved you... could I have said such a thing out loud?" With that Thomas darted open his eyes.

Talia leaned a little closer.

"What did you say?" She asked.

"Did I say something?" He responded.

"Yes. I knew it, even though you denied it when we were kids, I knew it!" Talia laughed.

"Are you sure? I am not sure that I knew it," Thomas responded.

Talia raised her eyebrows as if to tell him not to try and deceive her because she had heard it. He knew she did.

"Ah yes... I guess I did say something," Thomas confessed. "I... think it is... time, time, time I went to bed." Thomas stammered as he got up and went to his bed. Papa's and his bed were much smaller than he remembered and he marveled at how two had ever fit in it.

Talia smiled as she watched him and she turned and petted Lowen.

Some hours had passed before Thomas opened his eyes to look across the room. By the light of the dying embers on the fire, he could see Lowen curled up where he had left her. Talia was in his Papa's small bed. She sleeps a lot quieter than my Papa did, Thomas thought. He rolled over in bed and smiled. Little did he know Talia couldn't sleep either.

Thomas' movement caused her to turn in bed and look at him across the room. He is asleep she thought. She rolled back on her side and the words of Thomas played in her mind, "I have always loved you," that's what he said. She smiled and closed her eyes attempting to get some rest but she couldn't.

"Are you asleep?" Talia asked.

"No," Thomas answered without rolling over to face her side of the room.

"It's getting chilly in here."

"I could stoke the fire."

"You could do that," Talia responded.

She slipped out of Papa's bed and snuggled beside Thomas.

"There's hardly room for me," Thomas said.

"We'll just have to make it work," Talia replied.

As almost on cue, Lowen leaped up in Thomas bed and lay on top of Thomas and Talia.

"LOWEN," they groaned in unison.

The next morning Thomas awoke and saddled their horses. Talia got up and went to the door.

"I didn't have the heart, you were sleeping so well," Thomas said.

Thomas swung his leg over his horse.

"Why not wait here, let me scout the area and I will return shortly," Thomas said.

"Not a chance, I am coming!" Talia exclaimed.

Talia hurried back inside, got her armor and mounted the horse that Thomas saddled for her. He knew that she would not stay behind, that's why he prepared her horse. Off they went and Lowen ran after them.

As they passed through the tall grass the merriment of the Festival of Harvest carried on in the valley below. A celebration that never rested, thought Thomas. Soon they were by the old oak tree at the base of the mountain pass.

Beneath the brooding tree, Thomas saw that the Gatekeeper was sitting there. At the Gatekeeper's feet was the lamb that Thomas had rescued, although now it was fully grown. The strangest sight of all, the brooding tree that never had any leaves, was in full bloom. In all of Thomas' memory he had never seen this old oak tree so full of leaves!

Thomas and Talia dismounted their horses as they arrived at the tree.

The Gatekeeper had a fire going with fish cooking and fresh loaves of bread. He was wearing his hood again, like he had in all other places except the garden where they were trained. Thomas and Talia instinctively knew there was probably a very good reason he was again concealing himself, that they would come to discover in due time.

"Welcome, always room at the fireside for a traveller," said the Gatekeeper.

Thomas and Talia joined the Gatekeeper round the campfire. Lowen was soon behind them. The Gatekeeper greeted Lowen with a good rub behind the ears.

"The aroma of your breakfast is inviting," Thomas said.

"Today you will face that which you long hoped for," the Gatekeeper promised.

With that the Gatekeeper handed Thomas and Talia, bread and fish. Lowen stood off to the side and wagged her tail. Thomas threw her a piece of meat.

"When do we meet the Good King? What's our battle plan?" Thomas asked.

"Our army is gathering," the Gatekeeper responded.

They heard the sound of approaching horses. Thomas turned to see three warriors approaching. The warriors pulled their horses to a stop, Samuel, Jason and Aaron dismounted. Although they were much older, Thomas recognized them immediately and threw his arms around them.

"Good ole' Samuel still carrying a tattered satchel like a security blanket," Thomas teased.

Everyone laughed except Samuel whose face dropped in sudden seriousness. The others had not seen what Samuel saw approaching them from behind, it was Meesay coming down the mountain pass. Samuel unsheathed his sword and readied it in defense against the giant. Samuel swung his sword above his head ready to strike Meesay. Meesay threw open his arms and raced toward them... Thomas turned just in time to be caught up in the giants' arms.

"Toomas, Toomas... Meesay!" Messay exclaimed.

Thomas laughed and the giant let him down.

"Samuel, put away your sword... if it weren't for this friend's rescue long ago I may not be with you today," Thomas said.

Thomas slapped Meesay on the side. Meesay drew his hand back in the same playful gesture but Thomas cautioned him.

"No, no my friend, it wouldn't work as well if you slapped me with that force," Thomas admitted.

Everyone laughed and enjoyed each other's company for the next few hours. It was a grand reunion.

Once everyone had settled down and caught up with each other's adventures, they discovered that the Gatekeeper had rescued them all. Each had been providentially out of their village when the Queen and her troops attacked or were rescued from her henchmen.

"The Queen knew this day was coming. That's why she swept through your villages at the time she did; if she could have eradicated all of the warriors, who would be left to stand against her? The Queen knows her time is short," the Gatekeeper said.

The Gatekeeper unrolled a scroll with a map of the kingdom and he began to share the plan for attack with the group.

"The armies of the North shall be under your command Thomas, the armies of the west, under Samuel's, the armies of the east under Aaron's and the armies of the south under Jason's command. Each of these armies shall be engaged in a siege on the Queen's palace. Meesay shall go with you Thomas and the battle plan shall become clear once you reach the palace gates. Talia you shall come with me and on the first horn we shall break open the Gates of Mourning and set the captives free. This is not our only objective, each of your warriors must thrust their swords into any mythamöhre tree, not one should survive. Each has their own mission and must stick to their task at hand. For this to succeed we must all do our parts. You will hear the sound of the battle horn, it's at that call we all engage the enemy simultaneously," the Gatekeeper told them.

Samuel spoke up first. "Why does Thomas need Meesay the giant beside him?" He asked.

The Gatekeeper looked at each of them solemnly before finally resting his eyes on Thomas.

"Thomas will enter the chamber of the Queen and face her directly. Once she withdraws into her chamber, the only way to reach her is for Meesay to toss Thomas up and into the palace window," the Gatekeeper replied.

"I think I should be there to help Thomas combat the Queen... maybe we should all be there!" Samuel encouraged the others to join in.

Jason, and Aaron nodded their head in agreement.

"It does make good sense." Jason piped in.

Jason looked at each of his companions.

"I have always been the best at our games as children... the most athletic... the most..." Jason continued

Aaron interrupted him. "Yes we could only help," he added.

"For the reason you question this plan, is the very reason that I have decided that it shall be Thomas as the only one to deliver the final blow to the Queen. Stay to the plan, work together and we shall succeed. There shall be enough glory in that for you," the Gatekeeper interjected firmly.

They were all respectful of the firm statement the Gatekeeper delivered with absolute authority. He paused and let his words sink in. The Gatekeeper looked around the group as he delivered the final details. "Now ride with the instructions I have given you and in your place you shall find the armies I have gathered under your command." The Gatekeeper nodded his encouragement to send them on their way.

Jason and Aaron were first to their horses. Samuel turned to go but took a moment to touch Thomas' arm and get his attention privately.

"Save some of the spoils for your old friends," Samuel said. His eyes darted over to Talia and lingered on her as she spoke with the Gatekeeper. Thomas followed Samuel's gaze and knew he desired her. Thomas looked back at Samuel defiantly. Samuel smiled slyly and mounted his horse. Samuel's horse stood on its hind legs and whinnied as he turned it around.

"On to victory!" Shouted Samuel as he took off.

Aaron and Jason broke away in full stride as well. They rode to the near horizon together and then split away in their separate directions.

Thomas turned to Talia and the Gatekeeper.

"How did the Queen capture my village? I need to know," Thomas asked.

"Thomas, although your village knew the truth and they had all of the defensive resources at their disposal, they didn't understand the whole truth. It's not the truth you know that will hurt you, it's the truth you don't know," responded the Gatekeeper.

The Gatekeeper put his hand on Thomas' shoulder and drew him closer.

"There's something else for you to know. The Littlewood name came because of your ancestors seed of little faith," the Gatekeeper said.

Thomas looked down embarrassed that Talia could overhear this conversation.

The Gatekeeper looked at Talia to include her in his story. "But the rest of the story which you do not know, Thomas, is that your ancestor's little faith was enough. He met the Good King that night and took him at his word. The little firewood he collected, burned all night... and symbolically, it still burns in you. Never doubt it Thomas." The Gatekeeper hugged Thomas and smiled at him.

Thomas turned and walked to his horse. Lowen stood up and went to his side. Talia looked over her shoulder at the Gatekeeper and then ran to the side of Thomas' horse.

"For all these years we have not been apart. I need you to promise me that you will return to me Thomas Jacob Littlewood."

He looked deeply into her eyes.

"I will always come for you Talia," Thomas replied.

They kissed passionately.

Thomas slipped on his helmet and smiled. He stepped into the stirrup and mounted his horse. The Gatekeeper approached and held a closed fist to Thomas as if he would, to give him something.

Thomas reached out his hand open palmed to the Gatekeeper.

"I've held your treasure, Thomas... for this day."

The Gatekeeper released his grip on what he was holding and dropped Thomas' purple pebble into his hand. The same purple pebble he sacrificed on the first night he met the Gatekeeper outside of his house.

The Gatekeeper put his hand on Thomas' leg and on Talia's shoulder as a father would and smiled at them.

Thomas reached down and touched her hand, they looked at each other for a moment, which seemed like an eternity and then he took off.

Thomas dared not turn around or say anything more to her because she would hear the crack in his voice. His heavy heart and the pain in it would surely betray him.

Thomas rode away as fast as his horse would take him with Lowen in hot pursuit. Talia stood there watching him ride away for as far as she could see him.

Chapter Twenty-Three
THE BATTLE

The sun seemed to dance on the horizon as it rose above the mountains. Thomas' horse stepped left and right in anticipation of what lay ahead. Thomas let the horse dance under him but that did not distract him. His face was set at flint with a determination for the task before him. Behind Thomas, a massive army in similar warrior vestments mounted their horses and readied themselves for battle. The Queen's ambitious cleansing of those that resisted her, had not been as successful as she believed. This army was made up of the survivors of that cleansing. Young men and women from across the land were the warriors behind Thomas. They were warriors that the Gatekeeper trained for this day. All of them had stories of seemingly circumstantial events that saved them from being captured. Meesay stood to his feet and came to Thomas horse.

"Meesay's brothers will fight for Queen." Meesay said.

Meesay looked worried as he said this.

"I don't expect you to fight your family Meesay, I understand that." Thomas responded.

"Meesay's brothers wrong, they hate Toomas people but Toomas Meesay's friend... right?" Meesay questioned.

"Of course you are my friend. You saved my life. I trust you." Thomas encouraged him.

"Queen told brothers to kill Meesay because Meesay is different then other mountain giant people."

"And I am different than you Meesay, but that makes each of us all the more special." Thomas responded.

"Meesay like Toomas."

"And I like you too Meesay."

****

On the west ridge of the valley a mighty army gathered behind Samuel. On the east side an army gathered behind Aaron. Horses pranced as the warriors got in formation. On the south a tremendous army stood ready behind Jason.

****

The Gatekeeper and Talia approached the Gates of Mourning. The Gatekeeper moved his horse close to Talia's horse. He leaned in close to Talia.

"As I blow the battle horn, be brave and remember what I taught you, keep your eyes on our goal and we will prevail."

Talia nodded her head and placed her helmet on. She unsheathed her sword and it glistened in the sunlight. She looked toward the Gates of Mourning and could hear the mass of lost souls moaning and moving about behind the massive doors. She tried her best to be a brave warrior but to keep her mind to the task was no easy matter. Somewhere to the north she knew that Thomas and Lowen stood ready for attack and in her mind played the words of Thomas, "I have always loved you," and then there was his kiss and gentle touch when they last stood together. Had he not wanted to say something more to her before leaving? Why hadn't she told him that she loved him? Would she see him again, she wondered?

The sun was poking in and out of clouds. The shadows of the clouds moved on the land. Talia shivered when the clouds covered her. The temperature between the cloud covering and direct sunlight was significant. The Gates of Mourning remained clouded. Talia noticed it first, slowly and specifically the clouds in the sky seemed to gather together. Their size continued to shrink and the sunlight formed a straight line across the ground in front of her. The sun beat down on her and the Gatekeeper. The Gatekeeper raised a ram's horn to his lips. As he did, it was as if the sun was at his command because the clouds receded and the sunlight began to cut a path directly for the Gates of Mourning.

Talia moved forward on her horse and furrowed her brow in unbelief of what she was seeing. As the Gatekeeper inhaled the sunlight raced faster across the ground. He began to blow the battle horn. The sound of the horn began with a low resonate tone, the sunlight chasing the pitch of the sound, and suddenly the sunlight hit the gates and the blast from the Gatekeeper's horn was deafening.

At that moment the Gates exploded! Darkness oozed out of the opening where the gates once stood. The blast and flash of light was seen far across the kingdom.

This was the signal that sent the armies of the north, south, east and west on their charge.

****

The Queen ran to the courtyard of her chamber. Her Gargoyle Guardsmen floundered about running to and fro; hearing the sonic boom and seeing the Queen upset made them uncertain of what to do.

"To your posts idiots, he has returned!" The Queen screamed.

****

In no time, Talia found herself riding through the Gates of Mourning, the Gatekeeper ahead of her. The mass of people spread like a wave before them, as did the darkness of this place. Talia had felt cold before but this darkness was such that it could be tasted. The Queen's mountain giant guards at the gate moped around like blind men, looking for their weapons. Once the Gatekeeper reached the center of the mob he spun his horse around.

"Talia turn your horse around and lead them through the gate!" The Gatekeeper shouted.

Talia pulled her horse around. It whinnied and danced as she watched the Gatekeeper's horse stand on its hind legs.

The Gatekeeper removed his cloak and the bright sunlight caught his uniform, brilliant light, white, gold, silver shone and caused a dazzling rainbow of colors... it was the vestments of a king. The Gatekeeper, now revealed as the returning King, withdrew his sword and yelled with a mighty shout.

"Freedom is yours, be free!"

The sunlight catching the King's outfit caused a ripple of light to break out in waves repelling every inch of darkness. Talia's horse backed up at the awesome sight. She held her sword out and turned to the broken Gates of Mourning. A shout of the people went up that sounded like the roar of many waters. The people fell in behind Talia and began to run for the opening. Talia's horse was on the charge for the opened gate, leading the mass of people out.

The guards at the opening had just regained their sight from the blinding flash of light. The first giant gathered his spear and pointed it at Talia. He began screaming a war-cry. Talia swung her sword above her head and kept up the charge. The giant thrust his spear and Talia neatly deflected it swinging her sword back and bringing it across the giant's midsection doubling him over. Talia could hardly believe that she won the first battle when suddenly her horse threw her over its head and onto the ground.

Her sword went flying in one direction and she in the other. She took a moment to catch her breath and stood up to see that the second guard had thrust his spear into the ground tripping her horse. Talia only had her shield for defense. Her staff was on her horse. Her sword was out of her hand. The giant began to run toward her with his spear held in front of him, aiming at her.

Suddenly the rumble of the ground shook as violent as an earthquake, it was as if the very foundations of the earth had given way. The giant stopped in his tracks and wobbled trying to keep his balance from the tremors. Talia bounced off the ground from the rumble and then she saw it... the mass of lost souls were now free and dashing toward them.

The giant stopped and looked behind him at the stampede of people charging toward him. He momentarily looked back at Talia, dropped his spear and sprinted away for fear of being overrun by the people racing for their freedom. Talia knew she could not escape the flood and believed, this is it; she would be trampled. She bent one knee, closed her eyes and readied her shield in front of her for protection against the onslaught of the charging people. Thoughts of her love for Thomas raced through her head. She never imagined that she might be the one not returning. The crowd was close and she could not escape their enthusiastic charge. Suddenly, the Gatekeeper King swept her up onto his horse.

The mass of people ran around them separating like waves in the sea against the bow of a ship. The giant still running away from the throng, tripped and fell. The stampeding people trampled him under their feet. Talia's horse came beside them and she transferred onto it. The Gatekeeper King passed Talia her sword.

"Well done brave warrior," he said with a smile.

Talia smiled at him and they joined the charge of people over the hill and into the valley of the mythamöhre trees.

****

Thomas' troops where firmly inside the palace courts of the Queen. Battle raged all around. Gargoyles that adorned the walls of the palace took on flesh and began to join in the fight against Thomas. Thomas was engaged in battle here and there but he kept his push toward the Queen's chamber. The Queen stood above the courtyard as if to preside over the battle. In the flash of battle Thomas could see her. Her milky white skin and black eyes, although Thomas had aged she had not. She was still a twelve-year-old child.

****

Across the east, west and south battles raged. Giants in hordes fought the approaching King's armies. Gargoyles flew in and attacked the King's armies from the skies. The King's armies fought on and pushed back the Queen's militia. Archers from both armies fired a volley of shots into their opponents' forces.

As Talia and the Gatekeeper King entered the grove, Talia saw Lowen entangled in a mythamöhre tree. As if the tree were alive; the mythamöhre tree was trying to squeeze the life out of Lowen. Lowen had a branch in her mouth and was fighting with all she had. Talia jumped off her horse and noticed the Little Lies, the Imps running like scared mice for the trees. The Hunter, Old Lady and Chef entered the tree that held Lowen. Talia looked around her and other Little Lies were scurrying for cover under the mythamöhre tree bark.

Talia gritted her teeth and lifted her sword high in the air. "I see you and I know you for what you are!" She sunk her sword deep into the mythamöhre tree that held Lowen. The tree let Lowen go and began to shrivel up.

The Gatekeeper King also sunk his sword into the mythamöhre trees. The trees moaned, whined and shrieked as they shrank. As they dried up they became like ancient wood and began to dissolve. The mass of people freed from the Gates of Mourning, joined in the attack, pushing and pulling, breaking and snapping the trees until they began to dissolve.

****

In the courtyard of the Queen, Thomas continued to battle. He jumped off his horse, sheathed his sword and removed his staff for battle because of its long reach. He swung his staff with accurate lethal blows; just as he broke the stick man in practice, just as the Gatekeeper had taught him. He fought his way to the steps leading into the palace. Meesay fought his way to the wall beside Thomas.

Thomas shouted above the roar of the battle.

"This is our time Meesay! Toss me up to that window!"

Thomas pointed to the window the Queen had been standing in.

Meesay cupped his hands and Thomas put one foot in his hands and suddenly Meesay winced and slumped forward.

"Meesay my friend, toss me to the window," Thomas repeated.

There was no response from Meesay. As Meesay slumped forward a spear sticking out of his shoulder blade came into Thomas' view. Thomas saw the attacker. A giant who looked a lot like Meesay stood smirking at his strike.

The giant attacker looked mockingly at the mortally wounded Meesay.

"I told you little brother not to play with those mountain people. Your hands would get dirty!" The giant laughed.

Thomas withdrew his sword and swung it above his head. He leaped on the back of the slumping Meesay and jumped toward the offending giant. Just then a Gargoyle swooped from the sky and slashed Thomas' exposed back with its talon. Thomas fell to his back.

The Gargoyle swung around for a blow to kill. Thomas lifted his shield, catching the sunlight that blinded the eyes of the Gargoyle and in the blink of an eye the Gargoyle was swatted to the wall where it crumbled like the rock it was made of to the ground. Meesay had managed the strength to come to Thomas' aid and had rescued Thomas once again.

Meesay's giant brother swung his fist and knocked Meesay to the wall. The impact with the palace wall drove the spear deeper into Meesay. Meesay cried out in pain.

"You insolent fool!" said Meesay's giant brother.

Thomas rolled to his feet and drove his sword into the thigh of Meesay's giant brother, bringing him to his knees. As the giant fell to his knees, Thomas took a final swing with his sword into the neck of the giant and finished the battle.

Thomas ran to Meesay.

Meesay struggled to speak to Thomas,

"Meesay sorry Toomas... sorry Meesay not help you into window..." With a deep labored breath, Meesay closed his eyes.

Thomas' eyes welled up. The battle raged on around Thomas as he returned his focus to the task at hand. Thomas looked up the palace wall. Above him on the palace wall, gargoyles were gaining flesh and flaking off the wall into flight, and then joining the battle.

Thomas hopped up on the slumping Meesay and put his feet on Meesay's shoulders. He sheathed his sword, strapped his shield to his back and leaped for a transforming gargoyles foot. He grabbed the stone, as it was becoming flesh. It was gooey and slimy to the touch. Thomas swung his foot up to the next level. Climbing gargoyle by gargoyle, Thomas made his way up the wall. All around him gargoyles were becoming flesh and flaking off the wall. Undaunted Thomas climbed on.

It was then that Samuel and his troops entered the courtyard and joined in the battle to secure the area. Samuel saw Thomas swinging and climbing his way to the window high above the courtyard. Samuel's horse reared on its hind legs and he turned it round. It was then that a Giant lifted his battle-axe to swing it at Samuel that Nine sprang from the raging battle to the back of the Giant's neck. Nine sunk his canine teeth into the back of the Giant who let out a yell.

This warned Samuel who turned his horse around to face the Giant. Samuel sunk his sword into the Giant killing him with one thrust. Nine leaped from the falling Giant onto Samuel's horse clinging to Samuel's back. He leaned in close to whisper into Samuel's ear, "Come along you said, I will, I will, I will. Take what is yours, take what is yours, take what is yours, TAKE IT!"

Nine put both hands on the sides of Samuel's head and positioned it to face the Queens' Chamber window, "TAKE IT," Nine repeated. Nine leapt from Samuel's horse and disappeared into the battle.

Samuel began to fight with a new drive. Single blows from his sword, left and right, thrust and jabs, striking decisively into his enemy. Samuel dismounted his horse and fought his way to the base of the wall, battling gargoyles and giants along the way.

Samuel stood by Meesay and looked up as Thomas climbed and fought his way toward the window. Then Meesay took a shallow breath. Samuel leaned in close to him.

"Meesay you must throw me up to the window, Thomas needs my help... Meesay we must help him."

Meesay barely opened his eyes but moved to his knees and cupped his hands as he had done for Thomas.

Samuel slyly smiled and stepped up into Meesay's cupped hands. Meesay drew all the strength he had and tossed Samuel up the wall, past Thomas and up to the Queen's chamber window.

Once inside the window Samuel bent out looking down at Thomas. He reached his hand out for him.

"Come on my friend, a little further."

Thomas looked down and then up in surprise that Samuel had already made it into the chamber window. He swung his hand up but to no avail, he was too far away. Inside the window there came a loud boom. Samuel turned his attention and saw the huge fireball exploding out of the massive fireplace. Samuel held up his shield and ducked behind it. The fire consumed everything in the room.

The exploding fireball shot out of the window, raining ash on Thomas' head and across the battlefield below.

In the room: Samuel emerged from behind his shield unscathed. As he looked out from behind his shield he saw the Queen on a curving stairwell that hugged the palace wall, going to a room on a higher level. She seductively looked at Samuel and transformed into a beautiful young woman before his eyes.

Samuel watched her disappear from sight up the stairs and took a moment in disbelief at what he had just witnessed. Samuel knew he had to go after her. Samuel ran through the charred room with smoldering relics of its former magnificence, up the stairs and after the Queen.

Chapter Twenty-Four
IN THE CHAMBER OF THE QUEEN

A few moments later, Thomas fought off the talon of the last gargoyle to firmly grab the window ledge and swing himself into the chamber window.

Inside the decimated room, Thomas saw no signs of Samuel or any living thing. The air of the room was filled with smoke, which made it hard to breathe. Before Thomas was the stairwell going up to the higher level, a way of escape he thought.

By the time he made his way to the foot of the stairwell he heard Samuel scream. Thomas drew his sword and shield and made his way cautiously up the stairwell.

Thomas entered the chamber and found Samuel slumped by the door.

"Samuel are you alright? What is it? Are you alright?"

Samuel's armor was removed and scattered on the floor around him. Thomas shook Samuel, but Samuel shielded his eyes and slumped back against the wall. All Samuel could do was babble words that made no sense at all. Out of Samuel's hand crawled a piece of the mythamöhre fruit. Thomas sliced it with his sword, black worms poured out and the fruit shriveled up as if it was a living creature. A glow from the center of the room intensified and caught Thomas' attention.

In the center of the chamber stood one tiny mythamöhre tree and before it facing him, the Queen. On the walls of the chamber was a mural of men and women in the orchards of the mythamöhre trees and the image of the Queen in their midst. On the mural the people were worshipping her.

The Queen approached Thomas; she was in the form of beautiful young woman. Thomas had never seen her like this but nevertheless he knew who she was.

"You have admired me from afar and now we are finally together," the Queen said.

Thomas steadied his shield and sword. Although she was a strikingly beautiful woman, he would recognize her black eyes anywhere.

"Oh come now, do you really think I am that dangerous that you come at me with that sword and shield? I have seen you too Thomas Littlewood, high on the mountains wishing you were here with me. I too have desired you to be with me."

She held out her hand and presented the mural as evidence.

"See I am here and there you are... my king... Thomas open your eyes to the truth, you... are... the good king," she paused to let her words sink in.

The mural continued to illuminate as if it was presenting the story to him frame by frame. Indeed, there after the images of the Queen was an image of Thomas in his armor standing with his sword drawn beside a mythamöhre tree.

"You've enslaved my father, my family... deceived everyone..." Thomas uttered.

"Who enslaved who?" she laughed. "It was your father that enslaved you. He knew it was your destiny to come to me and be by my side, to be my king. It was always written that we should be together. Yes it is you that has been deceived by your father and the lying Gatekeeper. They were trying to keep you away from your rightful place and me. They are jealous because they cannot be with me. They are jealous that you are the rightful king of this kingdom."

She came closer to Thomas.

"Remove that silly belt and let me show you the truth. In my kingdom you won't need that shield, boots, sword or helmet either. You will be crowned king among my people and they shall finally respect and give you the honor you are due. Do I look dangerous to you?" She held open her arms. "How could these images of your glory be engraved on these walls if the prophecy was not true. See for yourself."

Thomas lowered his shield and sword.

"How can my image be on the wall?" He asked.

"Your family received the Littlewood name long ago, because of the little seed of faith which your forefathers had. It's clear that you are a greater man. Your faith has brought you here to me and to your destiny. People will call you Thomas-the-Greater, it is the prophecy foretold... Thomas it is you! You have to believe me, you are the good king and I am your queen. Come to me and see that it is good. Together we shall rule and turn back the attacking evil. I know what you want Thomas and I can provide it for you. In an instant, no waiting, your time is now and you deserve it."

The Queen held her hand under the tree and a ripe mythamöhre fruit dropped in it. Thomas walked up to the Queen and looked at her in the eyes. As he approached, her stature grew and Thomas saw glimpses of his mother, Talia and the Queen all mixed together. He wondered if his eyes were playing tricks on him and he ignored the sinking feeling in his stomach.

The Queen's body had firmly transformed into herself again and she was more beautiful than any woman Thomas had ever seen. Her lips were scarlet red and stood out against her milky white skin. Her eyes were dark, deep and inviting. The Queen pursed her lips as if to invite a kiss from Thomas. She held up the fruit between them.

"Let me give you more than you can imagine, more pleasure than you've ever experienced. It is what I want to do for you Thomas."

Thomas leaned in close to the Queen. The Queen leaned in close to Thomas to kiss him. At this close proximity he could see that there were living things crawling under her milky white skin. He leaned in closer as if to kiss her and then suddenly the Queen's eyes darted open with pain.

Thomas whispered into her ear as she stood gasping for breath.

"As water reflects the image of man so do the eyes reflect the soul. Wisdom is the truth that keeps me safe before your deception. When the Good King returns I hope he finds me to be his faithful servant."

Thomas withdrew his sword from the tiny mythamöhre tree and blood ran out of it as the Queen backed away from Thomas. She ran to the tree and caressed it.

"No... no... no... it is not my time, not my time!" She screamed.

The Queen continued to caress the tree as if it was a child. She was totally focused on the tree. To Thomas' amazement he saw her begin to take on the texture of bark, as if the tree was absorbing her or as if she was absorbing it.

The room continued to illuminate as the rest of the mural became clear. What was concealed in the shadows on the mural but now became apparent is that Thomas had cut the final mythamöhre tree down.

Thomas turned his attention back to the Queen she was now totally absorbed by the tree and melted away into the cracks in the floor.

Samuel began to stir. "Thomas," he said.

Thomas went to his side.

"Samuel my friend are you okay?"

"All of my senses became dull, my eyes were blind... she told me..."

Thomas interjected cutting Samuel short, "I know my friend but now we are okay, she's gone."

A great shout came from outside of the palace.

Thomas ran to the window and saw the Gatekeeper King on his horse. All of the gargoyles lay crumbled around the battlefield. The remaining giants and the overwhelming massive kings' armies were on one knee before him.

The Gatekeeper King turned his attention to the window and to Thomas. Talia rose to her feet from one knee and looked up at Thomas in the window. Beside Talia was her mother, father, sister and many others from the village including Thomas' Papa, Meesay and Lowen.

Meesay was all right, just like the time he brought Lowen out of the field when he thought she was dead. In the presence of the Gatekeeper King she was alive and so is Meesay.

Thomas smiled at the revelation that the Gatekeeper was King, living among his people all along. Somehow, something deep within Thomas suspected that to be the truth the whole time.

Thomas held up his sword and a great shout of victory rose from all that were gathered at the feet of the Gatekeeper King. The Gatekeeper King rallied his horse to face them.

"Come, not one stone of this palace shall remain. The groves of mythamöhre trees shall be charred to the ground for it is a new day where the kingdom has come to you!" The Gatekeeper King proclaimed.

A great shout went up from all. From the chamber window Thomas joined in the shout and held his sword higher.

In the chamber behind Thomas, something caught Samuel's attention. Between the cracks of the chamber's floor were little sprouts of mythamöhre trees growing. They were growing from the blood-like sap that had run from the final mythamöhre tree.

Samuel made his way to them and admired their glowing beauty. He took his tattered satchel off of his side and began to dig one of the saplings out.

Thomas turned to face Samuel who was now standing up right dusting off his hands. Thomas looked at the ground around Samuel and saw the many growing saplings.

"Come Samuel, the world will do well not to know what we have seen here. If our people were once enticed to believe in this lie, their desire for more will drive them to believe it again."

Thomas smiled and came to Samuel putting his arm around him. They left the chamber.

As Thomas and Samuel left the chamber the mural on the wall continued to illuminate, revealing more of the prophecy. It was of a time in the far future, beyond the time of Thomas and his people; a time of an advanced people and their desires of more.

Samuel adjusted the satchel on his waist containing the mythamöhre tree sapling. He moved it to his side so Thomas would not notice the satchel was getting heavier with every step Samuel took.

Chapter Twenty-Five
SAPLINGS SPROUT

IN THE KING'S CHAMBER:

"The long and tiring day of guiding sheep was coming to a close. Sweeps of deep red, orange and pink dashed the sky while shades of purple and dark blue covered the shadowed acres of the land. The sun was peeking her last rays of summer on us... and so began my journey. Signed, your appointed ruler by the Gatekeeper King: Thomas the-Greater " Thomas leaned forward in his chair and rested his elbows on his knees. His grey hair fell forward off of his shoulders. "Is it enough for now scribe?" He asked as he sat back in his chair.

"Yes your majesty, enough, enough. The stonecutters have the tablets prepared for the memorial as you commanded. Your story will be engraved and placed within the memorial so that no one in the kingdom should ever forget. I will deliver the scrolls to the cutters now," replied the scribe.

The scribe bowed and began to roll up the scrolls.

"Scribe?"

"Yes your majesty."

"There is much more to the story we've yet to transcribe; more giants, gargoyles, imps, dark creatures and Nine."

"Nine, an interesting crafty fellow," replied the scribe.

Thomas looked off in the distance and spoke his thoughts out loud, "Those I thought to be enemy were friends and others I thought to be friends enemies."

"I will be back tomorrow sir." The scribe rolled up the final scroll and backed away from Thomas the Greater until the King rose from his chair and walked to the window.

When the scribe saw the King's back to him, he turned around and shook his head and for a split second Nine showed his true identity. Quick to regain his disguise as the scribe, Nine exited the King's chamber chanting to himself, "Be back tomorrow, tomorrow I will, I will, I will."

Thomas the Greater looked out of the window on his kingdom and wrapped his hand around the handle of the sword that he has carried with him from the time he was seventeen. He whispered to himself as if he had heard Nine's comments and replied, "And I will be waiting for your return."

AT THE ALLEN ROOM PRESS CONFERENCE:

Dr. Elderidge smacked his lips together and cleared his throat.

"The final fragment begins..."

#

FRAGMENT FOUR

guiding sheep - coming to a close - shadowed acres - so began my journey.

----the---- Greater

****

"Signed something we cannot decipher, and then -- 'the-Greater', and so we have it." Elderidge looked over his glasses at the reporters.

"I believe it poses more questions for us. If this cave on Mangaia is the birthplace of these writings then could we speculate this island was actually once a mountain? Could we speculate that the chain of Cook Islands and the thousands of South Pacific Islands actually be the mountain range these writings refer to? Stop and consider the space between the lines. For example, if we took a person who journals and ripped a page out of his life, could we imagine what fills in that space that is created? What was his life like between the lines? Is there something to learn from these writings? What happened to his people? We only have these few fragments but what journey does he refer to? Is it some personal quest? Is it a quest on behalf of his people... we..." Elderidge stopped as he saw the little girl dart between reporters at the back of the room.

He slowly continued, "We know so little, yet we have enough information that... "

Dr. Elderidge stopped short when he saw the little girl dart back again. He furrowed his brow and tried to see where the little girl had gone to, but he could not.

The group of reporters murmured at Dr. Elderidge's apparent lack of ability to stay focused.

Dr. Elderidge cleared his throat and the journalists' whispers died down.

"Let me show you what I mean."

Dr. Elderidge went to a large canvas covering a wall type of structure. He removed the canvas and it showed an aged but fairly well preserved mural of people in an orchard, part of what appeared to be a little girl and part of what appeared to be a warrior. Cameras flashed around the room.

Elderidge searched his pockets for his extendible teaching baton; unable to locate it he looked over at Beth. Beth dashed to the podium and retrieved his extendible teaching baton from the podium in front of him. Dr. Elderidge smiled at her as he took it. Beth returned to the side of the room.

Dr. Elderidge looked out at the room of reporters and then up to the mural as he extended his teaching baton and used it to point to what he was talking about. "Here you will see that the people of this time appeared to be an agricultural group because of the trees that they are harvesting." Dr. Elderidge smiled and turned to look out at the audience. As he looked out he saw a little girl peeking out from behind the edge of the mural. Elderidge grabbed his heart and slumped against the mural. The reporters' rushed to flash pictures of the explorer slumped against his finding.

Beth dashed to his side, "Would somebody please call an ambulance? He may be having a heart attack!"

The crowd of journalists gathered around him. One reporter made a mobile call to emergency services. He hung up his phone.

"The ambulance is on the way," the reporter declared.

Beth loosened Dr. Elderidge's tie.

"Dr. Elderidge, you'll be okay, help is on the way," whispered Beth.

Elderidge focused on Beth, but then over her shoulder he noticed the little girl with dark eyes and milky white skin, as she moved closer to him. She smiled at Dr. Elderidge and wagged her finger in a mocking fashion. "No, no, no, it's not my time yet, you can't tell, you naughty boy... soon," the little girl whispered. With that the little girl's smile widened.

No one else seemed to be able to see the little girl or hear her. The little girl's gaze turned to Kip Somers. Their eyes locked. Kip could see her.

She would know him anywhere, or at least his type, even without his staff and gatekeepers robe, Kip Somers' type is the same throughout generations. It's the same type of dangerous characteristics that makes common shepherd boys believe that they can be heroes.

Kip paused and looked unflinchingly at the gaunt apparition that floated through the crowd. He was shocked at seeing her. He knew her, but from where? Was it from a dream? Something deep within his soul told him to be cautious. He felt uneasy; the scent of deceit is always the same, no matter how it is cloaked. Just as she came, the little girl disappeared into the crowd again.

Kip Somers shook his head, was he imagining things?

Jazz at the Lincoln Centre employees brought in a portable stretcher, just as the emergency medical response team arrived. The Paramedics went to work, asking questions and taking Dr. Elderidge's vitals. They secured Dr. Elderidge on their stretcher and the Jazz at the Lincoln Centre employees did their best to keep back the pressing crowd.

Kip got on his mobile phone trying to call his editor as the Paramedics lifted Dr. Elderidge's stretcher to its wheel extended position for pushing. Kip paused from attempting his cellular call to touch Elderidge and nod at Beth.

"I'm sure he'll be okay," Kip said as he looked reassuringly into Beth's eyes.

"They need to pick up... shoddy reception," Kip whispers to himself as he clicks off his cell phone.

Dr. Elderidge smiled at Kip. Beth looked at Kip's kind eyes and then back to Dr. Elderidge.

Josh pushed his way into the crowd beside Beth and caught Kip's attention.

"You got your 'always' good news story Kip?" Mocked Josh.

Josh began to reassure Beth as Kip's cell phone rang. Seeing it was his editor's number on his display he answered it before responding to Josh.

Beth tried to keep up as the medical team took Dr. Elderidge out of the room.

Kip's voice mixed in with the hum of other journalists talking and connecting with their news outlets.

Kip touched a finger to his free ear to block out the noise as he spoke into his mobile phone, "Yes sir, I called. Yes, I will be sure that I make it to the tree planting ceremony with the mayor in Central Park. I understand the significance of the Prosperity Tree... yes sir. Things wrapped up with an exciting lead story here... yes sir, as soon as I am off this call I am posting the story. I'll be back at the office before the end of the day... yes... I'll be back soon."

THE END

The Mythamöhre

ACKNOWLEDGEMENTS

The inspiration for "The Mythamöhre" came from the sad but true story of a famous Hollywood producer. He had reached the pinnacle of the movie industry and was riding the crest of success. Success meant he could live in excess without limits. It was that excess that ended his life.

A friend, John Garner was preparing to speak and asked me for information on the Hollywood mogul. The illustration John gave of a life lived without boundaries was thought provoking. It caused me to think of (the-myth-of-more) "The Mythamöhre" in tangible ways and Thomas' journey was born.

Perhaps no matter our age, 15 or 50, we find ourselves in Thomas: the potential of a King with the insecurities of a child. The armor always fits we just don't realize it. How often do we hear the voice of the Gatekeeper in our own heads giving us warning or advice and we choose to ignore it? Perhaps because it sounds like our own voice or we reason it away that often times we end up saying to ourselves, "I knew it, why didn't I listen?" Whatever name you give that voice, intuition, consciousness or gut-instinct - I believe every person on the planet hears it. So in that way, I also thought, what if that voice was personified? With the physical appearance of the Gatekeeper, would it make it any easier to follow him or would we still doubt? Our lives seem so intertwined it made me think long and hard about Thomas' journey and even my own. The subtext reveals that: The fate of many rests in the journey of one; at its deepest level I believe that to be true. Do any of us fully realize the significant impact we have on each other? If we could somehow zoom out of the atmosphere and see the chain of events and what our actions mean globally; I think we, like Thomas, would come to realize the journey is worth the cost.

There's more to share about Thomas' journey and perhaps I will pick that up in another installment. I would appreciate hearing from you and the encouragement to carry on Thomas' adventure. If the story inspired you please help me inspire others. The very best way to do that is to get the word out about "The Mythamöhre" especially if it is good and edifying: post on blogs, write a review on Amazon and other sites. Let pod-casters and broadcasters know about it. I would welcome the opportunity to share the story with larger audiences.

You'd be helping me and in turn you'd be helping others... isn't that what it's all about? Thanks for doing that. What started out as a way to share important truth with my children can be used by others to engage conversation and put the focus on what really matters in life... each other. We can all use encouragement and I hope you find "The Mythamöhre" an encouragement to your journey.

ABOUT THE AUTHOR

Christopher Mark Bessette is a multi-award winning motion picture writer/director/producer. www.christopherbessette.com In 2012 Bessette was honored with the province of Ontario Canada, Premier's Award nomination for outstanding achievement in the field of Creative Arts & Design.

Bessette has led an international career; while producing a program for Family Channel, Bessette worked with producers in 13 nations. He is the recipient of two best director awards, the first for his feature film "The Enemy God" at the 2008 ARPA International Film Festival in Hollywood. www.theenemygod.com The most recent feature film written and directed by Bessette was shot in Bangkok, Thailand. "Trade of Innocents" deals with the issue of human trafficking, specifically as it pertains to the sale of children. The movie stars: Dermot Mulroney, Academy Award Winner Mira Sorvino, John Billingsley and Trieu Tran. Among its recognition, it was awarded Best Drama and Best Director at the 32nd Annual Festival of Film Breckenridge and the 2012 ICVM Gold Crown Award for Best Picture, as well as Best Feature at the Toronto Cornerstone International Film Festival in 2012. For their roles in the film, Mulroney and Sorvino received Best Actor/Actress nominations at the 2013 Milan International Film Festival in Italy. www.tradeofinnocents.com

Bessette is married to his high school sweetheart Toni. They make their home on land deeded to Bessette's United Empire Loyalist ancestor, 200 years ago by the Crown of England. Their home is in southern Ontario, Canada. Christopher and Toni have 3 children: Rachel, Michael and William. Their son Michael and daughter-in-law Melissa are expecting. Christopher and Toni anxiously await the arrival of their first grandchild. "The Mythamöhre" is Bessette's first novel.

Connect with the author Online:
Twitter:
http://twitter.com/c_bessette
Facebook:
https://www.facebook.com/christopher.bessette.writer.director